THE NET

NOVELS BY ILIE NASTASE

Break Point
The Net

THE NET

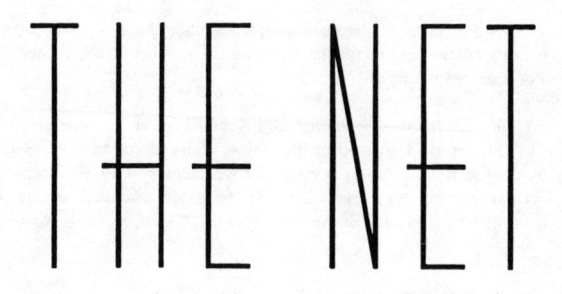

• A NOVEL BY •

ILIE NASTASE

Translated from the French by
ROS SCHWARTZ

ST. MARTIN'S PRESS
NEW YORK

This novel is a work of fiction. The events depicted herein have never occurred. Names, characters, places, and incidents either are the product of the author's imagination or are used fictitiously.

THE NET. Copyright © 1987 by Les Productions Robert Laffont. Translation © 1987 W. H. Allen. All rights reserved. Printed in the United States of America. No part of this book may be used or reproduced in any manner whatsoever without written permission except in the case of brief quotations embodied in critical articles or reviews. For information, address St. Martin's Press, 175 Fifth Avenue, New York, N.Y. 10010.

Design by Trish Parcell Watts

Library of Congress Cataloging in Publication Data

Nastase, Ilie, 1946-
    The net.

    I. Title.
PS3564.A846N4   1987   813'.54   87-16509
ISBN 0-312-01070-2

First Edition
10 9 8 7 6 5 4 3 2 1

THE NET

PART I

A murmur of disappointment accompanied his interminably slow approach to the net. A muffled protest from the astonished spectators made his leaden feet feel even heavier. He was sinking deeper and deeper into the quagmire. He was an underwater diver advancing through the silt, his arms outstretched toward the galleon laden with gold. But the sunken vessel, frozen there for three centuries, was receding, leaving only rocky masses and beyond them, the ocean depths. Miles away, Stuart Mill was roaring with laughter on the service line where he should never have ventured. This man, whom tennis star Istvan Horwat was to have slaughtered, was a long way off, and yet he seemed colossal. He shook his head. Strands of blond hair were escaping from Stuart Mill's headband. It was too late for Istvan now. Stuart wouldn't miss a thing, and the net was receding even further.

Suddenly Istvan was flying through the air, projected forward, winded. He could no longer control his arms or legs. He was being sucked into a whirlpool, a breathtaking fall into the abyss, caught in the net that was closing round him, imprisoning him, paralyzing him, strangling him like a giant squid. A deep-water squid, enveloping him in its ink. It was over.

His hand groped, running backward and forward over the buttons on the long panel that controlled the revolving bed, the lights, the air conditioning, the curtains, the French windows, and even Thieu, his Vietnamese valet.

Lying on his stomach, drenched in perspiration, Istvan suffered from a stiffness in his muscles that felt as painful as if the net in his nightmare really had closed on him. He turned over gingerly as if he, Istvan Horwat, the ex–number-one world tennis champion, still seeded fifth at thirty-two, were as fragile as a porcelain Dresden figure. On the shelves, those selfsame little white figures, which his old friend Countess Balanska had given him one by one to celebrate each new victory, danced and chased each other among the trophies.

He pivoted his circular bed so that he was looking out of the window. The linen curtains parted smoothly, and the metal blind rose to reveal an exceptionally blue sky for Paris at the beginning of October. He pressed another button to open the bay windows, drew several deep breaths of fresh air, and slid out of bed. He had too much respect for his body to inflict sudden movements on it.

In the bathroom, he walked round the swimming-pool-cum-bathtub that, like the bed, was round and black. The tub was where so many girls had the habit of lingering, playing with the countless combinations afforded by the gold-plated taps. Enervated by the water, which was usually too hot, and by the smell of the bath salts, they would climb out slowly, often pausing when they reached the top of the low steps, as if ascending the terraces of a stadium. Istvan preferred the shower, which was power-

THE NET

ful, almost violent—set that way to match his own strength. He had insisted on fitting a shower cubicle in a corner of his sumptuous spa-bathroom, despite the interior designer's protests. It clashed with the luxury of everything else. He liked that.

He abandoned himself to the sizzling jets of water that washed away the perspiration brought on by his nightmare. There again, nothing sudden: neither too hot nor too cold. Suddenly he shivered at the recollection of the vortex of the heavy net drawing its waterlogged weave tautly around him. Suddenly he remembered it all—the Iberia Airlines jetliner that had plunged into the Mediterranean the previous afternoon. As he collected his thoughts, he had some difficulty in breathing. The shower water left a salty tang on his lips—the presence of the sea in his tears as he remembered the news bulletins. . . .

"Màrton Kotany, long-standing international tennis star, was on board with his wife Jane. Kotany was the coach of Patrice Martinez, the French number one, and had been accompanying him to the Barcelona Tournament. After beating Richardson, Martinez had decided to stay in Spain a few days longer. That's what saved him from this disaster, another in the long line of air crashes over the last few months. The Navy is carrying out a search, but no life jackets have been spotted so far, despite good weather. Unfortunately, it appears unlikely that there will be any survivors.

"The search will continue for several days. Then it is expected that there will be a memorial service for the victims in Barcelona, followed on Sunday morning by a ceremony at sea."

* * *

Màrton, his childhood friend, born like him in Hungary. Màrton, who had telephoned from Orly just before leaving for Barcelona . . .

"Of course Jane's coming with me! You know what the press says. 'Màrton Kotany's devoted wife!' What about you, I don't suppose you're worried, you're busy with your flock of girls?"

"On Tuesday I've got an exhibition tournament in Lyon. I'm taking my latest girl friend."

"What's her name?"

"Mercedes . . . 450."

"All the same, try and arrive in some kind of shape, will you?"

And with these oft-repeated words, Màrton had rung off. Never again would Istvan hear those warm, cheerfully ironic inflections. He concentrated on his bathrobe belt, but it took two attempts to tie it. He knew he had to get a grip on himself. He strode across the room to the balcony that overlooked the Bois de Boulogne and the private domain of Roland-Garros. He tried to do his usual breathing exercises, but the feeling of suffocation was getting even stronger.

Furious with himself, he tried to concentrate on the routine motions, without thinking about anything at all. He automatically glanced at the Celsius thermometer outside; it showed seventeen degrees. The low sixties. Warm.

In the dressing rooms that Thieu had such a hard job keeping tidy, he rummaged for something to wear. As he slipped into his moccasins, he realized that he was dressing any old way—he who had been voted most elegant man of the year by the readers of *Vogue*. He stared wearily at his reflection in the mirror and saw that he had forgotten to shave.

THE NET

* * *

Istvan went down to the seventh floor by the interior staircase. In the dining room with gray velvet walls, Thieu had laid the oval marble table for breakfast. The sun streamed through the windows, picking out the shapes of the silver service, from the potbellied teapot to the subtle curves of the egg cups.

"Thieu!"

"Coming, monsieur. The eggs are ready."

"Well, you can eat them."

Puzzled, Thieu appeared from the pantry. He stood stiffly to attention behind the table and looked searchingly into Istvan's face.

"I know, I haven't shaved. I haven't got time. I'll shave in the car. Give me my orange juice and my tea. That's all I can swallow."

"Uh, the accident . . ."

Thieu, a "boat person" who had escaped capture by pirates in the Gulf of Thailand, had thrown in his lot with Istvan. He had no other family. The pirates had raped his wife before throwing her overboard to join their two tiny children. He had never understood why they had let him go drifting off. Perhaps they were low on ammunition. It was thanks to Istvan that he had gradually regained the will to live. He was thrilled when Istvan won, bemused when he notched another female conquest. Thieu looked after the apartment with meticulous care. He poured the tea and murmured:

"The suitcases are in the trunk, monsieur. It's so big in there that it looks almost empty, but everything's aboard. You ought to eat something, you know."

"Thank you, Thieu, but no. I'll telephone you from Lyon."

ILIE NASTASE

* * *

The car nosed its way through the inevitable traffic jams at the Porte d'Orléans. Istvan turned up the volume of the cassette player to drown out the concert of car horns. The six loudspeakers played Listz's *Mephisto*. He discovered notes of sadness that he had never heard before. True, he had not begun to love classical music until two years ago, thanks to Inge, the singer he had met in Berlin after winning a Davis Cup match. Inge, who was being compared to Callas, and who was to drag him into a tumultuous affair that was luckily now over.

He was quick to spot a momentary gap in the sea of indecisive drivers, and he glided the large Mercedes through in a flash. Even when he was young, he already loved powerful, luxurious cars. While his friends vied with each other over their low chassis and convertibles, he sought old Bentleys, which made him feel as if he were traveling in a drawing room. But now, he only liked things that smelled new, the smell of leather. He shot over to the right toward the verge, well ahead of a slow-moving huddle of cars. The entrance to the autoroute to the south was five hundred yards ahead. He pulled over by a gray house with boarded-up shutters, the planks nailed in the shape of a cross. A building contractor's board advertised that it was to be demolished. He looked away. The mute facade with its peeling plaster evoked death. Almost everything did now. He picked up the telephone, dialed a number, and absently watched the cars he had just passed drive by while the telephone rang in the suite at the Plaza Athénée where Frank Fenwick, his manager and friend, was staying. Frank did not like offices, and had transformed his pockets into a filing system that accompanied him everywhere.

THE NET

"I tried to call you yesterday evening," said Fenwick, after answering on the first ring.

"I was out. I was wandering around. I was thinking about Màrton."

"What a terrible accident. I don't know what to say. . . . When your best friend . . ." His voice trailed off.

"It's all right, F.F. There's nothing to say."

"You be careful. Don't drive like a lunatic on the autoroute. Accidents come in threes, you know."

2

A light fog dispersed the autumn sun into a cold light. The fields alongside the expressway no longer had a definite outline, no longer had boundaries. Istvan was approaching the heart of a mysterious domain. He switched on the fog lights. On the exotic wood dashboard, the dials of the gauges shone reassuringly.

He kept to the left-hand lane, passing the cars that became few and far between the further he got from Paris. He cruised like a shadow in the ghostly, late-morning light. He tried to keep his mind blank, to concentrate on feeling the vibrations of the new car. Despite the dealer's advice, he had turned down the automatic transmission, preferring to have tight control over the engine's power.

He pulled into a service area. As soon as he had requested a full tank, he raised the power window and found his Visa card among his credit cards. The curly-haired boy who filled him up and then went inside with the card barely glimpsed his face, but when he returned, he asked for two signatures, one on the charge receipt that bore the name Istvan Horwat, the other on a loose leaf

THE NET

from a notebook. Istvan signed quickly, forced a smile, and asked where he could buy a bottle of water. The boy pointed to the shop, a hundred yards away, stuffed the autograph into the pocket of his green overalls, and then walked off toward the diesel pump where a wine tanker had braked to a stop with a sigh like a locomotive's.

Several cars were clustered outside the shop, but Istvan found a space just in front of the door. The chubby-faced cashier looked up at this tall, handsome fellow who measured at least six-feet-three with black hair and dark green eyes. He made her forget the characters she had been reading about in the movie magazine, who seemed pathetic in comparison.

"Where's the mineral water, please?"

"At the back on the left," she replied.

She gazed after him as he walked past the display of car accessories and reached the toy counter. She had never watched a tennis match, so he could only be a famous actor—but who? She decided that she had seen him in a TV series, but she would never dare ask him which one.

The toy counter was empty. They obviously had not replaced the stock after the summer selling season, when children get bored sitting in overheated cars and trailers crawling along the congested roads and manage to wangle anything they want from their short-tempered parents. Two Barbie dolls, one in pink, the other in orange, had survived the holidays. Istvan, who had never understood the appeal of these stiff, glittering models, contemplated them with tears in his eyes. He could hear Natty going into raptures:

"See, it's written 'Dreamtime Barbie' on the box. I'm going to call her 'Dreamy Barbie.'"

Natty . . . Natasha . . . Màrton and Jane's daughter, born

in New York at the end of August one year, in the stifling heat during the U.S. Open at Flushing Meadow. Natty had been a daughter of tennis. Now it had made her an orphan.

Five years earlier in Paris, Istvan Horwat had not yet bought his apartment on the Avenue Robert-Schuman, close to Roland-Garros. For a year, he had rented a small private mansion in the Rue de Boulainvilliers. It was impractical and badly heated, but he liked the chaotic little English garden. "My country retreat," he would call it, while making it clear that he tired quickly of the country, especially in winter.

He had lived there for three months with Julie Charrière, the fashion photographer whose whims were the talk of the international press. One day, he carefully assembled all the equipment she had stored in the attic and piled it up on the garden path, then checked into the Ritz. As intended, the exhausting Julie had thereupon vacated the premises. She was surely disappointed at being deprived of one of the epic scenes she so loved, but she did not bear him any malice for this peaceful yet eloquent method of getting rid of her. She was subsequently to take photos of Istvan for *Vogue*. One of them, in which he looked as if he were emerging from an Irish castle dressed from head to foot in tweed, even appeared on the cover. Left alone, he had invited the Kotanys, who were in Rome, preparing to return to New York, to make a detour via Paris. Natty could play in the garden. She had been five at the time. Pale blond hair covered her shoulders, and she had huge gray-blue, almond-shaped eyes. One afternoon when her parents had gone to the movies, she got tired of watching Madame Reine, the governess, ironing laundry. Madame Reine was very talkative, but Natty

THE NET

only understood a few words of French. She decreed that she was sleepy and was going to lie down with Istvan. He had indeed announced that he was going to have a siesta while Màrton and Jane set off for the Champs-Elysées in a taxi; but he had not mentioned that he wouldn't be alone. The wife of Councillor Müller, who had the discreet knack of dropping in to see her lovers without compromising herself, burrowed under the sheets in panic as the little girl hammered on the door.

"Wait for me downstairs, Natty!" shouted Istvan. "I'll be ready in five minutes. I'll take you out for some ice cream!"

He laughed as he pulled on his clothes, which annoyed the disappointed councillor's wife even more.

"I'm not going to stay another minute longer in this nursery," she said testily.

"Wait until we've left, at least."

He opened the door carefully and found Natty sitting on the landing, hugging her knees.

He abandoned the councillor's wife in the bedroom then, and in the parking lot in the Place Vendôme he forsook the black Daimler he was preparing to sell so he wouldn't have to tune it all the time. He and Natty made their way down the Faubourg-Saint-Honoré. No matter how quickly he walked, she trotted by his side, her hand in his.

The passersby turned to stare at this unusual couple. Such a blond little girl beside a tall man with such black hair. At twenty-seven years of age, Istvan had never held a child's hand. It felt good, something he was sure nothing else could rival at that moment. At the same time awkward and responsible, he looked down at Natty as if he might lose her. But he felt his hand being gripped as firmly as a racket handle. In fact, he was looking at her because he was surprised to see her there. It was a strange feeling, such a far cry from his more familiar role as a champion—and lover.

"You'll see," he said, shouting to make himself heard above the traffic. "It's the most terrific toy store in Paris."

"What's it called?"

"Le Nain Bleu, the Blue Dwarf."

"Ah . . ."

The name had a dreamy sound—exotic and just scary enough to be exciting.

Idle rich women who had ventured out of their lairs en masse to be pampered in the boutiques of the Faubourg honked their horns as he and Natty walked along. A platinum blonde, thrilled at recognizing Istvan, turned to stare after him and had the misfortune to smash the hood of her Autobianchi into the indifferent bumper of a Rolls Corniche. Istvan was amused by this defeat of David by Goliath, but Natty worried that the lady might not be able to drive off. He had expected her to burst out laughing, especially as the scatterbrained driver extricated herself from her dented vehicle to insult the chauffeur who, having stepped out to assure himself that the Rolls was not scratched, was already back behind the wheel, sitting impassively, waiting for the light to change.

When they reached Le Nain Bleu, their exploration of the first two floors turned out to be more thoroughgoing than Istvan had anticipated. Natty lost all sense of time. She was enthralled. There was everything a child could wish for. But Natty, who had let go of Istvan's hand to dart from one counter to another, wanted nothing. For her, this luxurious shop was like a fun fair. Istvan was not prepared for that.

"Choose anything you like," he told her.

THE NET

"Wait, we haven't seen everything yet!"

Clients from neighboring Hermès came in to salve their consciences by spending money on their offspring who were shut up in school at this hour. Less discreet than the well-trained sales assistants, they did not hesitate to take out their diaries and ask with a dreamy look in their eyes:

"An autograph, Monsieur Horwat . . ."

"Is that your daughter?" asked the boldest.

"One of them," Istvan corrected her solemnly.

"What's her name?"

"I can't remember, I get them all mixed up."

A pale-complexioned redhead in a blue mink coat spelled her name aloud so he could write it on perfumed notepaper. When he handed it back to her, duly signed, she held out her visiting card in exchange: Nadine Bellini. It was a piece of intelligence he would put to good use a few days later.

Natty had vanished. He took advantage of her disappearance to make his getaway. A sales assistant found her for him, standing in front of a wall of dolls. They were in all sizes, shapes, and colors, as haughty as romantic heroines or as plump as Renoir's bathers.

For a few awkward seconds Istvan was reminded of the tiny breasts of Martha Möhl, a much-sought-after nymphomaniac who would only make love in front of her collection of antique china dolls, lined up as if on parade, their real hair peeping out under lace bonnets, their impassive eyes contemplating their cavorting patroness.

"Which one do you want? You can have two if you like."

"Oh no! You can't love two new dolls at the same time!"

Istvan got caught up in the game, as if he were judging the fashion show of a Miss World contest. He compared the cut of their clothes, their features—and, to himself, the curve of their thighs, disregarding the creatures that were too down-to-earth, their nakedness too realistic for comfort, or the baby dolls in boxes announcing that they drank their bottle, cried, said "Mommy," and peed. He suddenly found himself giving advice.

"That big one over there, dressed as a horsewoman with the boots, riding hat, and whip, she's beautiful, isn't she?"

"I like the blond one in a long tennis skirt, like they used to wear."

She's five years old, Istvan thought, and she even knows how Suzanne Lenglen used to dress!

"Well, take that one!"

"I've already got her at home."

"There must be one you don't already have."

"Come here and see the one I want."

She took his hand and led him to where, set apart from the name-brand examples of femininity, were rows of boxes containing straight, impossibly stiff, slender bodies, decked out in a collection of clothes that would not have been out of place in a third-class operetta. The one to which Natty was pointing, in a phosphorescent blue dress, struck Istvan as the least appealing of all.

"Do you like her?"

"Don't you?" She turned her suddenly inscrutable face toward him, giving him a look of wariness, of reproach.

"Of course I do, why?"

"She's a Barbie doll. Look, it's written on the box. Nobody will give me a Barbie. Mommy says they're too American, and she's American herself! You'll let me have one, won't you?"

Istvan picked Natty up to kiss her, astonished to find himself moved to tears without knowing why.

THE NET

"I'd be delighted to, but it's not much of a present. I mean, I'll buy you several."

"No, that one! But we can buy other clothes, if you want, and then I can change her. It says Dreamtime Barbie on the box, but I'm going to call her Dreamy Barbie."

As they walked under the arcade in the Rue de Rivoli, she clutched the elegant Nain Bleu bag containing her new treasure. At Angelina's, the tea salon the old Parisians still call Rumpelmayer's after the famous confectioner who opened it during the Belle Epoque, all the tables were full. Istvan, still holding Natty's hand, tried to find a table in the back room. He towered above the seated fashion models, who interrupted their chatter to stare at him, then at Natty.

Two waitresses, who had been busy a moment before, rushed over, both talking at once:

"Monsieur Horwat! If you could wait a few minutes, someone's asked for the bill."

While he smiled his acquiescence, Natty said something to him.

"What did she say?" chorused the waitresses.

A young woman with dark hair and a chalky triangular face had overheard. "She said it's too long to wait, she'd rather go elsewhere."

Then, as Natty was pulling Istvan toward the door, the woman said, "I love children, Monsieur Horwat. My friend and I would be delighted to share our table with you. You see, these two chairs are free."

She held out her hand to Natty and addressed her gently in English. "Do you want to sit with me?"

The child stared at the two smiling women warily, in silence. They were curiously alike. Istvan did not know how to interpret Natty's discreet squeezing of his hand.

Was she telling him she wanted to leave, or stay? The women were obviously using the child to lure the prince of the courts, which they would never have dared to do so brazenly had he been alone. He examined each one in turn. They were beautiful. . . . They would do well as future nocturnal companions. But—and this was another new sensation he attributed to Natty—he had not the slightest wish to sit at their table.

He looked at these two creatures who were hoping to horn in on this privileged moment.

"Look, Istvan," Natty said, "there are some people leaving, over there!"

Once again he felt like sweeping her up in his arms and hugging her. In his deep voice with its indefinable accent, he took leave of the two adventuresses at the table.

"Thank you for your invitation. Some other time . . ."

Natty seemed unaware of the stares that followed her as she threaded her way around the tables, brandishing her bag like a trophy. She sank laughingly into a chair, her nose level with the lipstick-stained teacups and jam-smeared plates left behind by the departing group.

"It's dirty," she said, pointing to the full ashtray.

"It'll be cleared in a second," the flustered waitress assured her.

Istvan, sitting next to the child, had an idea. "Look at those huge ice creams. Do you want one?"

"I don't like ice cream very much. Do you think they've got strawberry tarts?"

"Of course," replied the waitress between two flicks of her silent butler. "Strawberry and raspberry tartlets."

Natty had taken the box out of the bag and was contemplating the doll through the cellophane packaging.

"I'm going to ask for a knife so I can free Dreamy

THE NET

Barbie," said Istvan, going a little soft in the head and enjoying it.

"Careful, it's her house."

And the tall, oft-televised champion obediently applied himself to slitting the top of the box carefully, all the way across, melting the hearts of the women at neighboring tables and of the waitress who stood there, spellbound, holding her tray laden with tartlets. . . .

Istvan remembered that day five years ago as if it were yesterday. But he had forgotten for a moment where he was now, until a voice interrupted his reverie.

"You've got children, monsieur," said the cashier in the Total shop, slipping the two Barbie dolls into one bag and the two bottles of mineral water into the other.

She was convinced, now, that she had seen him on television, and that was the only thing she could think of to get him to talk.

"No children," replied Istvan. "I collect dolls."

Istvan flicked his turn signal, then pulled out of the slow lane and accelerated. The engine responded instantly. He no longer bothered to look at the tachometer, or the odometer either, for that matter. During the two hundred and eighty odd miles he had just driven, he had had time to familiarize himself with the car. In the dullness of the hazy hours, memories executed their dance of harassment while he sat alone with his grief.

The fog grew denser as he approached Lyon. Istvan had driven through this town maybe a dozen times, without seeing it, on his way to the south. The name, reduced to signposts on the motorway, was associated with Hollywood-style parties given in Saint-Tropez by Charlie Berton, a producer old enough to be his father and utterly devoted to him. He planned his private flight schedule according to Istvan Horwat's match program and never failed to present him with the most dazzling girls in his court. This stretch of the highway would always remind Istvan of Berton, and the architectural extravagance of the villa in Pamplona where pleasure reigned.

At the tunnel, the sodium lights along the road cut through the fog. Istvan only had to follow the signs straight to the Sofitel. These international hotels were all alike. You could find your way there blindfolded. You followed the signs until you reached a commissionaire, a porter, or a bar.

3

From the window of his sixth-floor room Istvan stared at the dark waters of the Rhône. The gray weather of that Saturday in mid-October suited his morose thoughts. He had not been able to sleep. For part of the night, images of Màrton kept coming to mind, jumbled memories . . . The beach at Ostia where they had slept when they had played in their first tournament in Rome, where they had gone without any money . . . the doubles in the international matches they had fought together . . . the family scenes where Istvan, who was always invited with his latest girl friend, posed in his perennial black track suit beside Màrton, who was always dressed in white, to the delight of Natty—she called them the domino brothers. No doubt she had come across the expression in a book. Although Màrton was four years older than Istvan, he seemed younger and more fragile due to his slighter build. It was that blond, almost delicate figure who haunted Istvan like a ghost.

Later that morning, at ten o'clock, the car drew up alongside the stadium caretaker, who almost put his nose against the tinted window to identify Istvan, then saluted him respectfully. Normally training took place behind closed gates, but already a few curious onlookers had managed to slip in among the groups of professionals to get a close-up glimpse of their idols. Istvan had never felt so little motivated as he did for this invitational in Lyon. He brushed aside a few early-morning autograph hunters with uncharacteristic ill humor before ducking into the changing room.

Though there wasn't quite the full-scale invasion tolerated in the afternoons, the spectators were already in place beside the courts. Some even preferred the training sessions to the actual match because it made them feel closer to the players, let in on their privacy. As he joined the Yugoslav, Vlado Franulovic, with whom he was to train that morning, he met Benson, assistant to his manager, Frank Fenwick. He had insisted that Istvan play in this tournament, a minor one with a prize of twenty-five thousand dollars.

"The Adidas people are here," he said. "They want to show you their latest racket, the one you'll be signing."

"I'll see them at lunchtime. That'll do, won't it?"

"They aren't alone," said Benson. "A horde of other sponsors has come too. Mainly French. Since you only play in France three or four times a year, they're taking advantage of our being here."

"That's your job," replied Istvan, walking away. "Taking advantage. Tell them I'm meditating."

Istvan was fond of Franulovic. Both men were from Eastern Europe, were of the same age, and had often played together. Franulovic, too, was irritated at the degree of disturbance in the stadium during training—the crowds of admirers on the warpath, children brandishing auto-

THE NET

graph books and pencils, sponsors already jockeying to set up the following year's contracts, and so-called sports lovers who came only to be seen. "The marriage of money and ostentation," as Màrton would have said.

The tournament organizers had invited four top-level players, to make the event more than just a local one. Behind Istvan was the ex-champion, the Italian, Panatta, currently ranked eighth, whose beautiful style worked wonders at exhibitions. There was the Spaniard, Orantes, and the American, Roscoe Tanner, who was to play with Franulovic that afternoon.

Istvan did not outshine the Yugoslav as brilliantly as he usually did. The deaths of Màrton and Jane Kotany, which nobody dared mention in front of him, hung in the air. As he lunched without appetite, Istvan spoke absentmindedly to Benson and the men from Adidas who showed him an eerily perfect reproduction of his own signature on the new graphite composite tennis racket that was about to be launched on the market.

"I'm going out," he said. "I need a breath of air."

Benson stared after him with a worried expression as Istvan made his way to his car.

"He needs to get a grip on himself this afternoon against Panatta," he said to himself, looking puzzled. "He looks like he lost the match already."

As soon as he returned, at around three o'clock, Istvan, whom everyone greeted as the star of the tournament, showed his irritation openly. He brushed off a laughing group of girls who were crowding around him. He turned to apologize, furious with himself, to meet the astonished gaze of Orantes who was scribbling his signature indifferently on cigarette packets, métro tickets, and banknotes.

Obviously perturbed by the spectators, he made the

public feel ill at ease. The first ball he served got stuck in the net. Several times, he rose to Panatta's attacks but was beaten back. He could not bring himself to concentrate, and this match against Panatta, whom he would normally have beaten, was heading for disaster. Istvan missed the easiest shots, and the few rare strokes he made that were worthy of him were followed by double faults. Panatta was surprised to see him miss every other backhand passing-shot, usually one of his most certain, one of his most indisputable strokes. Istvan, the relentlessly reliable champion who so rarely made a mistake and who almost always returned the ball, seemed to be allowing himself to be taken by surprise without responding. Returning Panatta's service, his shots were so inconsistent that his opponent had no difficulty whatsoever in concluding the match.

Consternation reigned among the businessmen of tennis as they watched him slide toward defeat. His admirers did not understand, either. Someone started a rumor that he had injured himself that morning while training with Franulovic. But the players and the coaches guessed the truth. They could feel the oppressive atmosphere in this stadium, with the spectre of Màrton hovering over it. None of them wanted to be there. As good professionals, they had all come because the hall had already been hired and their participation publicized. It was out of consideration for the spectators that they were taking part in this exhibition at all.

After concluding the last game, which saw him win by a crushing 6–1, 6–1, Panatta murmured as he grasped Istvan's hand: "You must get a grip on yourself. We all have to. I loved him, too. But think of something else, until this is over."

"You're very kind, Adriano," replied Istvan.

THE NET

He drew away after giving the winner a friendly touch on the shoulder.

"Do you realize the position you've put us in?" grumbled Benson. He was beside himself. "I've just called Frank. He's in a hell of a state. Of course, he agrees with me, you can't scratch. You're top of the bill, and everyone's waiting to see you."

They walked away from the local TV cameras, surrounded by a cluster of locals anxious to get their faces into the picture. When a journalist asked him a coldly calculated question, whether he felt in top shape for the next day's match, Istvan did not reply.

"You've made a commitment," hissed Benson, drawing Istvan away from the knot of reporters. "You've got to keep to it. How do you expect me to tell the organizers that you've withdrawn? If there are only three players left, what are *they* supposed to do?"

"I can't help it. It's the first time it's happened to me. I just can't keep my mind on the game. . . ."

"I've never seen such a thing, Istvan. Professionally, it's a serious offense." Benson sighed. "Personally, I feel lousy, too."

Three times the car was left parked up on the sidewalk, right under the noses of policemen who took pains not to notice. And three times Istvan was disappointed by the luxury boutiques, at the fateful hour just before seven o'clock on a Saturday evening when the assistants are raring to get home. As he walked out of Yves Saint-Laurent, he despaired of finding the formal black suit and accessories he wanted for the Spanish ceremony the following day. He was about to pull away in front of a group of young bikers, deaf and dumb in their helmets, when he saw the sign over the boutique on the corner. His car was blocking the door. "A la Grande Maison," the sign said. He backed up a couple of feet to be able to get into this old-fashioned den—his last chance at this late hour—and pushed open the door. His entrance set off a peal of chimes that sounded like a herd of alpine cows.

The head of a little bald man emerged from behind a long wooden counter that shone from generations of wax polish.

"Can I help you, monsieur?"

Istvan caught himself speaking in a monotone, just like that of the ageless man before him in his grayish overall.

"A black suit, a black tie, and a black coat."

The chimes on the door ceased ringing, as if silenced by this sign of bereavement.

"I've only got a cashmere overcoat left in a large, and an average-quality flannel suit. You have a very nice car, monsieur, but you shouldn't park in front of my door, if you'll forgive me."

"I'm sorry, I'm in a hurry."

"A recent bereavement? First of all try on the trousers. I'll have to adjust the cuffs. Do you want it all this evening? I can have it delivered to your hotel in an hour. You're only passing through, I take it? Now let's see . . . now let's see . . ."

As Istvan indifferently tried on the clothes, he was lost in thought once more. He pictured his father's funeral in Budapest. The gray-clad groups huddling under umbrellas. The same groups, the same rain as for his mother's burial, two years ago.

"So you'll deliver it all in an hour to the Sofitel. My name is . . . on the check."

* * *

THE NET

In the lobby of the hotel he spotted a group of well-known faces next to the reception desk. The nomadic little world of tennis that had come to Lyon for the tournament had, of course, bivouacked at this hotel. He paused for a minute and pretended to be absorbed in a window display by the entrance. He waited, drifting behind a giant indoor plant, until the herd of players, managers, sponsors, and journalists had dispersed in the direction of two bars, one on the ground floor adorned by a tropical jungle, the other on the eighth floor overlooking the river and the rooftops of the city beyond.

He did not feel like talking to anybody. He emerged from his hiding place, asked for his key, gave instructions for his dinner to be served in his room, and directed that the parcels he was expecting be brought up to him. He did not want any calls to be put through and requested a wake-up call at four o'clock the next morning.

4

The tramontane wind swept the headland, plucking at the flowers in the bank of wreaths laid out facing the sea. The surplices of the three priests flapped like flags. The waves boomed in, crashing against the rocks. Jets of foam rose up menacingly, then fell back and were sucked into the eddies. The somber crowd, gathered in front of the mass of multicolored flowers made dazzling by the sunlight, stood overwhelmed by a mixture of awe and horror at this Mediterranean sea that had swallowed up, somewhere out there, an Iberia Airlines Boeing.

The flotilla of boats provided for the funeral service had had to put back into port. The high tide had peaked at a respectful distance from the families and friends of the deceased, but the officiating priest's words were drowned by the squall. Losing his balance, Istvan struggled forward, winded, his new black coat billowing like a sail. He had misunderstood the directions he had been given in Barcelona and had wasted more than an hour looking for this remote part of the coast. He had had to give up the idea of finding a florist's.

THE NET

Holding the flaps of his coat firmly against his legs, he turned around for a moment to look despondently at his car, which gleamed among the hundred or so others parked haphazardly in the desert of pebbles and burnt grass. Exasperated by his lateness and at arriving empty-handed, he had had no hesitation in getting as close as possible and had driven halfway down the slope without thinking about what the shale was doing to his tires. He turned back to face the ceremony. Now he could make out the ropes, the ends held by men dressed in black, which imprisoned the flowers against the rocks.

Natty must be right at the end, near the priests. He elbowed his way through, murmuring "Excuse me." He stood out among the bowed heads, the shoulders bent with grief.

Her blond hair flew around the collar of the navy-blue cape. She kept it fastened and had her arms folded in the attitude of a demure schoolgirl. Istvan had been looking for a tiny figure. Natty looked tall to him. She held herself erect, riveted to the ground between the priests and the flowers, as if the fury of the wind did not affect her. It seemed as if the inaudible Latin words of the small, dark-haired priest in the purple surplice were addressed to her alone, and not to all the families of the other victims who stood in a row a yard behind her.

Istvan kept his eyes on the back of Natty's bare neck. The wind made her hair dance against it. He wanted to stroke the fluffy blond down to let the child know he was there. Now he was a step from Natty, but it was a step he did not dare take. He was paralyzed by the dignity of Màrton's daughter as she stood facing the watery grave. He could see nothing other than the obstinately upright nape of her neck.

* * *

ILIE NASTASE

The youngest of the three priests spoke in turn, in Spanish. His voice rose, high and shrill, piercing the barrier of wind. Istvan understood that the wreaths were going to be thrown into the sea; there was a rustling among the crowd. Istvan held his arms out to Natty, who had not budged, but a gray coat stepped between him and the child. The woman, wearing spectacles and a bun, was holding a little gray felt bag and a navy-blue hat in her left hand. She placed her right hand on Natty's wrist. The girl jumped, turned around, and saw only Istvan, who towered above the interloper. She pushed her out of the way and rushed into the big open arms that swept her off the ground, hid her face in the crook of Istvan's shoulder, and burst into tears. He could feel her small body quivering against him. He stroked her tousled hair. The woman in gray looked at him, dumbfounded.

"Mr. Horwat!" And as he looked at her, she explained: "We flew in from London last night. I am Mrs. Campbell, the mother of one of Natasha's friends at Roedean. The headmistress asked me to take charge of her."

"Roedean?"

"Natasha's school."

The girl gradually calmed down.

"Look," said Istvan.

Men and women were advancing. The howling of the wind drowned the sobs. Nobody claimed the wreath they had brought to fling into the whirlpool, like a flower into the tomb that is about to be sealed. They helped each other offer the flowers to the sea. The confusion and the anonymity made this nightmarish ceremony all the more poignant; once again, Istvan entertained the illusion that the mass ceremony was for Màrton and Jane and for them alone. He did it to maintain the privacy of his grief. That

THE NET

these mountains and these flowers were for them only. He no longer felt ashamed at not bringing some himself.

"Wait!"

They made way for a young man in a black leather jacket and trousers who rushed up to the flowers they were preparing to throw into the sea. Everybody froze. He frantically scanned the inscriptions on the wide ribbons. He was Patrice Martinez, the French number one, winner of the Barcelona Tournament the previous Sunday.

Istvan set Natty back on her feet. She took his hand and stood close to him. He walked a few steps toward the distraught boy rummaging through the wreaths.

"What are you looking for, Patrice?"

"Ah, you're here? I'm looking for two wreaths, the one from the Federation and mine. I've just got here from Ibiza. We nearly turned back because of this bloody wind. Help me! We'll find them."

"Impossible among that bunch. They may already be in the water. Everybody's throwing them in at random. It's better that way. Anyway, look."

As soon as the flowers landed on the crest of the waves, they began to float toward the south, then disappeared, sucked under by the rolling current in this place.

"I may as well leave," said Martinez. "Who's that little girl?"

"Natty, Màrton and Jane's daughter. She's at boarding school in England. Haven't you ever seen her?"

"Màrton had only been my coach for a year," said Martinez, kissing Natty's forehead. "This accident was a terrible shock to me. Fellows like him ought not to die."

"Nobody should die," said Istvan as Natty began to cry again. Istvan was a lost child himself for a few moments as he drew her to him.

"Damned dust," he said rubbing his eyes.
The last wreaths had disappeared into the foam.
"Could you go for a trip in Ibiza, Istvan? In that direction it'll be plain sailing, we'll have the wind in our sails."
"Impossible," replied Istvan. "But we'll see each other soon, don't forget: the Davis Cup in Budapest in two weeks. When I think I was supposed to be playing the doubles with Màrton . . ."
He took Natty and the Englishwoman and walked back to the cars.
"Can I give you a lift somewhere?"
As soon as he opened the car door, Natty slid gently in back without even tipping the front seat forward.
"Well, that is . . . yes please, we came by taxi. We're not putting you out?" Mrs. Campbell sounded grateful.
"Not at all. Tell me where you're going."
"To the British Consulate in Barcelona. The consul's wife is a friend of mine. We're having lunch with her."
"I want to stay with Istvan," said Natty from the back of the car.
"We are going to the consulate, Natasha," said Mrs. Campbell. "We're flying back to London this afternoon."
"Not flying," said Natty, and Istvan winced.
Mrs. Campbell's reply was drowned by the jolting of the car as it lurched down the rocky slope. The woman let out a couple of little cries, then sighed. When they reached the road, she said,
"You need a Land Rover, Mr. Horwat."
She rummaged in her handbag and took out a hairbrush, lipstick, and an oval compact with a mirror in the lid and arranged her hair. She adjusted the strange hat over her bun, which the perplexed Istvan examined out of the corner of his eye. It looked like a cross between a

THE NET

cowboy hat and cloche. He swung the sun shade down on her side, revealing a rectangular mirror.

"You can see yourself better."

Mrs. Campbell thanked him with a thin-lipped smile and began to apply her lipstick, apologizing. She turned around and handed the brush and powder-compact mirror to Natty along with the little navy-blue hat.

"Make an effort, Natasha. If your headmistress could see you! Do you realize, Mr. Horwat, she's always refused to let me braid her hair. My daughter's always looks neat and tidy."

In the mirror, Istvan watched the movements of the brush through the long hair, and the grimaces Natty made as she checked her part in the mirror. She ruffled her bangs a little—apparently it was too straight for her liking.

"Now your hat."

"Oh no. It flattens my hair. Anyway, we're in Spain, not England, aren't we?"

"In Spain especially, women wear hats," said Istvan. Then he caught himself smiling for the first time in what felt like ages. "But not in cars," he added.

"Don't answer back, Natasha. Put on your hat."

"Maybe this isn't the time to insist, Mrs. Campbell?" Istvan asked gently.

Mrs. Campbell's small round eyes blinked under Istvan's scrutiny. She knew he was right, and had the grace to say, "I suppose that's true enough. I was saying it out of habit, wasn't I?" But then, so as not to lose face: "Very well, not in the car. But as soon as we arrive at the consulate . . ."

"I'm not *going* to the consulate," said Natty stubbornly.

"Perhaps it won't be much fun for her," offered Istvan.

"With your permission, Mrs. Campbell, I'll take her out for lunch."

Natty, in an acrobatic posture with her feet on the backseat and her knees on the carpeted floor, slipped her arms around Istvan's neck without saying a word.

"No one ever refuses you anything, do they, Mr. Horwat?"

"Rarely," he replied equably. "What time does your plane leave?"

"Ten past five."

"What airline?"

"I wanted to fly British Airways, but we had to leave London yesterday afternoon, and to make their return flight we would have had to be at the airport by now. It wasn't possible—"

"So it's Iberia."

"Really, I don't see the impropriety of that. I mean, the company isn't being blamed."

"Nobody said it is. We'll be at the airport at a quarter to five. Or we can stop by and pick you up at the hotel if you wish."

"At the airport will be fine. My friend will drive me there. I'm sure you're a punctual man."

Istvan no longer felt the child's hands on his neck. He missed their warmth.

"Natty."

"Leave her alone," whispered Mrs. Campbell, glancing back. "You haven't got any children, have you, Mr. Horwat? One has to learn a few things about them. I wonder whether it might be better if she stayed with me."

Curled up on the backseat, Natty was asleep. Her face looked as if it had been washed by the rain. Istvan clenched the steering wheel. This well-meaning woman's presence was becoming unbearable. Behind her horn-

THE NET

rimmed spectacles, she was watching him with an unbecoming curiosity. As if he were a kidnapper. He opened the glove compartment, took out a pair of dark glasses, put them on, and turned slightly toward Mrs. Campbell.

"Do you know why she's asleep?" he asked. "Because she is reassured. Reassured to know that I'm taking her with me so she won't have to wear her hat and be a credit to her school in front of the consul's wife."

"I don't think she's very hungry," replied Mrs. Campbell evasively. "Still, if you have the patience . . ."

"I am very patient. I have to be in my profession."

5

"Istvan, can I have some more crayfish?"

"They're not crayfish, Natty. Remember what I told you? They're gambas, giant prawns. Wipe your mouth, you've even got cocktail sauce on your nose."

"When I grow up, I'm going to be a clown."

"That's a good idea," said Istvan, trying to attract the attention of the head waiter at Caraccolès, where only the name Horwat had been able to secure a table on such short notice. He managed, by simply frowning, to silence the waiter with a swashbuckling mustache who started talking to him about Màrton's death while Natty had gone to wash her hands. She went off, hopping from one foot to another, neatly avoiding the platters of sea food being carried at the same height as her head. He had only caught glimpses of the child on four or five occasions since she had been at boarding school. Jane had said that she was very tall for her age and Istvan, watching her across the room at a gallop, so long-limbed in her navy-blue dress, remembered the Adidas advertisement she had

THE NET

posed for at the age of two, with a downsized tennis racket made especially for her.

"It's not a toy," Màrton had said proudly then. "She knows how to use it."

"You're not eating anything, Istvan! At least finish your sole!"

He was no longer surprised at the behavior of the child who had gone from tears to sleep and was now dissecting the gambas of her second course as if the tragedy had been a bad dream. So, he was learning. Maybe he was a quicker study than Mrs. Campbell had given him credit for being.

Her clear eyes looked up at Istvan, seeking a compliment.

"You're behaving very well," he said. "Congratulations to your school." That made her laugh.

"Yes, but the food's awful at Roedean. So when I go to a restaurant, I make up for it. Mind you, I hardly ever *go* to one . . ."

She let the gamba fall onto her plate and hid her face in her napkin. Quivering with sobs, she kicked under the table, her whole body rebelling. Istvan saw the image she had just evoked, suddenly in the middle of the lull. Who took Natty to restaurants, other than Màrton and Jane when they visited her at Roedean, between planes? Màrton would be seated here, opposite his daughter, where Istvan sat now. What would he have talked to her about? His last tournament, the coming holidays, his friend who bred ponies in Ireland and who had given Natty a foal named Crazy that she would be able to ride the following summer? She would laugh, and then begin to sound wistful because the holidays were still such a long way off.

Màrton would know what to say. He would tell her that she had to be patient to deserve such a lovely pony. And if he could see her now, her head buried in her napkin, what would he do?

Istvan, his confidence shattered, poured himself a glass of Bordeaux—"your diet wine," Màrton used to say. Natty's head emerged from the napkin. Without looking up, she went back to her prawn and, without peeling it, bit into the shell.

"Do you remember one day in Paris," Istvan ventured, "when you were very little? You told me you liked strawberry tartlets."

"I don't remember. But I'd like a strawberry tart. Listen, Istvan, do you know what I really want? Not to take the plane. Yesterday in London, when we took off, I was frightened—I was *shaking*—and the stewardess gave me a pink pill."

"You mustn't be afraid, Natty. We'll have to work on that. You've got to take planes for the rest of your life."

"But I am afraid. Especially . . ." Her voice trailed off.

"We've got another two hours ahead of us."

"That's not the point. I don't want to go back at all."

"What about school?"

"I can't help the way I feel about that place."

"You see . . ."

But Istvan suddenly saw. He understood what was going through her mind. He had known too many women to be mistaken. Good lord, did they start this young? Yes, a woman would go about it in the same way. She wanted to stay with him as long as she could. She wanted him to drive her back to Roedean. She was waiting for the decision to come from him. So she smoothed her napkin. She counted the strawberries on her tart. She pulled her socks up to her knees. Then she put her elbows on the table and

THE NET

rested her chin on her clasped hands, confident in the power of her knowing young eyes.

"Well, I'm going to have some ice cream, since we've got plenty of time," said Istvan.

He breathed more freely. The vision of the plane taking off from the airport from which Màrton had flown to his death seemed inconceivable at that moment. He realized that deep down, he knew he could not let Natty go like that. He glanced down at his watch, then looked at it again incredulously. Time flew by too quickly. And Natty's eyes were offering him the answer she wanted to hear. Feeling light and free, he just wished she would come out and say what she wanted. Blurt it out. Isn't that what children were supposed to do?

"Plenty of time?" she said ingenuously. "We haven't got long."

As if she didn't know that the decision was already made. Istvan decided not to give in.

He calmly finished his ice cream. Finally, she murmured something.

"What did you say, Natty?"

"With a car like yours, we'll get there almost as fast as by plane," she said, humble in her victory.

6

The net closed around the choking, tortured man. Istvan once more had fallen into the trap in deep ocean water. But the shrieking of the ocean elements suddenly ceased. In the unexpected calm, the din of the cataracts was no more than a lapping—splashes from dives, children laughing and shrieking. Istvan recovered his breath and opened his eyes. He was lying on the bed, fully dressed. A bird appeared out of the low sky and tapped on the bay window with its beak. The video recorder clock showed eleven. I should never have lain down after driving all night, he thought. Sleeping for an hour or two never does me any good.

In the bathroom, the unusual racket sounded like a school playground. Istvan pushed open the black laquered door to find Natty diving again and again into the round bathtub to retrieve a heavy gold bangle that Livia Fabiani patiently kept throwing in the water for her.

"What are you doing here?"

"I called you at around ten," replied Livia. "Thieu told

me you were stopping off on your way to England, and that you had a female guest. I wanted to see her."

Natty's gaze followed the bangle as it sank to the bottom of the bathtub.

"Watch me, Istvan!"

She had no swimsuit on, just her panties. Natty glided across the surface of the water, arched her hips as soon as she touched the bottom, and emerged triumphantly a moment later. The bracelet glistened in her hand. She laughed, carried away by the game, but Istvan knew from the previous day that a moment of despair could just as easily follow this laughter and exhilaration.

"She's a born sportswoman," said Livia.

"I'm not as beautiful as you," said Natty.

"That's enough," grumbled Istvan.

But it was true that Livia, his latest discovery, was striking. A blond Corsican, with dark skin and black eyes, she had moments when she was unbearably bad-tempered yet managed to wangle forgiveness with a smile or a gesture. Istvan resented his weakness, which this young woman brought out in him. In fact, she hadn't even made a pass at him. For once he was the one who had taken the first step, six months ago, during the French literary television program "Apostrophes." The show's host, Bernard Pivot, had just finished a segment on one of the current bestsellers, the memoirs of Larry Wilson, the number-one tennis player of the sixties until the rapid rise of Istvan Horwat. Istvan had been about to switch off the television when Livia Fabiani appeared on the screen, talking about the second volume of *Game, Set, and Death,* the romantic adventures of a tennis hero. Already it was planned to be a TV miniseries. The next day, Istvan wrote to her in care of her publisher, enclosing an invitation to Roland-Garros.

From then on, she had taken the initiative. He found himself spending the weekend in an old house that Livia had inherited from an aunt, a real little museum of the Napoleonic era. You could not open a wardrobe without coming across genuine dresses that had belonged to the Empress Eugénie, who had stayed there on several occasions. Scattered around the house, busts of Napoleon the First and Napoleon the Second stood guard. This was where Livia withdrew to write for six months of the year. Until Livia, Istvan had never been to Corsica, had not known the unique flowers and smells of the Corsican scrubland in the spring.

Since their first weekend there, Livia had had a tendency to think Istvan belonged to her. Carried away by the success of her book and by her not inconsiderable Corsican pride, she felt herself to be his equal. Clearly, she expected to last longer than his other women. In Paris, sometimes, she dropped in on him without warning, making the journey from the eighteenth-century mansion in the Rue Jacob where she lived in a converted loft to what she called "the den of the ladies of the night" in record time.

"Dry yourself and get dressed, Natty. I want to take a shower. Have you had breakfast?"

"Ages ago. Thieu went out and bought me croissants. He's so nice. He put me in the blue room. He wanted me to lie in a little longer but I wasn't sleepy. I'm enjoying myself. It's a pity your swimming pool's so small."

Livia wrapped her in a bath sheet.

"She's luckier than I am with your Thieu. He almost wouldn't let me in. Naturally, I insisted when I heard that. So . . . I'll dry Natty's hair and I'll wait for you downstairs. The three of us could go out to a restaurant?"

"We've still got quite a long way to go," said Istvan.

THE NET

"You're not going back on the road now?"

"Oh no, I've had enough of sitting in the car," said Natty. "Couldn't we leave tomorrow?"

"I'll phone and find out the times of the ferries from Dieppe," suggested Livia.

"Tomorrow morning then, as early as possible. You can tell Thieu there'll be three of us for lunch."

Natty was sulking. Istvan had refused to let her sit in the front seat. How long was she going to stay like that, her face impassive, acting the part of a stranger, a hostile captive? He could see her in the mirror, rigid and remote because she had not got her own way, and because she wasn't next to him. Istvan, his nerves on edge, had almost lost his self-control in the traffic jam in the Saint-Cloud tunnel.

The traffic was flowing now. Istvan recalled the indoor courts at Roland-Garros the previous afternoon . . .

Livia had offered to take Natty to the zoological gardens, an idea that had hardly filled her with enthusiasm.

"Why don't we go and play tennis?" Natty had countered.

"I'm not very good," replied the author of *Game, Set, and Death*.

"I want to play with Istvan."

Natty was already rushing to her room to fetch the little suitcase that Istvan had taken from Mrs. Campbell at Barcelona airport. She came running back into the dining room, and flung the case onto the table, knocking over two crystal glasses. She took out three pairs of panties, a pair of Mickey Mouse pajamas, then two sweaters, finally unearthing a sky-blue track suit and brandishing it with a flourish.

"I take it everywhere with me. That'll do to play tennis in."

"You could hit some shots against the wall," said Istvan.

"What about you?" asked Livia.

"I'll find a partner at Roland-Garros."

"I'll keep score . . ."

In the car, Natty was very excited. Then suddenly she moaned: "I haven't got a racket."

"We'll find something."

Livia, left behind, had walked slowly, watching them as they ran side by side toward Roland-Garros five hundred yards away.

"Go ahead," she called after them. "I'll join you! I hadn't planned a sporty afternoon!"

Livia thought the pair had an unusual grace, and she noticed that their bodies were not unalike. They both had very long legs. They could have been related. She was sorry she didn't feel like running with them, they looked so free.

Mabrouk, the head of the maintenance crew at Roland-Garros and the clay-court specialist who had followed the fortunes of the players for thirty years, was delighted to do Istvan a favor. Istvan always slipped him a few francs to thank him for his kindness, while others who had it made never gave him a sou in tips. Mabrouk had some small rackets that had been given to him for his children. He chose the best for Natty. It wasn't very accurate, but Mabrouk didn't think that would matter.

Livia played the part of mother well. While Istvan, who normally never went training without booking a partner,

THE NET

set off in search of one, she took Natty over to a practice wall.

"Watch me," said the child.

She began to demonstrate her know-how, and Livia, unaccustomed to children's prattle, told herself that she was going to need a lot of patience. But Natty charmed her and was doing a surprisingly good job of controlling the ball.

Istvan spotted Yannick Noah, the eighteen-year-old French hope, chatting with a young woman. Noah did not appear to have a partner, so Istvan signaled discreetly, and the young man came over.

"I was about to leave," he said. "Jean-Paul Loth just phoned. He's stuck in Rome—the air traffic controllers are on strike."

"I dropped in on the off-chance," said Istvan. "I just got back from Barcelona."

"I know," replied Noah. "I saw the Lyon Tournament on television. They talked of nothing else but your scratch. Everybody was sympathetic, you know . . ."

"Will you come and hit a few volleys?"

For half an hour they exchanged very long shots from the back of the court, with neither man trying to make the other run, or tire himself either. Then, gradually, as their muscles warmed up, their game took on an increasing precision. Istvan thought back fifteen years, when he had been the same age as Noah. He had no doubt that the young Frenchman would go right to the top of world tennis. The rhythm of the forehands and backhands accelerated. After a series of smashes and services, they decided to play a one-set match.

Istvan had forgotten all about Natty when he spotted

her in a crowd of a dozen people. He had managed to keep up with Noah's very fast and confident game, and concluded their friendly match 6–4 with a beautiful crosscourt backhand volley.

Livia was standing close to the little girl. He waved to let them know he was coming over to join them. Noah thanked the great Horwat with a smile and the latter spontaneously offered to meet him at the same place the following Monday.

"And who is this future champion?" he asked, pointing to Natty, who was still holding her scale-model tennis racket.

"Natty, Màrton's daughter."

The young Frenchman was no longer smiling. He nodded, almost a little bow. "See you Monday," he said, his eyes suddenly sad.

He shook Istvan's hand again, turned on his heel, and walked away.

Natty ran over to Istvan clamoring, "I want to play too."

"She certainly deserves to," said Livia. "She's been waiting for this moment for two hours!"

"I'm sorry," replied Istvan, "I didn't notice the time. What have you been doing?"

"She was fed up with practicing against the wall. I took her to the bar. She told me her life story."

"I see," said Istvan. "Come on, let's get on with it!"

Istvan stood opposite Natty, pretending to look very earnest. He winked at Livia. He expected a rather boring fifteen minutes ... and yet he was soon caught up in the game. He knew that Natty had played a little with her parents, but at ten years old, she couldn't have played very seriously. He saw at once that she was very gifted.

THE NET

He marveled at her judgment and her touch. She never stopped moving. He, who owed his greatest successes to his legwork, saw that she instinctively had that essential quality, too. He concentrated on not making her run, returning the ball gently, and noted the exceptional sureness with which she positioned her body in relation to the ball. She had no technique. She had never really learned, or tried to. But she had the qualities to become a first-class player, perhaps. If she had the heart for it.

He glanced at Livia, who raised her hand giving him a thumbs-up sign. She had seen the same thing.

Natty hit all the shots from the center of her racket, never off the wood. Her vision of the game was as good as her concentration. With the right coaching, thought Istvan, she could go a long way. Why didn't Màrton do anything about it? But he felt ashamed for criticizing his dead friend. He knew that great champions rarely make their children play. Besides, Màrton had not seen much of Natty since she had gone off to boarding school. Istvan felt very close to her at that moment with her roughly strung miniature racket. He smiled at her.

But she had eyes only for the ball.

7

The windscreen wipers, on maximum speed, flung veils of muddy water to either side of the car. The driving rain had forced the workmen to abandon the stretch of highway under construction, and traffic was reduced to a single lane. Istvan turned up the heater.

"I don't want to take you back with a cold!"

"I'm never sick. When I was little, I had all the usual children's illnesses. Now I can relax. Istvan, are you very fond of Livia?"

"What? Yes."

"Is she your fiancée?"

"No."

"Have you got a lot of friends like her?"

"A few."

"I've only got one friend, Anne Campbell. Daddy only had one friend too, and that was Mommy."

Istvan feared the recurring cycle of tears and despair, but once again, Natty took him by surprise. Leaning on the back of the front seat, she smiled dreamily, as if remembering times she had spent with her parents in the

THE NET

days when they took her everywhere with them, before they decided to send her to boarding school so that her education would not suffer from what Màrton used to call "a performer's life."

Istvan was thinking he should call the Plaza. It was the best time to catch Fenwick, who must have been wondering what was happening. But he did not want to spoil the magic of that moment. The warmth of the car forging through the rain insulated them from the drenched countryside and from the road strung with red taillights.

"It'd be nice if you married Livia," said Natty suddenly. "You've got a big house."

"But Natty, Livia's got her own house and her work . . ."

"So you'll never have any children?"

"Are all young girls as nosy as you?"

"Am I tiring you?"

"No, you amuse me."

He turned over the rock music cassette. Natty would never understand if he told her that the lifestyle she was dreaming of would never be his. He was resistant to any long-term relationship and was always ambivalent about waking up in the morning with a woman in his bed, propped up on the pillows with a tray of croissants on her knee.

"The main difference between you and me," he used to say to Màrton, "is that I find my strength in solitude."

"Relative solitude," Màrton would reply ironically.

Natty's light, high-pitched voice broke into his thoughts.

"What are you singing?"

"The story of Cinderella in the pumpkin-turned-into-a-carriage by the good fairy. Your car's the carriage, with the rain pouring down the windows . . . Look, anyone would think it was dark outside. Is it much farther to the boat?"

"Not far."

"I wish I could have stayed with you in Paris for a few days."

"Yes, but what about school!"

"Will you come and get me for vacation?"

"That depends on my own vacation. In fact, I almost never have any."

"Daddy used to say, 'Istvan's the best.' So you can do whatever you want, can't you?"

"That's what you think."

Once again he felt uneasy, as if he could not find the reply the child expected from him. He guessed, in his confusion, what he ought to say: "Yes, we're in a pumpkin-carriage, in a spaceship, and then you'll be back at school, with your friend Anne, you'll spend weekends with the Campbells and order will be restored."

But what order? That of Istvan, whom Countess Balanska called "Istvan the Terrible," a bad pun referring to his fierceness and intransigence? She explained it once with a commentary: "I've met a few egocentric men in my time, but you are the czar of selfishness."

Then, that little creature, the passenger in the back who had begun to sing again, what planet had she hatched out on, what UFO had she stepped out of?

The stormy English Channel did not seem to remind Natty of the service in Barcelona. Istvan told himself he was a fool to have been apprehensive about it. He drove the car up the ramp of Townsend Ferries.

On the way over, she swayed to the rhythm of the pitching ship, and laughed because an elderly lady lost her scarf over the side.

THE NET

"Once upon a time you weren't like that," said Istvan. "She's seasick. Once upon a time you'd have said: 'Oh, poor thing!'"

"I've aged."

Istvan did not like that word in the first place. He didn't know whether to laugh or cry, hearing it—apparently without irony—from the lips of a little girl.

Perhaps he really didn't know how to handle her. Maybe children weren't for him.

And it saddened him to hear Natty talk as if her childhood were already over.

Istvan did not like driving on the left, and had never been behind the wheel in such a thick pea-soup fog. Despite the fog lights, he could barely see a thing. He had the unpleasant feeling of being asked to navigate by radar, but without the radar. As he drove along the coast road, he recalled the headland in Barcelona, and the storm. He had no wish whatever to drive off the edge of the road and make the queasy leap into the deep black waters that had tormented him enough already. With his eyes fixed on the road, he couldn't see Natty, and he didn't hear her, either. He felt as though they were progressing a foot at a time. These last three days seemed as if they had taken place outside his own life, in parentheses.

As he approached Roedean—according to his calculations, since no signpost was visible—the child's silence became a reproach. He counted the minutes, cursing the English roads, the English fog, and the English in general.

From the window of the headmistress's office, Istvan watched Natty recede in the direction of some buildings whose massive shape he could make out only indistinctly. Earlier, before taking Anne Campbell's hand, she had accepted his kiss on her forehead and then walked off with her friend as if Istvan were already far away. He could hardly see her now as she made her way through the fog, leaning toward Anne to whom no doubt she was telling everything. She gave a final wave in the direction of the window behind which she knew Istvan was sitting. That was all. Still, Istvan breathed more freely. He was going back to his usual world. Being with the child had disrupted his rhythm and had broken the chain of reassuring habit. Already the feeling of strangeness that had made him feel so ill at ease was dissipating.

"Mr. Horwat, I must tell you first of all that I am one of your admirers. I was at your last match at Wimbledon. Absolutely outstanding . . ."

The headmistress broke off for a moment out of respect, then added:

"Màrton Kotany's death is a great loss to the tennis world."

"It's a great loss to Natty," said Istvan.

"Of course, of course . . . As you must have guessed, I asked you to come here to talk about Natty. Did you know that this little American girl has no relatives left in the States? Her mother was an orphan herself. There are some destinies—"

"I didn't know. Màrton never told me."

"It's all in her file. Her only surviving relatives are her paternal grandparents in Hungary."

"In Bablona. I know them. Màrton and I were childhood friends."

He allowed his gaze to wander over the paneling that reflected the golden glow from the lightshades onto the bookshelves and the leather armchairs. He conjured up the village school he had attended when he was Natty's age. A very simple school, the one Màrton had attended,

THE NET

too. The headmistress's voice seemed far away as she went on in her Oxford English.

"In short, Mr. Horwat, this unfortunate event has put us in an extremely embarrassing situation."

"A question of money?"

"The fees for the summer term haven't been paid, Mr. Horwat. And after that . . ."

"I don't know anything about Màrton's financial affairs. You'll . . . we'll have to see what Natty's inheritance amounts to. Meanwhile, how much did he owe you?"

"He was twelve hundred pounds in arrears."

"I've only got credit cards. But I can transfer that sum to you tomorrow."

"There's no hurry, Mr. Horwat. I'm waiting for instructions from the family for the future . . ."

"In ten days I'll be in Budapest, playing the Davis Cup. I'll go and see her grandparents. I'll talk to them. Don't worry. Natty isn't alone in the world."

8

At the Budapest Hilton, reserved for distinguished visitors and this October full for the Davis Cup, the most alert of the uniformed porters was puzzled. He had just overheard the order that the Hungarian idol, who was due to face the French number-one player the following day, had given to the chauffeur of the Ziss put at his disposal by the Hungarian Federation:

"To the bus station."

"Where do you want to go?"

"To Bablona."

To the porter, choosing to go by bus rather than in the official limousine was one of those mysterious Western caprices that showed that comrade Horwat, the international star, was irredeemably eccentric.

As he often did when he played in Eastern Europe, Istvan had decided not to travel inside the country by car. The Mercedes 450 would bespeak a lifestyle foreign to his compatriots, and suspicious to the authorities constituted by the state to protect them. Creating envy and arousing

THE NET

jealousies had unforeseeable, potentially dangerous consequences. And so he had resigned himself to this decision while still in his seat on the Malev plane from Paris to Budapest, watching the slightly thick ankles and tempting thighs of the hostess with blond braids—charms that fell short of making him forget the smell of leather and the privacy of his luxurious coupe.

There was only one seat left on the bus, all the way at the back. Istvan settled in without being particularly surprised at his luck; he had already noticed that there was always, everywhere, a seat for him. He waved at the chauffeur of the Ziss he had just left, who seemed as puzzled as the hotel porter had been. What was the great Horwat doing in that dilapidated old diesel bus, surrounded by peasants in their Sunday best who had come to the town and were on their way home with their purchases?

Seeing them pile their packages onto the already-overladen roof, Istvan relived scenes from his childhood. In vain he fought nostalgia; he pictured himself as a child, braving the capital for the first time. He had been so afraid of getting lost that he clung to the trousers of his father, a colossal Magyar with a peasant mustache and a mane of black hair. No doubt he had looked something like the little boy who was falling asleep in the lap of the elderly lady on his right as the bus started out. Part of the reason he had given up his official car was so he could retrieve this kind of image.

Every time he returned to his native land—always for professional reasons because he had no family left—he was plunged into the past, and his memory violently awakened. Accustomed to money and luxury, he re-

ILIE NASTASE

spected the utter simplicity, poverty, and harshness of his parents' lives—the life that would have been his had it not been for tennis.

Above the din of the swaying bus with its worn-out shock absorbers, he listened to his native language. He amused himself by closing his eyes, letting himself be lulled by those familiar inflections, then opened them to find himself in the middle of a film set, the extras these men in soft, wide-brimmed hats with dark, double-breasted suits buttoned over white shirts. They were tieless. The black kerchiefs emphasized the solemnity of the women. A multicolored scarf brightened up the picture; it framed the cheeks of a young girl who had already turned round several times to stare at Istvan. The fourth time, he smiled at her. She blushed. To disguise her embarrassment, she rubbed her plump hand over the misted-up window.

The plain was covered with snow. The inky shapes of trees stood out in the black-and-white landscape revealed by the girl's hand as she set about wiping the whole window. In the summer, the narrow rutted road cut across the puszta, the vast, deep green prairie. Now it gave way to a white desert that would shift restlessly across it for many long months.

He alighted beside a ditch bordered by snowdrifts. He raised his hand to wave at the girl, who dared to flash him a shy smile from behind the glass that had already misted up again. When the driver accelerated, a gray cloud from the faulty exhaust pipe tarnished the virgin snow. Istvan set off on foot under the leaden sky toward the potbellied buildings whose yellow and white tones blended with the snow. Istvan could not imagine any other country that could offer this gradation of pastel shades, this baroque

THE NET

architecture, comprising both nobility and paunchy elegance, displaying its incongruous charms in the middle of the countryside. Istvan could feel the biting chill and turned down the earflaps on his chapka. In bygone days, he had not been afraid of the cold. Today, he was careful, and he protected himself. He cautiously breathed the frozen air. He slackened his pace to take in the beauty of this place, which seemed unchanging.

On the stud farms of Bablona are bred the finest Hungarian stallions, several times winners of the world driving championships at Aachen, Germany. It was a universe of rites and of discipline. Istvan contemplated the stallions at work on the paths. On the snow broken by clumps of black trees, dotted about like markers, the silhouettes of the one-, two-, and four-horse teams went past.

A few hundred yards away, Istvan spotted a huge platform on wheels that looked straight out of a western. He stopped to get a better look at it. It was a long time since he had seen an eight-horse team. The eight horses all had the same gray coat. Their trotting was perfectly synchronized in a symphony of black: the varnished black of the carriages, the black-lacquered wheels, the harnesses with black blinkers emblazoned with the stud farm's initials, shoes dipped in linseed oil shining darkly in the snow. But the studded shoes collected too much snow underneath. A heel formed and hindered their movements. Istvan suddenly felt ill at ease, as if he, too, were weighed down by leaden soles. He took several deep breaths of frosty air to dispel the phantom sense of oppression.

He watched the grooms moving, with the precision of ballet masters, in their gray-green uniforms, black rubber boots, jodhpurs, sleeveless fur-lined jackets over the coats, and riding hats—a legacy from the Austrian army of bygone days.

At a distance from the tracks left by the teams, he recognized Sandor Kotany, small, brittle, with a gray mustache barring the way to his gaunt face. Màrton's father did not appear to have seen the spectator standing in the snow about thirty yards away from the circle, around which he was leading a gray stallion. A ring of dung prevented the horse from slipping. Sandor, the handle of the lunging whip in his gloved hand, was dangling it toward the ground, making the stallion trot in a circle in front of him. Istvan was loath to distract him, but finally coughed loudly to signal his presence. The horse, on edge from the cold, shied suddenly.

Màrton's father looked up and shaded his eyes with his hand, for Istvan was standing with his back to the light in the pale sun reflected by the snow.

"Horwat Istvan! I didn't hear your car . . ."

"I came by bus. It dropped me by the road."

"By bus! Would you believe it! Erzebet is watching out for a big car coming along the road. Come!"

9

While Sandor masked his grief behind a fatalistic facade, Erzebet cursed the demons who had killed her son. The light came into the small, two-roomed dwelling through bull's-eye windows. Like the other grooms' homes, it was a conversion over the stables. There was only a thin planked floor separating them. That way they received the benefit of the warmth from the animals, and a little wood stove was sufficient to boost the heat.

Istvan's arrival had opened recent wounds, and Erzebet's invective rang out in the narrow room. Sandor's soothing words were powerless to calm her.

"Leave her," said Istvan. "It does her good, do you understand?"

He poured the tokay into the crystal liqueur glasses. Sandor pointed out that it was Màrton who had brought the set back from Prague for them, along with the octagonal carafe. He placed a glass in Erzebet's hand. She stopped her lamentation long enough to drink to their guest's health.

"I love tokay," said Istvan, "but I'm playing tomorrow."

"I know," replied Sandor, "and you should have been playing the doubles with Màrton."

And this time it was Màrton's father who broke down, and Erzebet took over, relieved, perhaps, at an opportunity to be the braver.

"Tell us about Natasha . . ."

"She's not doing too badly. I've heard from her school. She seems to be working normally."

"They didn't bother to write to us," said Sandor. "Perhaps they think we're illiterate."

Istvan recognized the pride of Sandor's special class—a poor caste composed of the grooms of the Hungarian stud farms who were ennobled by their knowledge of the horses they cared for and trained.

"Not at all," said Istvan. "The headmistress knew I was coming to see you, to discuss Natty's future."

"Meanwhile, let's eat," said Sandor. "Erzebet has prepared her special paprika csirke with lecso."

Istvan tried to tuck his long legs under the dining-room table as he was served steaming pieces of chicken with paprika, and tomatoes stewed with sweet peppers. His head almost touched the ceiling. He was aware that he was temporarily sitting in their son's place; Màrton did not have any sisters or brothers.

"So I can only offer you the water jug, Horwat Istvan?"

"I'm afraid so."

A sudden tenderness made him feel close to this small, brittle man who was pouring water into his glass with all the affection of a wine waiter giving him a famous vintage to taste.

"How lucky you are to have such a good cook for a wife, Mr. Kotany!"

THE NET

Erzebet bowed her head as was fitting, but all three knew that this exchange of hopeful little courtesies was meaningless. He was here to talk about Natty. They seemed to have foreseen what Istvan was going to say, yet he himself was not sure. Even in the bus, he had not had a very clear idea of the outcome of their discussion.

When he telephoned Sandor Kotany a week earlier, he had simply said that he would make the most of the Davis Cup tournament in Hungary to bring him news of Natty. He had felt vaguely then that his life was about to take an unexpected turn. And what he had refused to spell out clearly to himself was now staring him in the face, blindingly obvious. From the peasants in the bus to the linoleum of the two small rooms, from the snow-covered plain to the baroque architecture of the yellow-and-white stud farm—it was clear his childhood universe could not possibly suit Natty, a little American girl.

"Natasha could live here," said Erzebet, as if in rebuttal. "We'll manage to get a closet to make a room for her . . ." Her voice trailed off uncertainly into the silence.

"She's already been here at the stud farm twice," said Sandor. "When she was two, and when she was six. The second time, I took her trotting. She seemed to be very fond of horses, like all children. But of course . . ."

"Of course"—the loyal Sandor had uttered the word. Istvan could not change his mind now. What was obvious was that there was nothing for Natty there, outside of school vacations.

"Màrton chose to live in the West," he said finally, "that's where he and Jane raised Natty."

As he spoke these words, he felt giddy. He had come to Bablona with the simple thought of discussing Natty's future with the Kotanys, to help them without treading on their dignity. At no point had he imagined that he would suddenly be born to fatherhood.

From then on he felt carried along by an inescapable logic. He soon stopped asking himself if the decision to take Natty into his care made him happy or not. He almost snapped at Erzebet, who repeated that it would be a heavy responsibility and asked him if he realized just how heavy—after all, he had never married. Well, he'd be a single father, that wasn't so uncommon; there was no other solution at the moment.

Sandor begged him to think carefully about it. "At her age, she is still young enough to adapt to our way of life, but it'll be harder later, if things don't work out with you."

"It's already too late!"

With these words, uttered with a kind of fury, Istvan rose to press his face to the bull's-eye window through which he looked out over the white waste. The horse teams were invisible. The grooms must have been at lunch. He pictured the window in the headmistress's study at Roedean, Natty's figure disappearing into the fog. He did not turn around immediately, because he did not want Sandor and Erzebet to see his eyes full of tears. Near the black trees, a few hundred yards from the stud farm, the tracks made by one of the teams were in the rough shape of a question mark, a half-obliterated figure eight.

"Màrton would have done the same for me," he finally said. "I'll take care of her. I'll bring Natty back to see you. I'll take care of everything."

10

Enzo Medioli had caught a cold six days earlier, the minute he arrived in Budapest. The umpire of this Davis Cup tournament was not particularly impressed with the Hungarian sports complex built on Margarethe Island in the middle of the Danube, despite his good will and his indifference to political systems. Moreover, this southern Italian, transplanted to Milan, could not stand the cold. Snow before the fifteenth of October really was unthinkable. Yet he had to see something of the place other than his hotel and the indoor courts. His sheepskin parka had not been much protection. He was coughing. He knew he presented a miserable picture of a physical education teacher, of an umpire who had qualified with the International Federation, who had managed, at the age of forty-five, to reach the rank of chief officiator for this Davis Cup match.

This team competition, the only one of its kind in international tennis, should have delighted Medioli, a tennis enthusiast who hated stardom and money. He did like the fact that in the Davis Cup, the names of the countries were announced rather than the names of the players. He was also delighted to appear in Budapest as the supreme being, with his little crowd of Hungarian line judges. He chose them because he liked the look of them, trying hard to believe in their impartiality. He also rather liked being treated as a VIP, staying in the Hilton like the champions, and being driven to Margarethe Island in a black limousine whose size reflected his temporary status. It made a pleasant change from his three-room apartment in a Milan suburb, and the secondary school where his pupils preferred cigarettes to gymnastics.

With meticulous care, he had checked the quality of the courts, the lighting, and the composition of the teams. He proceeded to draw lots for the singles matches. He answered the journalists' questions amiably, without committing himself. But to this man who loathed illness and the medicines that went with it, this cold, which he fought with the energy of despair, felt like a blow from fate.

As for the Hungarian spectators, their attitude disconcerted him. Anyone would think they were in a football stadium. It was the first time he had umpired in an Eastern European country. He had been warned; he had been expecting passionate reactions. But not such a display of chauvinism. At the first singles match on Friday, he had been deafened by whistles and shouts supposed to encourage the children of the nation, Istvan Horwat and Balazf Taroczy, who were playing against the French. When Horwat beat the French number one, Patrice Martinez, the cries of "Istvan! Istvan!" transmitted nothing but unconditional love. But when Patrick Proisy had the unfortunate idea of winning against Taroczy, umpire Medioli felt the crowd's despair so keenly that he buried his red nose in one of several handkerchiefs that cluttered

THE NET

his pockets. Throughout the match, he felt ill at ease up in his chair. The Frenchman's best shots had been greeted with stony silence. When Proisy had served a double fault in the fourth set, it had been applauded with insulting irony. The spectators remained rowdy after the score of that first day, Hungary 1, France 1.

On the second day, Enzo Medioli, clad in his parka and his customary dignity, could not help predicting, already, like the enthusiastic spectators, Horwat and Taroczy winning the doubles against Martinez and Proisy. He thought his final hour had come when the Frenchmen won, after a fierce fifth set. The fury of the crowd was at a fever pitch. In the evening, at the hotel, he waited an hour and a half for the escalope milanese he had ordered to be brought to his room, sadly contemplating the nose drops, pills, and lozenges prescribed by Doctor Szàbo, the doctor of the Hungarian Federation. Luckily he had been able to get through to his wife and three children on the telephone. They were football, not tennis, enthusiasts. It was cold in Lombardy, but it was not snowing, at least not on the plain. As he hung up, Enzo Medioli felt unexpectedly alone. The line judges had all gone home. The players, the night before combat, had withdrawn to their rooms, and in any case his duty forbade him to speak to them. There was nothing for him to do but await the following day, Sunday, to see what Hungary would do. So far, they were losing to France by two matches to one. He had difficulty getting to sleep. He lay there counting rallies. At the two hundred and third shot, he fell asleep.

Hungary's morale rose in the third singles when Taroczy beat Martinez in three sets. Medioli noticed that the French number one was not in top form. He remembered the rumors he had heard with half an ear, for he was a

ILIE NASTASE

modest man who shied away from the gossip surrounding the stars. Some people were saying that Patrice Martinez devoted too much time to women, and too little to training, perhaps because he was a victim of the star system that had gained dominance in the seventies.

Being satisfied with little, Enzo Medioli, like all umpires, agreed to be paid virtually nothing, out of his love for tennis. As far as he was concerned, that was all right. This post, as sporadic as it was honorary, raised him above his modest post of physical education teacher. Sometimes he thought of the fortune made by his countryman, Nicola Pietrangeli, a genuine ex-champion from the time when tennis had not yet become an industry. Roland-Garros champion in 1959 and 1960, Pietrangeli had played in the Davis Cup finals twice. Medioli, on the other hand, was considered one of the top umpires in the world. Was it possible that on seeing Istvan Horwat he did not think about the fabulous amounts the young man earned? He who had been one of the best ten players in the world, on whom every day bigger amounts of dollars are heaped. Was he able to consider these millionaire champions with equanimity?

France 2, Hungary 2. The fifth, decisive match was underway. Medioli watched Istvan Horwat, who should easily beat Patrick Proisy. Medioli had followed the Hungarian since his beginnings, when he won the Roland-Garros championship as a junior at eighteen. He considered Horwat the last tennis virtuoso. The Italian complained that the new champions had a violent, fairly unimaginative game. Proisy, for example, was not a very good player. He had never worried the great players of Horwat's caliber—except that he was only twenty-four, as opposed to the Hungarian's thirty-two. He ought to beat Proisy without

THE NET

any effort, thought the umpire, 6–2, 6–2, 6–3, or something like that. And yet he's losing the first set. He's trailing. He ought to take this match more seriously. He isn't concentrating. But all his exceptional qualities are there: his very supple, powerful service, with that scissor jump that gives an extraordinary extension to his movements. The forehands and backhands, executed with a unique grip, that he doesn't change, making a success of even the dullest shots, slicing or lifting with a double spin. And all that, despite the orthodox grip, solely from the forearm and the wrist. It was Pietrangeli who said that Horwat was one of the first to play in that very original way. His shots have never been very powerful but they take the opponent by surprise, they are well placed in a way that few players are able to duplicate.

But why doesn't he make the most of it? He could easily take Proisy unawares. He's not taking any risks, that one. He's staying at the back of the court. Horwat hasn't got a chance to place his famous smash. As usual, the Frenchman's game was regular, precise, calm, intelligent—everything you could wish for but not normally a threat to Horwat. The Hungarian could only be beaten by a very powerful player: Stan Smith, Newcombe . . . So what was going on? There had already been the infamous scratch in Lyon, two weeks earlier. What was happening to Istvan Horwat's game?

"Two sets all!" Medioli would never have believed it. That Horwat lost the first one, through negligence, as if this business had nothing to do with him, was fair enough. But then he got a grip on himself in the second and third. Yet now he's stupidly lost the fourth. Time is working against him. But perhaps I've never really understood his tactics, Medioli thought. Proisy looks tired. Was Horwat laughing at him, exhausting him with drop-shots

ILIE NASTASE

and lobs? It's as though he's taken the wind out his sails. There you are. The great Hungarian is winning 5–2 in the fifth set! He's only one game away from qualifying his country for the next round.

In the fourth game, after a lob by Proisy who was expecting a violent smash, Horwat sent a gentle ball across the court that was impossible to retrieve. This clinched the game and set the Hungarian crowd laughing and shouting, "Istvan! Istvan!" In this fifth game, in a lightning change of tactics, he had adopted a classic, attacking style, the first shot well assured, a powerful serve, very long backhands. He went up to the net. Proisy arrived a little later than the ball on the volley. Horwat was leading 15–0. He served to the left.

Then came a crosscourt serve, still to Proisy's backhand. Medioli could sense the Frenchman trying to relax. He could hardly touch the ball. "Thirty–love to Hungary."

It passed through Medioli's mind that Horwat was going to make the sponsors improve their contracts with him. He'll be able to buy himself a new car. They say he can never find one that is beautiful enough. The same with women . . .

Istvan was two points away from winning the match. His concentration seemed absolute. Proisy wasn't expecting that feeble serve. Caught unawares, he tried to attack. The ball was a few inches out. "Hungary forty–love."

Istvan clearly wanted to end on a brilliant note with an ace. But the ball was out: only a couple of inches too long. "Hungary forty–fifteen." The spectators groaned, then fell silent.

Intense concentration gripped the stadium now. Medioli could imagine telling himself that this is no time to clown around. Yes, his second service was very high, right to the back of the court. Then a long rally from the back

THE NET

of the court. Proisy was cautious. Neither wanted to risk a fault.

But Proisy tried for the initiative. He played a short shot and Istvan ran up to the net. Istvan managed to send back a very long, fast ball up the center, to Proisy's backhand, to take control of the game. Proisy tried the stroke he was most successful at, the backhand passing-shot along the line.

Istvan was lucky. He anticipated the passing-shot with a volley across to the right-hand side of the court. The ball touched the net and dropped down, on the right side!

"Game, set, and match. Six–two in the fifth set to Hungary!"

Enzo Medioli had forgotten to blow his nose in the excitement. The delirious crowd hailed the national hero as emperor. They applauded their country; they applauded themselves. Even the umpire was entitled to applause, as if he had had something to do with this victory he had come to doubt.

Soon after rediscovering the baroque architecture of the stud farm in his native Hungary, Istvan encountered the Victorian neo-Gothic. He had taken a minicab, a new Ford with seats smelling of vinyl, from Brighton, and he asked the driver to drop him on the coast road. He wanted to see Natty's school, which had been enveloped in fog two weeks earlier, from a distance. He had always liked approaching places this way, as if he were picking up their vibrations before submitting to their influence. On the eve of a tournament, he would breathe the atmosphere of a stadium like this, from a distance. Progressive knowledge of something gave him the confidence he needed.

On the other side of the road, the large buildings looking out to sea rose up with a majesty as stolid as the figure of Queen Victoria herself. Roedean's dark citadel dominated the dreary undulations of the deserted Sussex coastland. When it came to plains, he preferred the Hungarian puszta. He was half an hour early for the appointment with the headmistress he had arranged over the telephone the previous day. He had time to leave the road

THE NET

to go and dip his big toe in the water. It was neap tide. The sea was slack, but preparing to rise. He looked out at the waves with an old weariness, then turned away to study the school buildings. It was just as well they had been hidden by fog the day he had brought Natty back. If the gray mass intimidated *him,* what kind of life could a pupil lead in this breeding ground for well-brought-up young ladies? He imagined the secrets, the bursts of laughter, the heads bent over old-fashioned texts, the pens racing over the pages of exercise books.

Since his return from Hungary, Istvan had felt totally ensnared, but at the same time, deep down, he was pleased. And early that morning, clambering aboard the rented eight-seater jet that had brought him to Brighton, he had laughed for no apparent reason, wondering whether he was laughing at himself. He recalled Frank Fenwick's face when Istvan asked him to put his lawyer, Bill Carrington, in charge of the guardianship formalities.

"You're completely off your head, Istvan! You instruct Carrington yourself!"

Of course, two hours later, F.F. had telephoned to tell him the date and time of the appointment he himself had set for Istvan to see Carrington.

"What you're doing for the kid is very good, Istvan, but try not to complicate your life too much. It won't always be easy, you know, what you're doing."

"It makes everything easier," said the headmistress. "It's a great load off my shoulders, I must admit; I couldn't see any solution."

The light in the office was different from that of the day they had first met. The fog had given way to pale sunlight behind the iridescent panes. Istvan was no longer simply the family friend watching the child walk away. As

Countess Balanska, whom he always confided in before anybody else, had said:

"You who think of nothing but tennis rackets and women—you're going to have to make an effort. You could take private lessons with a Swiss nanny."

As Istvan shook the headmistress's hand, he was well aware his was the privileged status of the man who would now be paying the bills.

"I insist you tell Natasha the news yourself," said the headmistress festively. "She's playing hockey at the moment. I'll send for her."

"Let her finish the match," said Istvan.

"That's likely to take some time! It doesn't matter, she can leave the field. There are at least two substitutes who can't wait to play."

"Natasha, Mr. Horwat has got something important to tell you."

Istvan heard the child clomping down the corridor in the cleated athletic shoes she had not had time to change. He looked at her, breathless in her hockey uniform, a short white skirt, blue blouse, pullover, and knee socks. Beneath the fringe of blond hair plastered to her forehead with perspiration, her face was flushed. She presented her cheeks for him to kiss, and he wondered whether it was shyness or coquetry.

"I'll leave you alone," said the headmistress.

"We'd rather go for a walk around the grounds," replied Istvan.

He turned up the collar of his raincoat and asked Natty whether she was cold. She absently replied "No." He waited for her to give him her hand, but she kept her distance. He concluded it was the school that made her so reserved.

THE NET

* * *

"Can you hear over there?" she asked.
"Is it a playground?"
"No, that's my team beating King's. Come and see!"
"Stop it, Natty, keep still. I have to talk to you."
"Come on, it's this way."
"I went to see your grandparents in Hungary. Do you remember the horses?"
"Yes."
"The three of us talked about you."
They were coming up on the hockey field. In her hockey shoes, Natty was at a disadvantage on flagstones, and waddled like a duck. Istvan was deafened by the shrieks and exclamations that cheerfully defied the pompous Victorian buildings. A girl had just been hit on the shoulder by the ball. She was sitting on the grass crying. People crowded around her.
"It's Maggie," said Natty. "She's taking my place. She's going to make us lose. She always gets in the way of the ball!" She stood there for a few seconds, considering, then asked, "Can I go back to the game? We've almost won! You can talk to me afterward."
"No need. Look!"
The girl called Maggie had stopped crying, gotten to her feet, and had apparently decided to counterattack with a vengeance. She seemed to be the only one who had not noticed Istvan, the handsome man with the long black hair who might have captured everyone's attention even without being famous. The game slowed down and went on in comparative silence. Istvan put his arm around Natty's shoulder and led her away.
"So what we decided . . . are you listening to me, Natty?"
"Yes, yes—we've just *scored!*"

"Your daddy was like my brother, do you understand? So now, I'm the one who's going to look after you, your schooling, everything. . . . Do you want to be my daughter?"

"Yes, of course."

"Look at me! What I'm saying is more important than the hockey match. It's our life together that—"

"I am listening, really. Just . . . can I stay at Roedean? Oh, *look* at this. Another five minutes and we've won! They're playing so *badly!* They won't take their eyes off you. And they hardly know anything about tennis. They must think you're a film star. . . ."

"What I want is for you to be happy. If you like Roedean, you can stay here."

"I've got my friends here."

"Are you happy with the teachers?"

"Miss Elliot is too strict. You'll have to have a word with her—there, Maggie's been hit again!"

Istvan turned around. Natty had stopped, her eyes glued to the field. Maybe this game was more important to her than he had realized. She seemed to have only one desire: to pick up a hockey stick and run over to take her place. He heard himself say meekly, "Yes, I'll have to have a word with Miss Elliot, and the others. There are bound to be problems that need straightening out."

"We've won!" shouted Natty.

But as she flung herself into the midst of her yelling teammates, she stopped short, as if she had only just heard Istvan's clumsy speech and only just taken it in. She looked up at him. She remained motionless for a second, deaf to the shouts of her friends.

He read a great trust in her blue eyes, which suddenly seemed to be inordinately large.

She threw her arms around his neck. He closed his arms

THE NET

around her thin body whose weight he could barely feel. On the field, the shouts had given way to forced laughter. Istvan even heard two or three wolf whistles, loud enough to make one wonder if a few rowdy boys had infiltrated the flock of young ladies from good families. Natty's warm lips lingered on his cheek. He remembered a tune by Johann Strauss. He led the girl, whose feet no longer touched the ground, in an impromptu waltz.

12

"Sound okay? Right, let's go, roll tape."

Autumn had slipped into winter, spring into summer. Tournaments had come and gone. Another year closer to the final point lost, to the sponsors' eyes settling elsewhere. The attractive American standing before him cleared her throat.

"This is Mary Collins, CBS News, Paris. Our crew has just invaded the apartment of Istvan Horwat, whom we took by surprise as he was getting up. He's a little tired after Sunday's ball to celebrate the close of Wimbledon, followed yesterday—Monday—by a friendly get-together that Istvan tells us, went on until the early hours. Let me remind you that the ex-number one, today aged thirty-two, only surrendered to Borg, the current champion, twenty-two years old, in the fifth set of the Wimbledon finals.

"Istvan, you have just given an extraordinary performance. One could say that your defeat was a triumph. It's been—yes, ten years since your first Wimbledon final. Will the television viewers worldwide who've been

THE NET

watching you for two weeks see you in next year's final?"

"Perhaps in the semifinals, with a bit of luck."

"Modest as ever! When you lost the first two sets, I don't suppose you thought there'd be a fifth set, did you?"

"Well, I lost the first two sets, six–three, six–four, but I was in very good form. I could sense that Borg would have to play to a very high standard to beat me. If he slackened even a little, the situation would be reversed."

"Weren't you afraid of getting tired?"

"Playing on grass is a lot less tiring than on a hard court, which is a slower surface. Rallies on grass courts are shorter and therefore less of a strain. And so the difference in age was less significant."

"And then there was the incident with the umpire."

"An incident I didn't provoke."

"For once."

"You're very aggressive, Miss Collins."

"I'm teasing. Carry on."

"Yes, Borg did in fact lose his concentration after that incident."

"And yet you let him have the point. But that seemed to make his concentration even worse!"

"That enabled me to win the third set fairly easily."

"Six–four. And then?"

"Then, Borg never managed to concentrate during the fourth set. I played a few successful strokes that gave me a seven–five win, but in the fifth set, I did feel tired."

"Even though it was on grass! What about Borg?"

"Borg wasn't at all tired. After his six–two win, he could have continued for another three days. I'm especially pleased with the result because even when I was at my peak, he had already beaten me. After all, he is the greatest champion of the last decade."

ILIE NASTASE

* * *

Istvan then went out onto the terrace. Mary Collins asked him to sit in a canvas armchair, a present from his friend Jean-Marie Périer. The name "Istvan Horwat" was scrawled across the back. The Wimbledon finalist was irritated that he had not even had time to shave when the CBS crew took over his bedroom, much to Thieu's despair. Mary Collins practically asked him to pose in his bathtub, as if she were producing a bubble-bath commercial.

Fenwick had warned him about the early-morning landing of the American armada, but it had been a rough night and he was still asleep when Thieu shouted to him through the intercom: "Monsieur, monsieur, they're here and I don't know where to put them!"

He slipped into a track suit and dispatched Livia, who had clung to him throughout the evening at Régine's, into the bathroom. He felt steady enough—barely—to face the invasion.

"Show them up, Thieu. And bring my coffee up when you come!"

Inconvenience aside, it quite amused him to appear before the cameras with a beard that made him look more like a folk singer than the eighth-ranked world tennis player who had once again proved he was in great form. His somewhat tousled hair would disconcert the viewers, which was not such a bad thing. It made a change from his usual appearance. And so he had waited resolutely for Jim Thomson, an old hand at sports reporting for CBS. Istvan knew him well. They had already exchanged the same questions and answers a dozen times. But Jim had just broken a leg windsurfing, so instead of seeing his too-tanned, familiar face, he faced Jim's new assistant, an

THE NET

ample-breasted woman he had taken for the script girl. Confronted with Mary Collins, the night hawk beat its wings.

She was standing in front of him, out of camera range, leaning against the smoked-glass windbreak. She must have been aware that with her back to the sunlight, her white cotton net dress was transparent. He could make out the shape of her brief panties—an outfit altogether suitable for switching from sporting to amorous exploits. Mary Collins pivoted toward the bed in front of camera 1 while she interrogated the champion about his career, leaving number 2 in front of the bathroom door that remained steadfastly shut, in preparation for the inserts. And now, on the balcony, where they could hear the familiar pocking sound of the balls from Roland-Garros, she had no hesitation about probing his private life. With her Ray-Bans planted in her shoulder-length auburn hair, she kept her eyes on Istvan, who ended up asking her if she had come to interview a sportsman or a playboy. Her mouth, which was perhaps a little too large, broadened into a mocking grin.

"You must be aware," she said, "that Livia Fabiani has made you the model for her nocturnal hero of the sequel to her novel *Game, Set, and Death?*"

"There's a rumor going around, but it's absolutely false."

"Are you sure? Do you read the manuscript as she writes it?"

"Let's say that she sometimes asks me for technical advice."

"I've heard that she doesn't appreciate the following of women who surround you."

"Has that got anything to do with tennis?"

ILIE NASTASE

"No more than the latest cover of *Vogue-Hommes* that is devoted to you yet again, as the most elegant sportsman of the year."

"It's a title I didn't go looking for. I don't even know what panel made such a choice."

"You live in luxury. You've been compared to a character out of Fitzgerald . . ."

"I've never read Fitzgerald, but from the little I know about him, that too is totally untrue. I don't drink, I don't smoke, and I lead a regular life. I train every day, I don't have moods, I don't even know if I have a soul. Listen, Miss Collins, you are charming and you're wearing a very pretty dress, but I really do a lot better with Jim Thomson's questions. At least he understands competition tennis and he doesn't mistake CBS for the pulp press."

"Thank you, Istvan Horwat! We're going back inside your bedroom to talk about your plans. For, of course, your agent will make the most of your final against Borg. . . ."

The assistant director was trying to calm Thieu, who remained impervious to all his apologies. He could not stand "his" house being in the hands of these people who were deploying their equipment like a battery of heavy tanks. The boom operator had just knocked over two Sèvres porcelain figurines that lay on the carpet in pieces.

Livia, immaculately dressed and groomed, was playing the role of mistress of the house. She knelt down to pick up the fragments and put them on the shelf with the care of a museum curator. Livia caught a murderous glint in the Vietnamese's eye.

"Come on, Thieu," she said, "you know what the television people are like. The last time a crew from Antenne

THE NET

2 came to my place, they managed to do twice as much damage with half this much equipment."

"I'm terribly sorry," said Mary Collins, placing her hand on Istvan's shoulder.

"While they carry on wrecking the place," he said, "I'm going to have my breakfast downstairs. Are you coming, Livia? You too, Mary, of course."

"I'd like to ask Livia a few questions," said Mary. "Can we make the most of the occasion and talk about her next book? In your dining room, that'll give us a different setting."

"Oh, no!" groaned Thieu.

Istvan and Mary burst out laughing.

"There'll only be one camera, the tape recorder, and a couple of lights. While you have breakfast."

Her hand had not left Istvan's shoulder. He seemed unable to refuse her anything, but Livia leaped to her feet, abandoning the severed head of Diana the huntress on the carpet.

"It's out of the question! You'll be asking to film us in bed in a minute."

"I thought you *liked* playing the part of the champion's fiancée," retorted Mary. "Didn't you start the marriage rumors?"

"I'd like to see the downstairs decor," said Tovani, the director, sensing trouble.

"Thieu, show monsieur around and ask these ladies what they want for breakfast. I'll have the same as usual. Give me five minutes to shave."

"No," said Mary, "it'll ruin the continuity. You look fine as you are."

Livia tried not to stare at Mary Collins and Istvan. She knew from experience how it would end. How many times, during the last few months, had she resolved to break off this relationship? Why should she, a novelist translated into twelve languages, continue to live in the shadow of this man? But her jealousy was even greater than her pride, and she found it difficult to ignore these girls who threw themselves at him, who assailed him with phone calls and cables from New York, Rio, and Rome, and whom even Thieu was unable to throw out!

"Well," said Mary, hoping to appear above the situation. "We'll stop for today. We'll wait for Istvan's next achievement . . . or the publication of your book."

"Come downstairs and have breakfast anyway," said Istvan. "I'll join you. I suppose I'm allowed to shave now since the onslaught's over."

Ten minutes later, the atmosphere around the table was frosty. Mary pretended to take notes in a large diary as she drank her tea. She's managed to sit with her back to the light again, brooded Livia. Of course he'll come down in battle dress; Lacoste shirt, white trousers (for a dash of twenties style), I.H. shoes . . .

"Thieu's happier now," said Istvan, who appeared dressed as Livia had predicted. "They've put everything back in place. They're leaving."

"I'm leaving too," said Mary, getting to her feet with polite signals of regret. "Would you like to see the recording before it's transmitted?"

"I'd like to talk about that this evening. I've just booked a table for two at Maxim's for nine o'clock. Is that all right with you?"

A buzzer sounded from beyond the room.

"I might not be free," replied Mary.

"There's someone at the door," remarked Livia, looking indifferent.

THE NET

"What on earth is Thieu up to?"
"He's supervising the removal of Tovani's crew," said Mary.
"It must be another one of your groupies," said Livia.
"Hurry up, she might leave."
Without rushing, Istvan went into the corridor, pressed a button, and questioned the intercom.
"It's me," came Natty's distorted voice.
On the doorstep, Istvan discovered a tall, thin girl standing between a suitcase and a bag.
"I know you never come and see me," said Natty, "but you do recognize me, don't you?"
"What are you doing here?"
"We're on vacation."
"You could have let me know!"
"I wanted to surprise you. At school they thought you'd come and pick me up by plane. But I got here all by myself. I paid for the British Airways stewardess's taxi, but she couldn't stay, she was afraid of missing the return flight. You know, I saw you on TV. You were in England and you didn't even come and say hello to me!"
"Natty, do you think that when you're playing at Wimbledon, you can just take off over those cursed English roads? Come on, don't stand there on the doorstep, come in. . . . You know Livia . . ."
"Who's the other one?"
Deaf to the maternal exclamations of Livia, who was gaining ground back from Mary, Istvan contemplated Natty with consternation. He had not seen her since Easter, and the change was dramatic. She had shot up. He could not help finding her ugly in her clothes, which she had all but outgrown. Her skirt revealed bony knees that jutted out from her long, skinny legs. On her nose, which was sunburned, there was a pimple that she had

scratched. But the worst was her hair. Istvan glared at Mary Collins, who was biting her lip to stop herself from laughing. Natty must have tampered with her sensible school hairstyle in the airliner's lavatory. Where the devil had she found that orange powder that made a shapeless lock, hastily cut into a punk shape, shine like a beacon?

"Did you have breakfast on the plane?" he finally managed to ask.

"No, it was foul."

"I'll make you some soft-boiled eggs," offered Livia.

"I prefer them fried."

"Thieu will take care of it," said Istvan. "In the meantime, I'll run you a bath. In the 'swimming pool.' And then we'll go out and buy you some clothes. How you've grown!"

"I know," said Natty. "Everything I've got in my suitcase is too small."

"I'll leave you to your family affairs," said Mary Collins. "What time will you pick me up?"

"We'd better put off our dinner until another evening," said Istvan. "I'll telephone you."

13

The Air Inter Caravelle was descending toward Calvi. Livia Fabiani went to sit by Natty's side as soon as the Corsican coast came into sight. Her passion for her native island prompted her to give Natty a frantic geography lesson. She covered every creek, and every beach, unusually empty for July.

"You can only get there by sea," she explained. "I'll take you in the Zodiac. We'll water-ski."

Istvan, sitting behind them, wondered whether Natty, whose nose was glued to the window as she sat in silence, was listening to the novelist's chatter, or whether she was remembering the sea near Barcelona, tormented by the tramontane, when the wreaths of flowers were swallowed up by the waves.

He was reassured by her ingratiating smile as she turned to ask him if he would teach her to water-ski.

"I'm not very good," replied Istvan.

"I'll teach you," said Livia. "Istvan can drive the ski boat."

"I'm not very good at that either," said Istvan. "I'm not

at ease on the water. I haven't even got a boat license."
"All my cousins have. They'll be delighted to pull Natty!"

Then she launched into a lyrical description of the smell of the scrubland, which would not fail to make their nostrils quiver as soon as they set foot on the island.

The Corsican bandit who looked as though he had just stepped off a film set glowered at the little herd of tourists disembarking from the Caravelle. He looked as if he suspected every one of these strangers of coming to Corsica to set fire to the scrub. As soon as he caught sight of Livia, his arms opened. He stood motionless, waiting for her to come and embrace him for a solemn triple kiss.

"This is Istvan Horwat," said Livia. "My cousin, Sampierro Fabiani."

"So happy you could meet us," commented Istvan frostily, noting the mustache that blended with the beard, the open shirt revealing suntanned skin covered with frizzy hairs, and the beige trousers held up by a large red leather belt.

"Sampierro is a great sculptor," said Livia. "He's exhibited in Paris several times."

"She made me," said Sampierro. "I don't give a damn about Paris. Is this your daughter?"

"In a way," replied Istvan. "Her name's Natty."

"Will you sit for me, Natty? I've been commissioned to do a child for Bastia High School. I'm looking for a very tall, thin girl."

They piled the suitcases into the red all-purpose Toyota from which the roof had been removed. Natty, standing up, was holding on to the roll bar.

"I've got the same car," said Livia. "I thought of you when I bought it, after your visit in the spring." She

THE NET

turned to Istvan. "I'll show you paths nobody ventures down except donkeys and shepherds!"

"I'll drop you off at the Ile-Rousse," said Sampierro, "and then I'll shoot off to Corte. The Union of Corsican Artists is demonstrating against the Ministry of Culture's policies."

"You ought to sit down, Natty," shouted Istvan as the Toyota passed a double line of tourists on mopeds negotiating one of the numerous bends on the coast road. "Hold tight!"

"Don't worry," said Sampierro. "I know this road like the back of my hand. I could drive it blindfolded."

"That's how he's already smashed up several tons of old iron," said Livia, who was holding on firmly to one of Natty's legs.

They sped past a campsite crammed with tents and caravans. Istvan put on his sunglasses. He did not open his mouth; he was waiting for the scramble to end. Since they left Orly, he'd been wondering how he could have let himself fall into this trap: two weeks in Corsica, without even a suitable partner to train with! The word "holidays" had never meant anything to him. Natty's arrival had caught him off guard. He felt guilty for not having made any plans, and Livia's suggestion had seemed like the lesser evil.

Out of his depth, he had let his hot-blooded consort take charge of the situation, listening to her arguments with only half an ear: this pale child emerging from England's grayness would blossom in Corsica. She would find children her own age among the Fabiani clan. She would run in the pure air of the deserted beaches where they would go and picnic by boat. She would swim in the cleanest water in the Mediterranean, polluted everywhere except in Corsica, according to Livia.

The only essential Istvan had grasped from her travel agent patter was that a woman would be better able to look after Natty than he would alone. Livia had already proved herself in buying Natty a new wardrobe, deftly choosing summer clothes that somehow flattered her gangly shape, her bony legs, and her chest. She had even taken her to Carita's for a facial and a new hairdo. Natty came back happy, almost pretty, with her bangs just brushing her eyebrows and wearing a Hawaiian blouse.

Sampierro pulled up in the courtyard of Livia's house next to a red Toyota, the twin of his own right down to the color. "I'll leave you here."

"Are you coming to dinner?" Livia asked.

"I don't know. In any case, I'll meet you at the Platanes for aperitifs. Everyone will be there, they know you're arriving today."

"Everybody knows everything in these parts," remarked Istvan, surprised at how aggressive he sounded.

"You'll find your fans at the Platanes," quipped Sampierro, pulling away. "I don't know a thing about tennis."

Natty shivered as soon as she walked into the hall of the old stone house, built as a fortress against the sun. An emaciated woman dressed in black rushed up to kiss her while Istvan and Livia unloaded the baggage.

"Your name's Natty! I'm Maria . . . Livia's told me a lot about you!"

Natty's cheeks prickled. She felt a dangerous temptation to ask the servant why she didn't shave her mustache. Finally, Maria left her to monopolize Livia, after greeting Istvan with a little curtsey.

THE NET

Leaving the two women chatting in Corsican, Istvan and Natty took a house tour and soon lost themselves in the maze of corridors. They clutched their suitcases like lost travelers. The house had been built contrary to mainland logic, and Istvan had forgotten the layout, although Livia had shown him around from top to bottom the previous spring. They opened squeaking doors to find themselves in musty, scantily furnished bedrooms that were obviously never used. Dark wooden statues of Christ guarded the entrances. Narrow windows were set in the walls at the base of which the saltpeter had formed yellowish blotches on the whitewash.

"What about me, where am I going to sleep?" asked Natty.

"I don't know what Livia's decided."

"Why? Is it always Livia who decides?"

"It's her house. Let me think for a minute and see if I can remember where my room is. Then at least we'll be able to put this stuff down."

He crossed an Empire-style drawing room, so vast even the huge pieces of furniture were dwarfed. Natty glued her nose to a glass cabinet containing rows of lead soldiers. The entire Imperial Guard. Another glass case was full of decorations and miniature cannons. From the walls, stern portraits of marshals aglitter with medals looked scornfully down on the man and child.

"It must be this way," said Istvan.

A double door opened into a smaller drawing room with dark-red velvet hangings. Books were piled on the console tables, on the couch, and on the faded carpets. Istvan could sense Natty's unease. His memories of the house had been rather vague. Otherwise he would never have brought her to such a sinister place for a holiday.

"Here it is," he said, crossing another corridor lit by two skylights that divided the dazzling sky into azure rectangles.

Natty burst out laughing at the huge four-poster bed. She leaped onto it and started jumping up and down. As she bounced on this improvised trampoline, clouds of dust rose up and rolled in the rays of sunlight filtering through the blinds. Istvan stowed the suitcases in front of the wardrobe, where three or four Second Empire uniforms hung and a pair of ankle boots that had belonged to the Empress Eugénie were kept.

"An empress once slept in this bed, Natty."

"Really, which one?"

"Her name was Eugénie."

"Was she Livia's grandmother?"

"No—"

Livia appeared in the doorway. "Stop jumping up and down, you'll break the slats," she shouted. "I wondered where you had got to. Really, Istvan, tell her to stop!"

"Your house is so *old*," said Natty, "and if you're not even allowed to jump . . ."

"Look at this dust!"

"You should keep it clean, then!"

"Listen," said Istvan quickly, "what about going out for lunch? I remember a restaurant overlooking the port—"

"Maria's prepared everything here," said Livia.

"Chicken and chips," suggested Natty.

"No, today it's mutton. Pick up your suitcase and follow me. I'll show you your room first. You're going to wash your hands."

Left to himself, Istvan gloomily contemplated the white leather bag where the three rackets he had brought, just in case, lay idle.

He opened the shutters and the windows, which the

THE NET

supposedly indispensable Maria should have done days ago to rid the room of its musty smell. Beyond the olive trees, past the green oaks and the flower beds parched by the July sun, his gaze followed two Chris-Crafts challenging each other to a race on the absolutely smooth sea. The monotonous screeching of the cicadas only added to his boredom. He knew exactly what he would do if it weren't for Natty's cursed holidays. He would go straight to New York and train in earnest for Flushing Meadow with Tanner or Connors, instead of going rusty on this island for two weeks.

Mary Collins had telephoned him the previous day to give him her address in the States, where she was returning at the beginning of August. He pictured her on the terrace with her back to the light in her transparent dress with her auburn hair and her impertinent eyes. He could hear the voice of old Jim Thomson, who had called to tell him what a success the interview was.

"I sent you a nice present, didn't I?"

A nice present, yes. Not that he'd done anything with it. It was all because of a ten-year-old. No, it was Livia's fault. But without Natty, Livia would never have been able to pull off the old-family-house trick again. Even in the days when he had not been able to escape the ubiquitous Countess Balanska, he had never felt so much a prisoner.

He jumped. Natty's hand had come to rest over his.

"Hurry up, Istvan, lunch'll be cold. Afterward we'll put the Zodiac in the water."

"It's even hotter in New York," said Livia, lying on her stomach in the sand.

Istvan, sitting up, watched Natty swim across the creek with a faultless crawl.

"New York, why New York?"

"You talked in your sleep last night. You said New York."

"I often talk in my sleep. That's why I prefer to sleep alone. At least I don't bother anybody."

"I was awake. I was writing. Were you thinking of Flushing Meadow?"

"I could have been. I don't remember dreams," he said, remembering The Net. Then, changing the subject: "Natty's an extremely good swimmer. Look how furiously she's swimming. She's crossing the creek for the third time!"

"Furious is right. She snapped at me because I put cream on her sunburn. She's peeling all over. These fair-skinned people . . ."

"Not all girls can be blond *and* Corsican, like you."

"She's grousing because she lost a ski yesterday. For once she managed to get out of the water! I thought cousin Charles was very patient. He'll be along soon, by the way. He's taking Natty fishing with Laetitia and two or three other children. The two of us will be left in peace for a bit. . . . Look, she's coming back at last. No, she's making for the rocks."

Natty was swimming a slow breast stroke toward the tip of the band of sand. She stood up, climbed the rocks, and sat right on top, taking no notice of Istvan's gesticulations.

"Leave her alone," said Livia, "she likes being on her own."

"Does she?"

"Yes. Little girls are like that."

14

Every day at dawn Istvan made himself swim in the bay for an hour while Livia and Natty were still asleep. He would take the Toyota and drive to a little beach that Livia had shown him, at the end of a sunken lane bordered by dwarf tamarisk trees that sloped steeply down to the sea. He knew perfectly well that tennis players were forbidden to swim but he made it a point of honor to overcome his repulsion and plunge into the whitish water that was still cool from the night. The rising sun gradually tinged the little waves pink; they seemed to be holding their breath in the silence of the dawning day.

For Istvan, it was a way of confronting the nightmare that tormented him in moments of tiredness or stress. He made himself open his eyes in the water. The salt stung, but that way he could assure himself that no sea creature lurked in the shadows, hovering in wait for him; that no drifting net was going to close around him. The rhythmic movement of his muscles reassured him. In the sea, which he had always thought of as hostile, he alternated a supple, perfectly timed crawl with a furious butterfly stroke.

His arms beat the water, as if in exorcism. Then he would glide onto the sand on his own momentum, his arms outstretched. Next, he devoted himself to his daily breathing exercises before slipping on his jeans and T-shirt, leaping into the car, and starting the serpentine climb up the hill. He reached the top, taking a shortcut across the scrub over barely discernible tracks, and arrived at the back of the house where Maria was listening for the sound of the engine before plunging the eggs into boiling water. He found Natty in the kitchen in her swimsuit. She had lost the liveliness of the first few days. She had succeeded in staying upright in her skis, but it was no longer a game and she had lost interest. She would sulk at the slightest provocation. She was annoyed with Istvan because he wouldn't volley with her on the tennis court that sat, surrounded by dilapidated fencing, behind the vast pink house belonging to Fabiani, Livia's cousin and the father of numerous offspring.

"Why don't you go and play with the children? If I start playing with you out there, then I'll have to give all the others a turn. It's no fun for me, do you understand?"

"It's no fun for me either playing with them. They're hopeless."

"Maybe you could teach them some."

"Because I'm a girl, they say I play badly."

Livia had been very patient, but she could not help losing her temper when Natty answered her back one time too many.

"For goodness sake, Istvan, tell her I'm a grown-up, not a chum her own age!"

"I haven't got any chums," Natty said, silencing them both. "Maybe that's my problem."

One afternoon she went so far as to cling to Istvan to keep him from taking a siesta with Livia. She ensconced

THE NET

herself in Livia's bed and refused to leave the room. Istvan, irritated, led Livia into the Empress's room, but Natty followed them stubbornly, humming a Christmas carol and saying nothing. The three of them ended up under the huge plane tree in the garden.

Livia pretended to take no notice. She sat reading Françoise Sagan's latest novel, looking up only to dart spiteful looks (that Istvan would not have believed her capable of) at Natty, who was playing solitaire on a seat. He shuffled half-heartedly through the sports pages of *Nice-Matin*. He felt he was wasting his time, not training and not able to rest either. Inactivity itself exhausted him, and he did not know whether he owed the feeling of boredom to Livia or to Natty. He had always sought the company of women, but he was used to quietly enjoying it at his leisure. Natty's presence disrupted his plans. Livia's nephews were not much help. Natty had decided that they bored her. On the other hand, to entrust her to their father would be an invitation for them to invade the house. He wondered how families coped.

In the evening, from seven o'clock onward, the terrace of the Café des Platanes was crowded with pastis drinkers. The small clans occupied the tables according to an evident protocol; the Fabianis sat at the edge, alongside the parking lot. Istvan, who was not talkative by nature, and moreover drank nothing but freshly squeezed lemon juice in ice water, had difficulty keeping up. The conversation always remained closed to him; Livia's cousins and friends talked only about people and villages he did not know.

"Tomorrow, we'll go to Monticello," said Livia. "There's a lovely view from there. You can take photographs."

Istvan had already used up several rolls of film, which the photographer in the port had taken his time developing. He had sent Natty to pick them up, and she had walked back very slowly so she could look at them before anyone else.

"I'm in nearly all of them," she observed, tossing the envelope of prints on the table. "But there aren't very many of Livia."

"I think there are plenty of me," said Livia with a half-smile. "It's odd, they're all a little overexposed."

"You have to beware of the Corsican sunshine," said Sampierro, with a sculptor's squint at the slant of light. "Haven't you got a light meter?"

"No," replied Istvan. "I don't like automation."

"Great champions are all manual," said a tall, red-haired girl whom everyone called Zaza and who kept looking adoringly at Istvan.

"Still, you need some brains," said Charles Fabiani, who had followed Istvan's career from the beginning and had asked for a set of autographs to give to all the patrons of Les Platanes.

Natty was standing next to Istvan's chair, shifting from one foot to the other.

"Natty," said Livia, "please stop fidgeting. You're tiring Istvan."

"No she isn't," said Istvan without thinking, regretting the words as he saw a gleam of triumph in the child's eyes.

Natty went to fetch a chair and sat close to Istvan, brushing against his knees.

"So," Sampierro asked her, "when are you going to begin sitting for me? Tomorrow morning?"

"You could do a bust of Horwat," suggested Zaza. "They could erect it outside Roland-Garros."

Natty glared at Livia and Zaza with equal animosity.

THE NET

What rights did these women think they had to Istvan, to vie for his attention like this? She didn't make a nuisance of herself all the time, the way they did. She left him alone. It would be so much better if they could spend their holidays together, just the two of them, in a place where there were good tennis courts, grass courts, like at Wimbledon. She had always wanted to play on grass again since the day her father had given her her first lesson on a court in Melbourne. Her eyes were filling with tears. Istvan looked at her; he was moved. He wanted to get up, wipe her eyes, take her mind off her grief. He had an idea about that, in fact. For the last two days, she had talked of nothing but Pinder's Circus, which the posters said would be opening the following Sunday.

"I'm nearly eleven," said Natty. "I'm entitled to know how you use makeup. Mummy didn't put anything on her face, she just wore a little lipstick."

Perched on the edge of the bathtub, she observed Livia's face under the row of spotlights above the twin washbasins. The foundation cream spread out and vanished under the skillful fingertips.

"But I'd really like to get ready on my own," said Livia.

"I know. But I'm *learning.*"

Livia smiled. She liked Natty's unpredictable replies, calculated though they often were. She was not taken in. She remembered what she thought when she was Natty's age: "These women need a lot of paint to make themselves presentable!" She felt the need to justify herself a little.

"It's a very chic party. I have to look done-up for it. You've seen the dress I'll be wearing."

"And I'm going to be left on my own in this creaky old house."

"Maria's here."

"Maria sleeps. I can hear her snoring from my room. A bomb wouldn't wake her up."

"Who's been telling you about bombs?"

"The children."

"They talk nonsense. There's nothing to worry about here."

"That's the trouble. Oh, Livia, can I try your eyeliner?" Natty stood up and went over to the washbasin. She put her face close to Livia's in the huge, illuminated mirror. She pulled back her hair, lowered her eyelids, and tilted her head to the left and to the right.

"You see, my blemishes have all gone."

"I took good care of them."

"Istvan says that with the sea and the sun, they'd have gone anyway."

Livia shrugged her shoulders. It was hopeless.

Natty followed the advance of the foundation cream toward the tiny wrinkles at the corners of Livia's eyes. "It's magic," she said. "How old are you?"

Livia accidentally elbowed Natty, who was balanced on one foot, her hands leaning on the edge of the washbasin. The girl swayed and knocked the vanity case off the table. The tubes, brushes, pencils, tissues, and little round and square boxes scattered over the pink mosaic tiled floor. A bottle of Arpège broke.

"Ooh, what a stink!" said Natty.

"You could at least apologize!"

"Sorry, but you pushed me."

Natty got down on all fours and picked up the materials that had scattered to all four corners of the room and put them back into the case higgledy-piggledy.

"Let me do it," sighed Livia.

Without a word, Natty gently shut the bathroom door.

THE NET

She ran through the maze of corridors to her room. The washbasin was nowhere near as well lit as the ones belonging to the mistress of the house.

She wiped the traces of makeup from her eyebrows. She splashed cold water on her face. She laughed to see her skin shimmering with droplets of water in the magic mirror. Livia thinks she's the most beautiful, she thought, but she's at least thirty. She's old.

The crowning diversion of the interminable last days of July had to be the ball given in Bastia by another of Livia's cousins, Pascal Rossi, a member of the Corsican Parliament and former minister. The illustrious Pascal had shared family fame with Livia since the success of her *Game, Set, and Death*. Istvan, whom Natty had embraced as if she would never see him again, stood watching the couples amble around the swimming pool.

Beside him, Livia was playing official fiancée. No matter how much he told himself that it was for Natty's sake that he was drinking the obligatory cocktail of Fabiani family and politics right down to the dregs, he could not get used to it. Sitting in a swinging seat under a moribund olive tree decorated with multicolored Chinese lanterns, he did not even feel Livia's hand on his thigh. And Livia was very beautiful that evening. Her black eyes shone, and her long blond hair, resplendent in a carefully cultivated tangle, moved lightly in the sea breeze. She had become gloomy for a moment when he had announced that he would not dance. Then she decided to play the role of the secure lover, and Istvan was irritated by her smile.

He was even more annoyed with himself for being disagreeable because she did not reproach him. Out of the corner of his eye, he saw her fend off some autograph hunters. The host himself walked away after a few polite words. His son Antoine, a local playboy in a white Mao jacket, contented himself with saying, in passing, that he trained every morning on the court of his father's estate in the hope that he would be ranked one day.

Istvan disliked the role he caught himself playing. Passing himself off as an indolent idol who keeps his distance, with a swinging seat for a pedestal, was not his style. But all these people were so far removed from him, from his regular partners, his spectators, his women, from the whole stylish entourage that followed him from one major tournament to the next . . .

Livia came over with two tulip glasses of champagne.

"No thank you," said Istvan. "I've already had three."

"Then I'll drink them. You can drive me home."

She looked him in the eyes, drained both glasses, and put them down beside the swinging seat, near the ashtray where her Dunhill filters were accumulating.

"You're smoking too much," said Istvan.

Livia was no longer smiling. She shook her hair, snapped the lid of the Cartier lighter Istvan had given her, lit another cigarette, and exhaled a long trail of smoke.

"You're not playing at the moment. You don't have to follow Natty's regimen. *I* certainly don't have to."

"What's Natty go to do with all this?"

"No tobacco, no alcohol, early to bed . . . She's a miniature version of you. Or vice versa."

"Am I supposed to laugh or what?"

"That would be nice for a change, at least. Since she turned up in Paris, she's been driving us up a wall. Don't pretend you don't know what I'm talking about."

"She's a child, doing things a child does. I'm just not a very good father yet. If I ever will be—"

"Well, you certainly can't be her father *and* her mother,

THE NET

too. She monopolizes you. She does everything she can to make it clear to me that I'm in the way."

"That's enough, Livia."

"I feel as if anything I do for her is useless. And you . . ."

"I'd like to slip away from here. Can we?"

"You only have eyes for her. Can't you see what she's up to? Whether it's me or someone else, it makes no difference. She's gobbling you up."

"Don't be crude. Listen, I'm going for a walk around the grounds. I'll meet you by the car. Apologize to your member of Parliament for me, will you?"

5

Livia stretched and moved her hand to caress Istvan's face, but did not touch him. He had fallen asleep sprawled across the bed after making love to her for three hours. He had made her promise to wake him up and send him back to the Empress's bedroom when he fell suddenly, as he always did, into a relaxed sleep with his head on her breasts, which made her happy. She never loved this elusive man more than when he closed his eyes like that. She stroked his black hair and smiled. He always said he wanted to sleep alone. Yet he had hardly used the four-poster bed in the guest room since their arrival in Corsica.

That night, he had not moved or spoken after their tumultuous reconciliation, the inevitable outcome of their tiff at Pascal Rossi's party. She liked to think she was taming him and that soon he would belong completely to her. She was waiting for the right moment to suggest that they send Natty to stay with her grandparents in Hungary during August, while she accompanied Istvan to Flushing Meadow.

THE NET

She had nearly brought up the subject that night in bed with Istvan. She was going to say that the pure air of the puszta, riding the horses, would do the child a lot of good. But she decided it would be better to prepare the ground first. All the more so since she had something else to tell him after his early-morning swim. She did not know how he was going to take it. In fact, she regretted having committed herself in the candlelit foyer as she took leave of her cousin Pascal and his son Antoine, while Istvan slipped away with a casualness not accepted easily by Corsican society. It was, of course, to obtain forgiveness for the departure of the star of the evening, her guest, for whom she felt responsible, that she had promised Antoine that Istvan would play a couple of games with him for half an hour in the morning. There was no going back now. Antoine, who was beside himself with excitement, had stopped dancing at once and gone to bed so that he would be in good shape the next day.

After all, she thought to reassure herself, she had seen him hitting a few with Natty at Roland-Garros. But, a few seconds later, the anxiety returned. Obviously, Natty was different. She didn't want to get them started on Natty again.

Istvan moved. Without opening his eyes, he pulled Livia toward him, took possession of her body, and she abandoned herself to him. Then, thoroughly awake, he sat up and looked around.

"What about the four-poster?" he asked with a smile. "Where is the Empress's four-poster?"

Well, how do you do, thought Livia. He's in a good mood. This will be all right.

"What time is it?" he asked.

"Nearly eight o'clock."

ILIE NASTASE

"Then my swim's done for. By the time I get to the creek, the picnickers will be there."

"I can take you over to the cliffs by boat."

"No, there's no point. When I haven't slept enough, I don't feel like doing anything. Did I talk in my sleep again? You should have—"

"You slept like an angel," she murmured, sealing his lips with a kiss, regretting the expression that made her sound like somebody's aunt.

"But the angel's hungry. The angel's going to have a shower and go down to the kitchen."

She told him over breakfast.

"You must be out of your mind," Istvan shouted, crushing the egg shells on his plate. "Natty, tell her she's crazy!"

"I don't interfere in your affairs," Natty said haughtily.

"Corsican hospitality is a two-way thing," said Livia. "It's a way of returning their invitation of yesterday evening."

"It was that fool of a minister who insisted on inviting *me!* And what's more . . . but who do you take me for? I don't play for my supper."

"If there was a decent court here, I would have invited Antoine anyway. When Richter came, he was happy to play on the Steinway in the drawing room."

"The difference," said Natty, "is that a pianist can play by himself."

Istvan turned to Natty, who was hanging onto the back of his chair again, shifting from one foot to the other. His anger was instantly transformed. He burst out laughing.

"You could have played a few sets with me," Natty said, "to show this Antoine how to play. How old is he?"

"Twenty," replied Livia, reassured a little by Istvan's

THE NET

laughter. "He's already been listed second rank. Just a half-hour, Istvan . . ."

"We'll have a good laugh," said Natty.

Some of the guests from the previous evening had not gone to bed. At ten o'clock in the morning, they were making an effort to put up a good show. A group of girls in the full blush of youth, who had fallen asleep in the drawing room, were spreading their skirts in a corolla on the dry grass around the old court with the worn fencing. It was only used during the holidays when Antoine Rossi came to the village for a month. His father had given up playing after a heart attack, and his sisters preferred to gallop along the seafront on the stalwart riding-club horses. First thing that morning, Antoine had gone into Calvi to buy a brand-new racket, hardly able to believe that Istvan Horwat would show up for a game with a player from the bottom of the second rank. And yet, there he was. If he had not looked so bad-tempered, Antoine's happiness would have been complete.

The whole town would be talking about what he insisted on calling a game, although Istvan had made it clear that it was impossible to play a set in that heat, and that they would have to make do with a few volleys. No matter. It would give them something to talk about for a long time in La Balagne.

Istvan did not even hear the applause that greeted his entrance on court. The head waiter passed around glasses of iced Muscat, which kept up the general euphoria. Istvan brightened when he was offered a glass, and smiled. Livia was reassured, a little, about having inflicted this chore on him. If he was furious, he was hiding it very well.

He did not think much of his opponent, and all the

impromptu spectators irritated him. His temper improved when he realized, during the first rally, that this was a great moment for Antoine.

Istvan literally gave him points. Antoine ran happily about the court, playing confidently before his little group of friends who saw him with new eyes as a prospective champion, and applauded him accordingly.

Natty, who was keeping herself busy making fruit juice cocktails, had lost interest in the show. Istvan, she knew, was making a commendable effort to hit the ball as gently as possible. He placed the ball at the center of Antoine's racket.

Then, he began to feel the effects of the Mediterranean sun. He wiped his forehead conspicuously. "Let's stop!" he cried. "It's too hot, you've worn me out!"

"What a pity," said Antoine. "I was just getting warmed up."

Livia went to join them by the net. "You see, Istvan, Antoine's good. You played some lovely rallies."

"Look at that," said Natty who was jumping backward and forward over the net, "for a brand-new net, it hangs like an old blanket!"

"I checked the height," said Antoine vexedly.

"Natty, haven't you had enough of this?"

"Enough of what, Livia?"

They were standing by the water, their feet in the band of foam, skimming pebbles without much enthusiasm. Natty broke off, dropping the flat pebbles she was holding.

"Do you want to leave?"

"Aren't you bored?"

"A little."

"Well, it's you I'm thinking of."

THE NET

"You couldn't stand the tennis game, is that it?"
"Partly, I suppose."
"Livia's got some weird ideas, hasn't she?"
"I wouldn't—"
"All you have to do is decide that we should go back to Paris. There's no risk. In any case, she'll follow us everywhere."
"What do you mean, *she'll* follow *us?*"
"Do you want to ditch her?"
"That's no way to talk!"
"Is that it, or isn't it?"
"It's complicated. You can't understand."
"Yes, I can."
"Livia's very kind."
"She's always yelling at me."
"I haven't noticed."
"And I'm fed up with all her ointments. The more she slathers on me, the more I peel. It's finished on my face, but everywhere else . . . By the way, what did you say to her about Hungary?"
"Nothing, it's none of her business."
"Doesn't she know that Erzebet is ill, and that Sandor is too busy with his work to look after me?"
"You could call them 'grandmother' and 'grandfather.'"
"I hardly know them."
"All the more reason to be a little respectful."
He took her hand. They walked in silence, oblivious to the droning of outboard motors. From time to time Natty would bend down to pick up a shell and examine it before throwing it into the sea.
"It's too bad they can't come back to life, even in the water," she said.
"What?"

"Shells."

"You know, shells and their problems . . ."

"I can't help them, but I can help you. Let's play the Hungary trick on her."

"What are you talking about?"

"You tell her that you're taking me to Budapest, and that you'll be back. She'll wait for you here and we'll stay in Paris. You can go back to your training . . . and from time to time you'll hit a few with me."

Istvan took Natty's other hand and spun her around, faster and faster, their arms outstretched. Her feet left the sand and she shrieked with laughter until they were both dizzy and Istvan stopped.

"And you know," she went on as she recovered her breath, "when she telephones, saying that she's tried to track you down all over the place, Thieu will tell her that Erzebet has been taken ill, and that you've stayed in Hungary to take care of me. It's almost the truth, isn't it?"

"You won't be able to pose for Sampierro, or go to the circus."

"We'll find other circuses."

6

Natty had forgotten her keys once again. She thumped the intercom, hardly heard Thieu's indulgent "I'll open the door," pushed aside two chairs, and flung *Pariscope* onto the dining-room table.
Istvan intercepted it as it slid across the marble.
"Well," said Natty, "that was clever of me, wasn't it? It was the last one. And this old woman wanted to snatch it away from me."
Istvan flicked through the weekly listings magazine and smiled, as if he found himself in familiar territory, at the memory of one of his first visits to Paris, with a student at the Ecole du Louvre, whom he had met at the tobacconists on the Quai Voltaire.
"Today," he announced, "I'm taking you to the Carnavalet Museum."
"Is it like a carnival?"
"There's no connection. It's a big seventeenth-century house where Madame de Sévigné used to live."
"The woman who sold chocolates?"
"No, the one who spent her time writing to her daugh-

ter. You'll see collections of objects, paintings, lots of things from the old Paris. After all, you're so fond of the city."

"Hold on, pass me the paper again, I half-read something in the lift . . . *Star Wars*. It's supposed to be fabulous."

"We've already seen lots of films, Natty."

"And museums. Yesterday we were at the Museum of Mankind. The day before that, the Maritime Museum. I've had enough, I'm suffocating."

Thieu coughed discreetly and smiled. Teatime. He poured the hot chocolate into Natty's cup from high up, to make it frothy. He watched the girl mischievously, as if the pair of them had rehearsed something for Istvan's benefit.

"It's true," he said, "you could go and see *Star Wars*. It's educational if it can help avert another war on Earth. I'm convinced," Thieu went on, "that children should see what war on a planetary scale is. There are other films, too. In one of them, I think the leading part is played by a monster. Children love monster stories."

"How do you know, Thieu?" asked Istvan.

"I had children, once."

Natty sensed that it was not the moment to ask about Thieu's children. This was the first time he had said anything about them in her presence. She contented herself with staring at him for a long time. She, too, had lost everything.

That last week of July, in a Paris invaded by tourists, Natty heard her mother tongue spoken more often than French, and the time went by too quickly. In the afternoons, she usually managed to drag Istvan to the cinema.

THE NET

But she did not have too hard a job persuading him because he was still child enough to enjoy the same films she did.

Natty was very proud to walk into a cinema when the poster outside proclaimed "Children Under Thirteen Years of Age Not Admitted." She made a sport of it.

"Luckily you're there," she said to Istvan. "I'm big for my age, but they'd never let me in if I weren't with you."

Istvan devoted himself to Natty, knowing that he would be leaving for Flushing Meadow at the beginning of August. He wondered what she would do with herself during his absence. For the time being, he was avoiding the question. Thieu was there to look after her. He had also discovered, during a walk in the woods, a children's home in a manor house near Chantilly. Natty had said, "They're an unlucky bunch, they've got to spend their holidays at school." But for one or two weeks perhaps . . .

Discouraged by Thieu's unbreachable wall, Livia had finally given up telephoning. In fact, it was a quiet period for the telephone. They lived as if on an island, on the seventh and eighth floors overlooking Roland-Garros. Thieu watched over them like a lighthouse keeper. Natty was happy. Istvan was, too. He thought, without impatience, of Mary Collins, whom he would see again in New York.

Natty woke up very early every day, at about five o'clock. She had gotten into the habit of going diving in Istvan's bathtub-cum-swimming-pool after kissing him good morning while he was still in bed. In the evenings, at nine o'clock, when he went to kiss her good night in the blue bedroom, she showed him one or two pages of the magazine she knew by heart as soon as she had flicked through it. In a sleepy voice, she would say, "Read this little story!"

That phrase enchanted him, he did not know why. When he had demonstrated his interest in the "little story," he would switch off the light. Natty closed her eyes. He gave her a parting kiss on the forehead and went to his own room. Thieu, already asleep, had switched on the answering machine. Istvan went to bed and played with the television remote control; then he, too, chose sleep.

In the mornings at seven o'clock, after Natty's diving session and Istvan's shower, Natty went into her room to fetch the white leather bag where she kept her towel, two boxes of balls, and the little Adidas racket he had given her on their return to Paris. To Thieu's great disappointment, he was no longer required to make breakfast; they made for the pâtisserie on the way to Roland-Garros. It was not open yet. They walked round the building to the side alley. The smell of warm bread wafted out of the small basement window. Natty gave her bag to Istvan, who ended up with a bag in each hand, pushed open the little tradesman's door, and returned triumphant with fresh, hot croissants that burned her fingers. Then they ate breakfast, walking along the still-deserted avenue in the cool of the early morning.

One day, Natty declared that she was irritated by the other players, who had come to train early on the open-air courts of Roland-Garros, questioning him on the progress of his "pupil" or his "daughter" during the private moments she wanted to share only with Istvan.

"Tomorrow, you'll have a surprise," was all he said.

The following morning, they finished their croissants in

THE NET

a different street, heading toward the Avenue Mozart. They went through a door. At the back of an apartment block, Natty discovered an indoor tennis court, a giant Mylar mushroom that grew there as if by magic.

"It's my friend Jacques's court," explained Istvan. "This is where he gives lessons, but the club is closed in summer. He gave me a key so that I could come and train in peace."

"It's wonderful, Istvan! Our own private court! Why didn't we come here sooner?"

"You've got to get used to playing in front of other people as well, Natty. And playing well."

"But it's better when there's just the two of us. I like Roland-Garros, but it makes a nice change to come here. It's weird playing in the middle of all these houses...."

The car glided along the forest lanes. In the late afternoon, after the cinema, Istvan and Natty liked to drive in the woods. They soon left Paris behind. When they reached the edge of a wood as magical as any in a fairy tale, Istvan would slow down, looking for a gap in the wall of trees, and find a promising lane. There, Natty was allowed to slip onto the front seat, next to him. They breathed in the fragrant, warm air, which brought in through the wide-open windows the smell of sunshine, held by the trees since morning.

"Don't you want to walk for a while?" asked Istvan.

"I'm tired. I like it when the car is silent. It's like a plane without an engine, landing in the middle of the trees."

"A glider. A plane without an engine is called a glider."

"Listen. Can you hear that noise, over there?"

"That's the sound of horses on the bridle paths."

Natty had been preoccupied for the last two days.

Sometimes she lost her on-court concentration completely as she stood facing Istvan, who never knew where to place his shots when she was acting this way. Disconcerted, he had tried to find out what was upsetting her. She had answered with an enigmatic silence.

That evening, as they drove around the ponds in the forest of Rambouillet, she seemed jumpy, starting at the slightest cry of a bird. He could see nothing of her but her hair. She kept her back to him, her chin resting on her arms, her head half out of the window, her eyes riveted on the trees that filed slowly by.

"Are you mad at me because we stopped playing this morning?" he asked. "We couldn't go on. You weren't even watching the ball."

"I don't care. Anyway, you're wasting your time with me. You'd do better to train for Flushing Meadow. You really should, you know. When are you leaving?"

"At the beginning of August."

"That means in two or three days."

"Look at me, Natty."

She drew her head in and shook her hair. He had stopped the car. The engine ticked over quietly. Istvan tried desperately to think of the right thing to say. He made her turn to face him and found her blue eyes full of tears, sadly defying him.

The door clicked open. Istvan's hand remained open as in a void. Natty ran, zigzagging through the freshly planted saplings. She stumbled, picked herself up, and kept on running, vanishing into a mass of dark oaks.

Istvan switched off the engine. He noticed that his hands were shaking for the first time he could remember. Shaking from . . . from what? He ran through the young trees, brushing against springy new branches as he passed. He did not shout after her; it was pointless. He

THE NET

knew by now that he would find her curled up and sobbing at the foot of a tree.

"Come on, Natty. Don't be silly. We'll take care of your ticket to New York. That's where we'll celebrate your birthday."

17

Mary Collins knew from the start not to make the same mistake as Livia Fabiani. She was just a journalist among so many others in the little group awaiting the landing of the TWA Boeing 747 carrying the tennis star. She pretended not to recognize Natty, whom she had only seen once. She contented herself with asking Istvan a few routine questions as she held out the CBS microphone—his physical condition, his training partners who would also be his opponents, his chances of playing as good a match as he had in July against Borg at Wimbledon.

Natty seemed unaffected by either jet lag or the sweltering heat of August in New York. She was sporting the radiant smile she saved for special occasions. Despite Istvan's efforts to persuade her that he would probably have difficulty surviving the quarter-finals, except for a miracle ("But you must never put your trust in miracles, Natty"), she was convinced that her champion would crush all those whom she indiscriminately called "the Americans."

"But you're American too!" he had told her. "You were born here, in New York."

THE NET

"During the Flushing Meadow finals, I know. That means that in three weeks, I'll be eleven."

Mary Collins was as discreet as her décolleté summer dresses were not. She showed no uncalled-for satisfaction when she learned, over the telephone, that Livia would not be accompanying Istvan. Surprised at seeing Natty by his side, she realized immediately that this rival would be much more formidable than any successful European novelist. Mary was much the wiser from her latest affair with a famous painter, who was single but came equipped with an eight-year-old son. The boy's constant presence had soured their relationship to the point of ending it. She decided the best course was to carry on as if children, big or small, did not exist. Livia, had she come to New York as part of the baggage, would certainly have acted as baby-sitter for Natty while Istvan trained. Mary, on the other hand, would only appear at the hotel when Natty was asleep and would leave well before dawn, not so much out of consideration for the champion's strength but because she liked to end the night alone in her large studio apartment where utter chaos ruled and she never entertained anybody.

Natty was already ensconced in the back of the limousine. Mary, standing by the door, shook Istvan's hand vigorously. She was ready with a suggestion.

"Betty, the sister of a friend of mine, is studying French literature at Columbia. She's twenty. She could keep your daughter company. They can perfect their French together."

"You think of everything," said Istvan.

"She wanted to be a hostess at the stadium, but she applied too late. It'll be a welcome little job for her."

"Okay, tell her to call me at the hotel."

* * *

ILIE NASTASE

After two days, Istvan was reassured. He congratulated himself on having brought Natty with him. She adored Betty, the plump French student. He had rented a car for her, so that she could drive around freely with Natty, whom she picked up at the hotel immediately after they had finished breakfast. This was a moment of intimacy that put Istvan in good spirits, as did dinner, which they also ate together, just the two of them, usually. It was a restful change from his training with his two American partners: Jim Gordon, a tall, fair-haired player with a powerful game, so elegant that he had been nicknamed Gentleman Jim; and Jimmy Connors, his friend.

Istvan was satisfied with his timetable, which assured his equilibrium and enabled him to feel in top shape on the courts. In the evening, he dined early with Natty, who always went to bed before nine o'clock. An hour later, Mary Collins appeared. Istvan temporarily locked the door that connected his room with Natty's. At midnight, Mary left, without failing to point out to Istvan that he was managing to experience the sweet intimacy of paternity without the constraints of married life.

"So far, everything's gone well," said Istvan, watching Mary as she stood naked in front of the mirror, brushing out her hair. "Natty's happy."

"And Connors says you're in great shape."

"She charms everybody. Except you. I sometimes get the feeling you're avoiding her."

"I've already told you, Istvan. From now on, Natty's your daughter, she's your business. I'm not avoiding her. I'm just making sure I don't interfere."

"Jim Gordon's wife adores her. She promised to play some sets with her."

"Cora's a good player. If she hadn't married Jim, she could have been a tournament player by now."

THE NET

"Jim didn't stop her playing."
"No, I know. It was her two miscarriages."
"You really *are* opposed to marriage, Mary. Why?"
"What about you? At thirty-two, you still haven't hauled down the pennant."

Mary didn't expect an answer, and she did not wait for him to go to sleep. His large frame was already sprawled across the bed. She shut the door gently, crossed the little corridor leading to Natty's room, closed the door that said 502 just as softly, and hurried to the elevators.

18

Natty and Cora Gordon were resting between rallies. Natty was checking her racket, which she spun like a top on the tip of her foot.

"Tell me, Cora. Jim isn't as good as Istvan, is he?"
"It depends. Some days he is, some days he isn't."
"Is he older?"
"They're the same age."
"Lucky you play with me. You can't rely on the men."

Cora Gordon burst out laughing, enchanted by Natty's precocity. The first time she saw her, it gave her a pang. Natty was so like her mother, Jane, whom Cora had known well. Màrton, Jim, Istvan, Jane, and she used to meet up all over the world, wherever the tournaments took them. For a time, they were inseparable, eating at the same table, celebrating the men's successes together. Neither Jane nor she had taken up competition tennis. They both remained good players who stayed in the background. They had taken the teaching exams, without really intending to teach, knowing they were destined to be tennis nomads.

THE NET

Jane and Cora were very much alike, both tall and blond, with blue eyes. But Jane's eyes, like Natty's, had been deeper and darker. During a South American tour, the highlight of which was the Buenos Aires tournament, Cora had discovered she was five years younger than Jane. Natty was then two years old, and Cora had told herself that when Jim was ready, they, too, would have a little girl.

As soon as she saw Natty again, the years started spinning inside her head. She had never been able to have a child. After one miscarriage, brought on by a car accident, she had had another, and the doctors held out no hope for her.

"Shall we carry on, Cora?"

"Let's go!"

She admired the precision of Natty's game. She was already a gangly adolescent, with thin legs and bony shoulders. She'll be even more beautiful than her mother, Cora said to herself. She couldn't recall seeing anyone center the shots on their racket so well at her age. Suddenly, Cora rediscovered the teaching methods she had learned but never had an opportunity to apply.

Betty, who was revising an Advanced French paper in the shade of a parasol, looked up from her file. She had looked after a number of children during the school year to earn pocket money. Usually they liked her. But she had never felt quite so maternal as she did toward Natty, even though the girl was nearly as tall as she was. She was ambivalent about Cora Gordon's monopolizing Natty more and more. "It's good for you, Betty," Cora had told her. "While I look after Natty, you can get on with your studies in peace." Betty smiled complaisantly, knowing Cora's connection to Istvan through her husband, but she felt that Cora was going too far. It was all right as long as she brought them both along for a tennis session at Flushing Meadow. But now she was interfering in their hamburger and hot-dog parties, telling Betty not to eat so many french fries and ice cream because of her complexion and large behind. Let her be Natty's mother if she wanted, but Betty was old enough to look after herself.

She looked up from her books and watched as a little motorbike pulled up courtside. On it was Mary Collins, who called out cheerily:

"Hello, Cora!"

Cora raised her racket in greeting and missed a shot that Natty had just sent over the net.

"Hello, Natty," Mary went on without getting off her bike. "Are you glad to be in New York?"

"It's okay. We're playing."

"So I see. I was just riding past, I don't want to disturb you. It's peaceful here. When I think of the chaos there'll be soon . . . Well, Cora, is Horwat's daughter any good?"

"I get by," replied Natty.

Every day, at the end of the afternoon, Cora Gordon went to fetch Jim after his training session with Istvan. One Sunday, Betty could not contain her excitement. She had been asked out by a boy from school whom she had not thought she would see again before the new term. Cora suggested she should go home, rest up, and make herself pretty. She would look after Natty.

Cora and Natty were sitting with huge glasses of fruit cocktail on the terrace of the bar overlooking the court where two of the top women players in the world were training: Billie Jean King and Rosie Casals.

"The men won't be long," said Cora. "They should be in the showers by now."

THE NET

"We're not in any hurry," replied Natty.

Cora looked up with interest. Natty was usually so impatient. Now she was following the ups and downs of the set between Billie Jean and Rosie with the relentless attention of an umpire. The same concentration as when we play, thought Cora. The girl really was amazing.

Natty was totally absorbed, as if nothing existed outside the rectangular court. The spectacle was worth watching. The two women played as if the tournament had already begun. Natty did not even seem to notice Istvan and Jim put their bags down on two empty chairs and order mineral water.

"Istvan wore me out," said Jim, kissing his wife.

"Well, Natty," said Istvan, "are you learning something? Not bad, eh? Real men, these women!"

"Yes," sighed Natty, "but they play so much more slowly than men!"

"You can't compare them," said Cora. "The best woman in the world would be beaten by the man graded two hundred and fiftieth! But women work harder."

"That remains to be seen," said Jim.

"Look," said Natty. "Forty-thirty! Billie Jean's going to win the first set! There! I knew she would. Rosie didn't run up to the net fast enough."

"We'll get Natty a job as commentator for ABC Sports," said Cora.

"I'm not interested," said Natty solemnly as Rosie Casals wiped her face and prepared to serve.

"What does interest you, then?" asked Istvan.

"You know very well. Holding a racket. One day, I'll be in Billie Jean's shoes."

"I hope not, for your sake," said Cora. "If you play tennis four hours a week, that's fine. To get to Billie Jean's level, you'd have to play four hours a *day*."

"So?"

"What about your studies?"

"School gives me a pain in the butt."

"Don't talk like that," said Istvan. "Anyway, you'll carry on with your studies. After that, we'll see."

"Then it'll be too late," said Jim. "If I had a daughter like Natty . . ."

He broke off and put an apologetic hand on Cora's shoulder, but she pushed it away.

"If we had a daughter," Cora said vehemently, with tears in her eyes, "she would not have done what I did, or what Jane did, that much I know."

"Mommy used to play very well!" said Natty, beginning to cry.

"Of course she did, better than me. Not only her studies but her whole life as a young woman. Friends, films, walks, dancing . . . At twenty, she understood. She decided to have you!"

She wiped her eyes and Natty's, then fell silent. All that could be heard was the sound of the balls on the court.

"What's the score?" sniffed Natty.

"Rosie's leading two games to one," Istvan replied automatically. "But it won't last."

"How do you know?"

"She's not relaxed today."

"Of course," said Cora, "women aren't reliable. It's a well-known fact."

"I didn't say that," protested Istvan. "I find you very aggressive."

"I'm sorry, Istvan, but you know, I was thinking about all that when I was out on the court with Natty."

"So tell me, is that going well?"

"Too well."

"What do you mean?"

THE NET

"She's not even eleven and already all she can think about is competing. I don't want you to turn her into a mass of muscles."

"She'll be a beautiful girl," said Jim.

"At Roedean, they tell me I'm a beanpole," said Natty.

"Precisely," said Cora. "You'll see."

"Game to Billie Jean," announced Natty.

"Besides," Cora went on, "Màrton might not have wanted her to become a champion. He had Jane's and my example. We gave up that idea very young. We stayed ignoramuses, uneducated. It was always ball, racket, racket, ball. And then we saw that we'd never make it. There's one woman champion every five years. If we'd thought of that earlier, we'd have had a normal youth."

"Don't go on about studies and all that again," said Jim.

"What about femininity, what happens to that? Natty will understand when she's older, but—"

"Oh, come on! I know about all that . . . and other things, too," declared Natty mischievously.

"Well I'm damned," said Jim.

"And she goes to the best school in England," said Istvan.

"Let her stay there," said Cora. "Try to understand what I'm saying, Istvan. Twenty percent tennis. Not a hundred percent."

"Yes, okay, you're right," Istvan said irritably.

He glanced at the neighboring tables, which had been empty earlier, and lowered his voice.

"Don't you think her father gave up everything too? Even though he wasn't a woman?"

"Yes, it's true. So have you. But you've been number one, you've made a fortune," said Cora.

"Now I'm only eighth and I can only go down from here, as you well know. As for a fortune . . . I'm thirty-two, Cora. The sponsors are still paying up, but what about later on?"

"We're in the same boat," said Jim. "But at least you've got Natty."

"And you've got Cora," rejoined Istvan.

"Thank you," said Cora with a sad smile. "The two of you make it sound as though that's not enough."

"You know what I wanted to be when I was thirteen or fourteen? An architect! A Hungarian Le Corbusier! I could already picture the plaques on great Western-style structures in the middle of Budapest: 'Istvan Horwat, architect.' Today, my signature's on shirts and shoes."

"And rackets," added Jim. "Your Adidas is very good."

"It's not 'my' Adidas. One day they'll put a different signature on a different model. Finished!"

"Billie Jean's amazing," said Natty, oblivious to the middle-aged debate about ill-spent lives. "You're not even watching! She's winning five–three in the second set! Cora can say what she likes, I'll play like her even if I don't have her muscles!"

"The career of a champion is very short and very monotonous, Natty. Tournaments all over the place, living out of suitcases, no family life, no time for a movie in the evening, no—"

"But there's tennis, Cora!"

"Your mother would have explained to you . . ."

"What her father would have told her," Istvan broke in, "would have been about his efforts, his anguish, his difficulty in getting motivated so that he felt like massacring his opponent. He couldn't keep it up. That's why he never gave all he could have given."

"I understand," said Natty. "It's no use being a good player, you've got to be the best."

THE NET

"You haven't understood a word I said," sighed Cora, disheartened.
"Yes I have, Cora," Natty said. "I understand. I just don't believe it."

19

In the Mercedes returning from Roissy Airport where she had seen Istvan off for the September Palermo tournament, Natty did not open her mouth. Thieu drove too slowly for her liking. She sat stiffly, her eyes barely level with the windshield.

Thieu glanced anxiously at her. This week in Paris, without Istvan, was going to be very long for Miss Natty, even though her schedule had been well organized. Every afternoon she would have a tennis lesson with Jacques, the coach and Istvan's friend, on the indoor court where they had gone in the mornings before Flushing Meadow. Everyone was returning from their vacations, Paris was full of people again, and the club was open. But what about the rest of the time? Thieu was reluctant to judge his employer, but he thought that Istvan could have taken Natty with him. No doubt he had his reasons. He, who had lost his three children, would not risk being parted from her, even for a few days, before she had to go back to her English school.

Natty, half-reclining between the two backseats, her

THE NET

legs on the armrests, was pondering all the possible forms of revenge on Mary Collins. She was certain it was she who had asked Istvan to go alone to Palermo where she was waiting for him. All that because one night, in New York, she had had a nightmare and been frightened. She fumbled around looking for the light for a moment, bumped into pieces of furniture in her room, finally found the door to Istvan's room, and realized it was locked. She called "Istvan," hammering on the door with her fists. He finally opened it, wrapped in a white bathrobe, hair disheveled. She flung herself into his arms and sobbed, but he stood there looking stern and did not even hug her. And he had been in a good mood the day before, not at all affected by being eliminated in the quarter-final by Vilas as he had predicted. Astonished, she looked up, seeking an explanation for his silence. She smelled perfume. Moving away from him, she rushed into the room and saw Mary Collins lying on the rumpled bed. Mary drew the blue sheet up to her breasts, but her legs were naked up to her stomach.

Natty spun round and fled to her room. Istvan made no attempt to stop her. Everything was ruined. The party planned for her birthday the next day meant nothing now. And yet she had found out from Betty, who could not keep a secret, that Istvan had hired a lounge at the hotel and that lots of players would be drinking champagne in her honor, and that she would be showered with gifts.

In front of Cora, Jim, Tanner, Jimmy Connors, and the two hundred guests, some of whom she knew by sight, Natty had forced a polite smile. She told herself that all these people had known her parents but did not dare mention them to her. Only Cora was able to talk about them, sometimes so naturally that Natty felt only a vague longing, as if they had gone away and would be back soon.

Mary Collins had the decency to keep out of sight after the incident the previous night. When Natty went over to blow out the eleven candles on the giant cake shaped like a tennis racket, she spotted the CBS crew filming her and Istvan. He was smiling the blissful smile of the fulfilled father, but Natty could only see Mary's nakedness in the rumpled sheets, and the CBS microphone they held out to her made her recoil. She refused to utter a word, which everyone took as an endearing sign of stage fright. The lights were switched out. It took Natty three attempts to blow out the candles, which did not improve her temper. She was so distraught that when the five musicians began to play "Happy Birthday," she put her hands over her ears.

Istvan did not dance. He withdrew into a corner with Frank Fenwick and pretended to be discussing business, forgetting how out of place it seemed at a party he was giving for his adopted daughter. Cora Gordon, sitting on a sofa, looked weary. Natty snuggled up to her as if for protection from strangers who came up and bowed ceremoniously, inviting her to dance. Betty began to unwrap the presents, but Natty decreed that since they would be going back to France it would be easier to carry everything as it was.

"It's not fair to Istvan or the other guests," protested Betty. "If I'd been given all those presents . . ."

"I don't care," retorted Natty. "Neither does Istvan. He won't even look at me."

Thieu parked the car in front of a shop that looked tiny but that extended back like a corridor and seemed to run the length of the old building.

THE NET

"Where are we?" asked Natty. "You know we had to buy the papers, I couldn't find a thing at Roissy."

"You can find newspapers everywhere, miss."

"I like you calling me 'miss.' What do they sell in there?"

"Spices for Vietnamese cooking. And incense to perfume the house, paper lanterns. Just look around and leave it to me."

Natty wandered around the corridor-shop. She recognized spring rolls, fresh mint, soybean sprouts, Chinese nougat, mangoes and lychees, which she had been wary of when Thieu first served them at the Avenue Robert-Schumann. But as for the rest, she found the vast array of cans and boxes with incomprehensible inscriptions as disconcerting as the unfamiliar language Thieu was speaking with a young man who was even smaller than he was. She had never heard Thieu speaking Vietnamese. He suddenly seemed very mysterious. He reassured her with a smile, pointing out the Chinese lanterns and the multicolored incense sticks. She felt a little dazed by the odor of pungent spices and fruits mixed with the sweet aroma of incense. Where had she felt this way before? She seemed to remember walking into a huge store, a long time ago, clutching her mother's hand. The shelves were too high for her to see, but the strong smells had made her feel sick. She reached out for a bottle of Nuoc-man and held it to her nostrils. A little of the brown liquid had run at the base of the cork. That was the mixture Thieu served in a crystal cruet. She remembered something Istvan had said:

"It's very energy-giving, but it's best not to know what's in it."

And as she insisted, he burst out laughing: "Ask Thieu."

But he had not wanted to tell her, either. She concluded it was a magic potion, a witches' brew concocted of secret ingredients, that made you play tennis very well. Today, she would find out. She interrupted Thieu's chatter and asked the little shop assistant, who replied that it was "fish juice."

"So the fish is rotten!" she exclaimed. "That's why it smells so disgusting."

Thieu shrugged and piled the exotic purchases into an empty carton with a peeling red label marked "Hong Kong."

"For lunch," she said, "you can make me steak and salad. I'm playing this afternoon."

To accustom her to Asian cooking, Thieu asked her to help him prepare complicated, colorful dishes, giving her the job of tasting them and perfecting the seasoning. That kept her busy for most of the mornings. He was astounded at his pupil's progress. When Istvan telephoned from Palermo every evening at seven o'clock for a report of the day's activities, Thieu was full of praise: "Miss Natty made the beef in a hot sauce all by herself." Or: "When you come back, she'll be able to make you lacquered duck!"

"But she's not spending all her time in the kitchen is she? What about her tennis?"

"I'll let Miss Natty tell you about that herself."

But Natty was not very talkative on the telephone. She simply replied yes or no. Thieu tactfully left her alone in the drawing room. From the dining room, all he could hear were long silences, punctuated by onomatopoeic sounds. He thought monsieur must have been disappointed, but he did not disapprove of Miss Natty—quite the contrary. He knew what chatterboxes Istvan's girl

THE NET

friends were. Natty had time to learn to babble. Anyway, why telephone home every evening? Wasn't Thieu there to make sure that everything was all right? As for the Palermo tournament, didn't Thieu read about Istvan Horwat's drive for the finals, which he should carry off with ease, in the sporting paper *L'Equipe?*

"Thieu? I'll hand you back to Istvan."

Once again, Thieu repeated that Miss Natty was no trouble, she got up early, went to bed early, and had not even asked him to take her to the movies. They had, however, bought several *Asterix* and *Lucky Luke* books. No, Madame Fabiani had not called since he had left. But Countess Balanska would soon be back from the Balearic Islands. In any case, the phone rarely rang, since everyone knew that monsieur was in Palermo.

Thieu hung up, relieved. The receiver gave him a headache.

As he made a clear soup with vermicelli for Natty, who insisted on setting the table by herself, with chopsticks instead of knives and forks, he tried hard to banish a certainty that had become increasingly apparent and of which he was ashamed: he was in no hurry to see Istvan return from Palermo. Life was so pleasant with Natty, so peaceful. She only made a mess in her room. Thieu tidied it indulgently when she went off to play tennis. He sighed as he piled up the scattered books, arranged the dolls on cushions, and washed her laundry. He kept some of the drawings she left lying around and took them to his room near the pantry on the seventh floor, which he always called "the ground floor," just as he called the eighth floor, where Natty and Istvan's rooms were, "the first floor." In the evenings, he would stare for hours at the drawings, which reminded him of the days when he had a family. He liked thinking of her as the mistress of this little house perched over the Bois de Boulogne. When he ironed her white tennis shorts and Lacoste shirts, he could picture her standing triumphantly on a podium one day.

"Read this, Miss."

Thieu spread *L'Equipe* on the kitchen table while Natty fumed because she had just spoiled a hot pepper sauce.

"You read it. What's happened?"

" *Istvan Horwat had an easy victory at the Palermo tournament in the absence of his usual major rivals. Yesterday afternoon in the finals, he beat a solid player, the Swede Holgersson, ranked twenty-fifth, by six–four, seven–five.*' That's why he didn't phone yesterday evening. I bet he'll turn up today and surprise us."

"What's going on, Thieu? Couldn't you hear the phone?"

"I was in the kitchen with Miss Natty, monsieur."

"Again! I'm at Roissy. I'll wait for you in the restaurant."

"Shall I bring Miss Natty, monsieur?"

"Of course. It'll be a change from the kitchen."

"May I congratulate you, monsieur. I read about it in the papers . . ."

"Thank you, Thieu. Hurry up. You will have lunch with us."

"Miss Natty's got her tennis lesson at three o'clock, monsieur."

"So she'll be a bit late for once. Jacques won't kill us."

Natty was standing in front of the wall mirror in Istvan's bathroom, debating whether to wear the red cotton top and matching embroidered dress he had brought her from Sicily. She did not like the pattern, but mainly it seemed much too small for her. Since Istvan's departure, she had got into the habit of bathing naked in the bathtub-cum-

THE NET

swimming-pool, taking care to lock the door. What was she supposed to do with this one-piece swimsuit? She had no breasts and could hardly see herself wearing the bottom half of a bikini. Another of Mary Collins's ideas, she thought. But she decided to slip it on. The result was disastrous. The shoulder straps were too long and slid down onto her arms, and the bottom cut into her buttocks.

"It looks like a leotard gone wrong," she sighed.

By this time she was furious and hurriedly tried on the dress to have done with the whole thing. No, Mary Collins couldn't have chosen that. A woman, no matter how stupid, could not have got Natty's size so wrong. It was Istvan, it had to be Istvan who had found this dress for an eight-year-old. The hem was hardly longer than a T-shirt and the bodice cut into her ribs and shoulder blades. It was as tight as a corset. She stood with her arms hanging by her sides, her nose pressed to the mirror, inventing the most grotesque grimaces.

"I'm really sorry," said Istvan. "You've grown so fast . . ."

Natty jumped and spun around.

"Thanks all the same," she said, "it's a souvenir. . . . Can I take it off? It's going to split. But don't look at the swimsuit, it's really pornographic!"

"What?"

"You'll see."

She lifted up the hem of the dress and wriggled out of the straitjacket. With her head buried in the embroidered material, she gyrated as Istvan looked on in horror.

"Okay, that's enough, anyone can make a mistake. We'll buy a big doll to put in the dress."

"Whew!" sighed Natty, red in the face. "I nearly suffocated."

ILIE NASTASE

And without a word of warning, she dove into the bathtub, splashing Istvan and leaving the dress crumpled on the floor.

"And with that bathing suit I'll drown, I can't move!"

Then, standing on the bottom step:

"It feels as if it's shrunk even more in the water!"

The material had become transparent, making Natty look more naked than naked. Istvan handed her his large white bathrobe with the initials I.H., but she was already writhing to get the swimsuit down to her ankles. She pulled her wet hair back from her face before wrapping herself in the bathrobe.

"Tell me, Istvan, it must have been lovely in Palermo at this time of year?"

"It was, almost too hot."

"So why are you so pale with great bags under your eyes?"

"Do you think I had time to lie on the beach and sunbathe?"

"Everybody says it was an easy tournament for you. That can't be why you're so tired. What does Miss Collins say when you wake up looking like that? You should be careful. It's the same for all sports. Over the age of thirty, it's harder to get your strength back. Jim Gordon said that at Flushing Meadow, and he's the same age as you."

Istvan could not believe his eyes when Natty's racket landed at his feet. The laughter of a few tired players watching him work out on a court at Roland-Garros made him both ashamed and furious. Despite Thieu's protests—he insisted on taking her side—Istvan maintained that the child had become unbearable since he had left her on her own in Paris for a week. And yet he had shown great patience with her.

THE NET

As she disagreed with all the well-meaning young women to whom he had hoped to entrust the task, he had ended up going from boutique to boutique with her himself to buy a new wardrobe for her return to Roedean. The assistants, always prompt to ask for his autograph, took pity on him in vain. After they had displayed their entire stock of pullovers, skirts, dresses, and navy-blue coats, as well as their assortment of white blouses, Natty always ended up declaring that everything looked too much like a uniform. One morning, in exasperation, he went on his own to a large department store and filled a suitcase with clothes he ended up hating himself. Of course, everything was too big, as opposed to his Sicilian present. Furious, he sent Thieu out to change everything. And then, with a huge, sincere smile, Natty had insisted on going, too.

Now, at Roland-Garros, he fought back the urge to jump over the net, put Natty over his knee, and give her a good hiding. But he watched her walk slowly round the court, her hair in her eyes. She walked over to him and picked up her racket without a word, waiting for him to walk toward the exit.

"Why did you do that, Natty?" he asked as they walked along the avenue.

She shrugged.

"I brought you to Roland-Garros to please you."

She stopped and looked him defiantly in the eyes. "To please me! You're always talking about pleasing me! Did you leave me alone in Paris and buy me ridiculous clothes to please me? Is it to please me that you push me so hard to play tennis when I'm tired?"

He strode toward the apartment, swinging his bag. He did not want to think about anything. He did not even turn round to see if she was following. He closed the elevator door behind him, pressed the top button, and stepped right into his apartment.

"Thieu, go and get Natty, she's downstairs in the avenue. She won't be eating with me. I'm going out."

20

The net closed tightly, in a night brightened only by the phosphorescent eddies of foam. Istvan's head, heavy and painful, was dragging his paralyzed body toward the abyss. Seaweed, bleached by the foam, made his hair look like an old man's. He dreaded it—that octopus of a net lying in wait for its prey—and yet he screamed only when the mesh crushed his lungs and his blood mingled with the whirlpool, tinging the water pink. As he struggled, his arm knocked the switch that made the circular bed revolve. He was still screaming when he sat up, adrift in the rotating movement.

The lights came on. Dazzled, he burrowed under the perspiration-soaked sheet.

"Istvan! Istvan! What's the matter? How do you stop this thing?"

He had never shown Natty how the bed worked for fear she would turn it into a merry-go-round. She shook him and yanked back the sheet he was clasping.

"I'm not feeling good," he said. "Go away!"

She found the stop switch, having first pressed the one

that opened the curtains and shutters. She picked up a pillow from the floor and slid it under Istvan's head. He opened his eyes and saw standing before him a tall girl with very short blond hair, dressed in a black velvet sweatshirt and white trousers.

"What time is it?"

"It's after midday. I've just been to the hairdresser's. I wanted to surprise you. Thieu told me to let you sleep, but I was in my room and heard you shout. What did you do last night?"

"Go and get my bathrobe from the bathroom."

Under the shower set to maximum strength, he recalled a few snatches of the previous night at Régine's. The music was still pounding in his head. He remembered Bjorn Borg shaking him, asking him what was wrong. A woman whose face he could not remember emptied the whiskey bottle into a champagne bucket to stop him from drinking any more. He still had the taste of whiskey in his mouth. What had gotten into him to make him drink like that? Normally he could hardly stand the smell of alcohol.

The water stung his face; his muscles smarted and tingled. He gradually came back to life. Why had Natty had her hair cut without consulting him? He made himself get out of the shower.

Natty, leaning on the balustrade of the balcony, was listening to the sound of balls hitting rackets that rose from Roland-Garros.

"Noah phoned. You had an appointment with him at nine o'clock. He doesn't mind. Everyone knows you had too much to drink at Régine's. He just said to call him back to arrange another day, when you're feeling better."

"What about your hair? Who did that to you?"

"Carita. I went there once before with Livia. They fitted

THE NET

me in between two appointments. I said it was urgent because the two of us were going away."
"You're completely mad. I suppose Thieu drove you there?"
"I told him that you had agreed and that we'd made an appointment. I'm sorry. He dropped me outside Carita's. I took a taxi back."
"Go and wait for me downstairs. Tell Thieu to make me a giant, hot, freshly squeezed lemon drink."

"It's not a good time to tell him about your plans, miss."
In the kitchen, Natty watched Thieu tip up the lemon-squeezer, pour the juice of three lemons into the thick, preheated punch glass, and add a third of a glass of boiling water.
"Will he drink it like that, without any sugar?"
"Above all without sugar!"
"What about the coffee?"
"Very strong, with two aspirin. Here, dissolve them in a little water. Now add some granulated sugar."
"You certainly know what you're doing."
"I used to be a pharmacist in Saigon, before—psst, he's coming down. Put the tray on the table. I'm shutting myself up in the kitchen."

Istvan adopted a casual air as he sat down opposite Natty. She saw that his face, with dark shadows under his eyes, almost matched his gray track suit.
"Haven't you dried your hair?" she asked him.
"The noise of the razor was bad enough."
He sipped the steaming glass of lemon without flinching. When he put it down, it grated on the marble

tabletop. His hand, which was shaking slightly, went for the glass of aspirin.

"What a mixture," he said with disgust. "I'm saving the coffee till last, it's the best."

"Istvan, I've got to talk to you."

"What about?"

"Something really important."

"You want to buy yourself a wig?"

"Don't laugh at me, it's serious. I'm fed up with tennis."

"Tell me about it later. There've been times when I've been fed up with tennis, too. And I've still got a headache."

"That's not all. I'm sick of Roedean too. I don't want to go back to England."

Istvan drained his second cup of coffee. He looked at Natty's determined face framed by her short hair. Her eyes, which all of a sudden seemed deeper and bigger, told him that trouble was only just beginning. The racket Natty had flung at him at Roland-Garros was not just a kid's display of temper, any more than his drunkenness of the night before had persuaded him that with the end of her vacation, new problems wouldn't arise. He sat and waited, too hung over to speak.

"Don't you want to know why?"

He raised his eyebrows inquiringly.

"Well," she began, "I'll ask you: why England? You're not English and neither am I. My parents often came to see me at Roedean. And in the summer, they took me on a cruise. In the winter, they sent me skiing in Switzerland, at Christmas and even at Easter . . ."

If she begins to cry, thought Istvan, all I can do is leave the room. But she did not. Her eyes were dry and her voice forceful.

"They played tennis, like you, but they never forced me

THE NET

to. I asked you to work out with me, okay. But now you use it as an excuse to get rid of me!"

"Don't exaggerate, Natty," sighed Istvan through his headache. "What do you want me to do?"

"Send me to a school where I can ski! We've got to hurry. The season is nearly here."

"You're off your head. It's too late. No schools anywhere are still enrolling new pupils."

"There'll always be a place for me. I'm your daughter, and you're you."

2

Edelweiss School in Gstaad did indeed agree to enroll Istvan Horwat's adoptive daughter as a special favor on the recommendation of Countess Balanska, whose children had done well at this very exclusive Swiss institution. Faced with Istvan's helplessness, his old friend the countess had taken charge of operations.

"Don't fall out with the headmistress of Roedean," she advised. "You never know."

Natty had retorted that she would never set foot in Roedean again, but the countess silenced her. "You don't know anything. At your age, you often change your mind. You used to swear by tennis, now all you can talk about is skiing. Since Istvan is weak enough to give in to your whims, leave things to me!"

She insisted on taking Natty to Gstaad herself, which would leave Istvan in peace with Mary Collins, who wanted nothing to do with the whole affair.

"I know Edelweiss very well, dear Istvan. Don't worry about a thing."

She launched into a glowing description of the com-

THE NET

fortable little dormitory chalets that each housed two boarders ("They're like little dolls' houses"), grouped around one large chalet where classes were held and another that was reserved for cultural activities, with a library, chess room, and television lounge.

"What about skiing?" asked Natty.

"The instructors are among the best in Switzerland." The glossy brochure confirmed the edelweiss to be "très cher"—a flower both expensive and rare, like the school itself.

Thieu was at loose ends, left to mourn Natty's departure in an atmosphere that mingled Istvan's relief with the countess's bustling and Natty's impatience. She could talk of nothing but schussing and slaloms, decreed that Paris was definitely unbearable, and said that she was sick of the city. Thieu wandered around the apartment, his head bowed, assuring for the umpteenth time that Natty had forgotten nothing. He had packed the suitcases so meticulously the day before her departure that she had to unpack everything to find something to wear.

"You really can't wait to get rid of me!" she exclaimed.

She was distressed when he looked up.

"Are you *crying?*"

"It's nothing, miss. When you come back, you can teach me Swiss cooking."

"You *are* crying! You're sad because I'm leaving! And I thought you never showed your feelings." She kissed his damp cheeks and added, "You're the only one. Istvan's perfectly happy to see me go!"

Thieu did not have the strength to play the devoted servant who always defended his master. Mary Collins had telephoned very early. Before Thieu had even had time to put her through to Istvan, she asked if Natty had left yet. So she knew the date of the Swissair flight, if not the time. That was all it took for Thieu to build the whole thing up into a melodrama with Natty as the heroine, the victim of a plot. He felt that Istvan had been too quick to jump at Natty's suggestion to send her away to ski. . . . As for Countess Balanska, who had been suspicious of him as long as he had worked for Istvan, Thieu had never been able to stand the way she behaved like a forty-year-old femme fatale. She was the chief plotter in this scheme to send an innocent soul to the cold, to the mountains.

"Thieu, I'll send you a photo of me, in my ski gear standing outside my chalet in the snow."

As the months passed, Natty's postcards became less frequent. At Christmas, Istvan decided to go to the Bahamas rather than explore the Edelweiss chalets. Thieu had shown him a photo of Natty, holding onto it as if he were afraid someone would snatch it from his grasp. It could have been any long-legged girl—her face was engulfed by a red hood and half-covered by goggles. As Istvan did not seem particularly moved by the sight of her, Thieu hid the photo in his room, under the drawings he had stolen from her.

But Istvan was out of his depth with Mary Collins, who had deserted her hotel for the apartment in the Avenue Robert-Schuman, despite Thieu's quiet but evident opposition to this invasion. Above all, Istvan had to cope with Fenwick's increasing pessimism as sponsors' offers became less and less frequent.

"After the tournaments, things were still okay," said Fenwick, taking his file cards out of his pockets and shuffling them like a pack of cards. "We've got to hang on, Istvan, we've got to hang on."

"I am hanging on!"

THE NET

"Too many women. Be satisfied with your journalist. Take more interest in your daughter. Yes! Now I'm the one who's telling you. You're thirty-three. It's time to calm down."

Istvan was only too well aware of that. But he was trapped. The career he had pursued to the top now seemed like a precipice. His inevitable fall made him giddy. So he made the most of the money he had left, and the royalties he was still earning. Sometimes, when he trained with much younger players, their admiration for him hurt. Didn't they realize that his genius was intact? It was his body that was being gradually overtaken. His body, not him . . .

In the spring, he agreed to see Livia Fabiani, who had stopped telephoning him three months earlier. Since then, bored with Mary Collins, he had been flaunting his new mistress, Carla, the top model of the moment, in the Bahamas, while Livia thought he was with Natty.

Livia had invited him to her apartment in the Rue Jacob. She was just back from a trip to Ireland. She intended to go and live there, more for tax purposes than out of love for wild ponies.

"I hope Natty's happy," she said.

"She's all right."

"In eight months, you haven't managed to make time to go to Gstaad for a week?"

"I don't think that's any of your business, Livia. I do what I can."

"Well, I went to see her. Champagne?"

"What? Yes . . . You did? I suppose she behaved abominably?"

"She was delightful. She showed me around the chalet

she shares with her friend Baba Bugatti. She introduced me to her ski instructor. She said I was her aunt."

"Did you see the headmaster?"

"He gave me permission to take her out to dinner."

"Did he say anything?"

"No, why?"

"She's goofing off. I'll go and see her after Roland-Garros. I've got to have it out with her."

"I don't understand. Can't she come back here for the Easter holidays?"

"So that she can start with the Vietnamese cooking and the tantrums again? I can do without that at the moment."

"Then I really don't understand. When your journalist was around, fair enough—"

"What have you got against Mary Collins?"

"She tried to come between you and Natty. But since you've kicked her out, like all the others . . ."

"Perhaps you're right, Livia. When are the Easter holidays?"

"In four days."

"I'll phone her. She'll come to Paris."

"Listen, Istvan. You may think I'm being ridiculous, after what happened between us, but I could go and fetch her."

"It's very kind of you, Livia. But she's traveled on her own before. In fact, this almost feels like she's coming to fetch me."

22

Natty was standing up very straight against the kitchen wall. Thieu slid a pencil through her hair at the top of her head, and drew a little horizontal line.

"Go and get the tape measure out of the drawer."

He measured the height of the line three times, while Natty looked on disdainfully.

"You're wasting your time. I told you, five-foot-two and a half."

"It isn't possible! You're as tall as me!"

"I'll be twelve this summer. So, it is possible. And now that I'm at school in Switzerland, I don't think I like rotten fish juice anymore. Will you cook me some nice chunks of steak?"

Thieu put the tape measure back in the drawer, appeased. He jumped at the sound of Istvan's voice.

"What are you up to, still messing around in the kitchen? Thieu, please go and put away Natty's things. As for you, come onto the balcony. You haven't said a word to me since you've been home."

As he looked at Natty standing with her back to the

light on the balcony overlooking the Bois de Boulogne, Istvan was reminded of Mary Collins's see-through dress when she came to interview him after Wimbledon the previous summer. Natty stood in the same pose, leaning against the smoked-glass parapet. Under her T-shirt, on which "tennis" was inscribed in different-sized capital letters, he could make out the breasts that had appeared during the last term. A headband held her hair. Istvan, who had prepared his lecture so thoroughly, no longer knew what to say.

Natty noticed him looking at her. "I suppose you think my legs are too long, like everyone else? In Gstaad they call me a beanpole. They're all warped, except Baba."

"Your legs are fine, Natty, but there's something wrong with your head. Do you remember what Cora said at Flushing Meadow? The most important thing is for you to do well in your schoolwork. You didn't want to go back to Roedean, so I sent you to Edelweiss. And now you're not doing any work at all. The headmaster phoned me three times last month."

"What more does he want? I get by in French and English."

"Yes, but have you seen your latest report? Math, C-minus. Natural science, D-plus. History, D-minus."

Natty sighed and pushed back a strand of hair that had escaped from her headband.

"And what about skiing? They think you get caught up in the slalom poles on purpose!"

"Skiing isn't a sport, it's just fun. You should see the idiots who take it too seriously, Istvan, really. Those elephant boots, those parkas like eiderdowns, those divers' masks! Besides, just about all the girls who ski are hopeless. In tennis, it's the opposite. At Edelweiss, the instructors are useless, too. They don't teach risks. I'm better

THE NET

than half of them. If you'd come and visit me, you'd see for yourself!"

"I thought you didn't like tennis."

"At one point I didn't, because I wanted to ski. But now—"

"This is no good at all, Natty. You're not making the slightest effort, and you're not considering me at all. I've got my training and my tournaments. How do you expect me to concentrate if I'm always worried about you?"

"I think if I went back to tennis and got some good coaching—really good, I mean—you wouldn't have to worry about me anymore." She smiled persuasively. "But you'll worry anyway."

"We'll discuss all that again when you start summer vacation. But this coming term, you'll just have to make an effort."

"What about afterward?"

"Maybe I'll surprise you. If you'll buckle down at school and surprise me."

Contrary to Livia Fabiani's pessimistic predictions, Istvan reached the quarter-finals at Roland-Garros. Even though he did not get any further, Fenwick was not too dissatisfied.

But when Istvan thought about the end of the school term, he felt helpless. He often telephoned Natty, who told him cheerfully that everything was all right. The headmaster no longer called Istvan; that was a good sign. But he was certain that this was only a respite. During his long periods of insomnia, he tried to reassure himself, thinking that Natty was at a difficult age, that all he had to do was be patient, but he always felt guilty. He no longer dared talk about her with anyone. He avoided Countess Balanska and Livia. What would he say to them? That Natty was vegetating at Edelweiss and he could see no way out of his predicament?

Some nights, while he lay awake listening to Carla's breathing, Marton's and Jane's faces loomed before his eyes. Were they frowning at him? Did he not deserve their reproach? If he had not had such a horror of drugs, he would have asked his doctor for sleeping pills to break this cycle he was in. Contrary to habit, he allowed Carla to stay and sleep with him because having her there in the dark kept at bay the nightmare of the net and the eddy sucking him in. But his thoughts about Natty's future haunted him no matter what.

Gradually he came to resent Thieu. Like Marton's and Jane's ghosts, the Vietnamese kept looking at him reproachfully, then quickly lowering his eyes, exasperating him with his silence.

Yet it was Thieu who, one morning, suggested an idea that should have occurred to him. Istvan went down to the dining room, leaving his bedroom to Carla. He felt weary and bad-tempered, having finally fallen asleep very late. He complained that the soft-boiled eggs were overcooked and the coffee lukewarm. From the kitchen, where he was cooking more eggs and putting the percolator back on the range, Thieu shouted something that Istvan did not catch.

"If you want to talk to me, come in here!"

"I'm keeping an eye on the eggs, otherwise they'll be too hard again."

"What did you say?"

"I'm coming!"

He stood in front of Istvan, who took a few gulps of scalding-hot coffee and dipped the thin fingers of toast in an egg: "Come on, out with it."

"Miss Natty's grandfather is in Aachen, monsieur."

THE NET

"Where?"

"In Aachen, Germany. For the world driving championship."

Driving at 120 MPH along the autobahn, Istvan felt relaxed for the first time in weeks. He was going to be able to talk to the brusque little man with the gray mustache about Natty, in Hungarian. He remembered the bus making its way along the uneven road toward the stud farm, over the snow-covered puszta. That day, which already seemed ages ago, when he had decided to take the place of Natty's father, there in the little groom's lodgings above the stables . . .

For the time being, he did not want to think about anything except driving. He passed a red Porsche convertible. Three girls, their hair streaming in the wind, waved to him as he drove past. He smiled. Sandor Kotany was going to be surprised. No doubt concern over the authorities who monitored mail had prompted him to say nothing about his trip to Aachen in the short letter he had sent two months earlier asking for news of Natty. Istvan had written back, even more briefly, that she was well. When he saw Sandor now, he could be more explicit.

The horse reigned for a week in Charlemagne's city during the greatest equestrian competition in the world. Istvan had not troubled to telephone the Kaiserhof, the massive, majestic palace where he had stayed during a tournament more than two years before. He knew that although all the hotels were full, there would always be a room for Istvan Horwat at the Kaiserhof, where he would meet the best horsemen in the competition and the masters of dressage. The town had been invaded by tens of thousands of spectators, and he nosed his car carefully through the crowds in the inner city to get to the hotel.

ILIE NASTASE

As he got out and turned the car over to the parking valet, he remembered how he had been awakened at about four o'clock every morning by the dawn because the rooms here were strangely devoid of shutters and curtains.

The porter managed to achieve a miracle. Herr Horwat would not have to sleep in his car. Without bothering to open the suitcase that Thieu had packed in record time, Istvan set off across town to find Natty's grandfather.

At the competition office, he was told that the Hungarian team was staying at the Hotel Muller. There was every chance he would find him there, since the day's heats were over. But the slightly homesick Hungarian delegation was not prepared to let Istvan Horwat, their national hero, leave so easily. He had to agree to have dinner with his countrymen.

The Hotel Muller, unlike the Kaiserhof, was in perfect keeping with Sandor's lodgings on the stud farm. Even with the address they had written out for him on a card, Istvan had difficulty finding it, situated as it was on a disorienting bend in a warren of streets near the railway station. The peeling facade bore witness to the hasty rebuilding of Germany after the war. A chubby girl at the reception desk, dozing over a copy of *Brigitte,* said laconically, "Room twenty-one." Then, looking up at Istvan, she added almost pleasantly: "Second floor."

In the dimly lit corridor, Istvan found room 21, next to the communal bathroom. He knocked several times, but there was no answer. He was on his way back down the hall, planning to return later, when the door opened and Sandor, in shirt-sleeves, suspenders, and jodhpurs, appeared sleepily on the threshold. Without a word, he opened his arms and embraced Istvan.

"I fell asleep," he said apologetically.

THE NET

"It's only seven o'clock."
"I know. There were heats this morning and this afternoon. Then I had to take care of the horses. To tell you the truth, I'm not in very good shape."
"I was counting on inviting you to dinner, but when I dropped into the office to find out where you were staying—"
"They requisitioned you, the way they dragooned our horses during the war! Anyway, we all eat together. I'll have you put near me."
"I need to talk to you in private," said Istvan.
"My room is very small," said Sandor, rapping his knuckles on the thin wall beside them in a gesture familiar to Eastern Bloc citizens. "We could walk a little."
"You're tired. Let's have a drink at the Kaiserhof bar."

Over chilled glasses of herbed vodka, Istvan poured out his troubled feelings about Natty. The old man listened quietly, until he heard about her performance at school.
"I *thought* she couldn't be doing well at school," said Sandor. "You've never mentioned her school work when you write."
"I don't know what Màrton and Jane would have done in my shoes. She's at one of the best Swiss schools—"
"They'd most likely have ended up having her back home with them," volunteered Sandor. "Jane mentioned it to me. She wanted to stop the tennis and look after Natty. She was going to, too."
He drained his glass and ran his tongue over his mustache. Then he considered for a long minute. Istvan respected his silence.
"Erzebet and I are constantly worrying about Natty's future," Sandor said finally. "We know you are doing all you can."

"No, I don't think I know how to go about it, how to do the right thing, the best thing. I don't phone her often enough, but I don't know what to say to her anymore."

"You people in the West, you attach too much importance to the telephone. Màrton always used to tell me that. Anyway, Erzebet thinks that Natty is too old for boarding school now. Nothing can take the place of a mother and father."

"So I'm finding. But what can I do, that I'm not doing already? I'm on my own, Sandor."

"What have you planned for the holidays?"

"Nothing yet, it's always a problem."

"She can stay with us. That'll give us all time to think about her fall term at school."

"Stay with you?"

"For July and August, if you like. If I recall, you won't have much time to look after her. There's Wimbledon, then Flushing Meadow. I'll teach her to handle the horses. That'll be a healthy change from tennis all the time."

Istvan stared at Sandor's hands, which lay crossed on the table. They were thick, strong, and worn. Rough as the life he led. Once again, silence fell between them and Istvan was even more confused. Suddenly, he felt afraid. Why had he come to tell all this to the old man? Did he subconsciously want to get rid of Natty, send her back to Hungary? Having made the commitment to be her guardian, he felt uncomfortable at the thought. He remembered his conviction, which had not changed: with her upbringing, she could not live anywhere else but in the West.

"Of course, it's only for the holidays," added Sandor. "Even though, afterward, if you don't feel up to it, Erzebet and I could probably manage to—"

"It's impossible," said Istvan. "Forget what I've told

THE NET

you. Natty's going through a difficult stage, that's all. If she doesn't like Edelweiss, I'll find her another school."

"It's not only a question of which school," said Sandor. "Affection and company are more important. I know how generous you are, Istvan, but it's not enough just to sign checks to pay tuition or to buy clothes. You're rich, but money isn't everything."

"I know, I'm sure Natty would be very happy with you this summer." He put two fingers on the sides of his empty glass, turning it back and forth on the tabletop. Then he looked up at Sandor. "I'll apply for a visa for her."

23

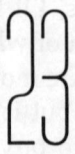

The months that followed Natty's vacation in Hungary were punctuated by her requests to leave Gstaad. But Istvan had decided to hold out for another year, all the more because he knew what Natty was getting at, even if she did not spell it out. She returned depressed from her stay with her grandparents, even though it had been reduced to one month. She did not want anything more to do with skiing. Now she did not want anything more to do with horses. When Istvan telephoned her, she asked him about nothing except the new tennis players:

"Have you noticed that the champions are getting younger and younger?" She complained that her teacher at Edelweiss was hopeless. "He's not even third-rank level. How do you expect me to improve?"

"Start by improving in math."

It was like a dialogue with the deaf, Istvan thought, and for his part he pretended not to understand that in Natty's mind it was no longer even a question of finding a new boarding school, but of coming to live with him in Paris.

THE NET

In case he had any doubts, his servant was ready with arguments in her favor:

"Miss Natty won't get in your way at all," Thieu told him. "I'll look after her. You'll make a champion out of her."

"You could also open a Vietnamese restaurant, and she can do the cooking!"

Since his mediocre showing in the first three tournaments of the 1980 Grand Slam, in which he got no further than the quarter-finals, Istvan had known that he had to get a grip on himself. All the more so because in February 1981, in the Davis Cup against England, he had lost two singles on the indoor courts at Eastbourne, to John Lloyd and Buster Mottram. The English had also beaten Istvan and his fellow Hungarian Taroczy in the doubles. Frank Fenwick was forever lecturing him, and no matter how hard Istvan tried to avoid him, F.F. always managed to waylay him, looking alternately stern and upset.

"All the things I keep saying, you already know, Istvan. I sometimes get the feeling you're running away from the facts. You're thirty-three, you can't go on living it up the way you used to at twenty-five! You need a quiet, balanced life, whatever that is these days. Just look at you, beaten in the first round of the Davis Cup, and you didn't get beyond the third round at Flushing Meadow last season! You, the record holder of wins in the Masters—but the last one goes back two years. Now you're seventeenth, just asking to be beaten by the thirtieth or fortieth in the Strasbourg and Clermont-Ferrand exhibition tournaments. You're going to have to find regional sponsors! I don't know a single one. There's no point dwelling on lousy results, but we have to learn something from this. Your gross take from your contracts has already gone down by more than half since you've been out of the top ten."

"Adidas is still a taker . . ."

"Yes, they're sentimental, but I had a hell of a job hanging on to that one. If you keep going like this, next year you'll be thirty-second, and when you're sixty-fifth, what will you do? You've blown all your money. All you'll have left is debts and a dependent child. Do you think you'll still be driving around in a Mercedes 450? I can just picture you at the wheel of a second-hand Peugeot!"

Istvan knew he had lived as if his life would end at forty. And Fenwick had reminded him all too often that he had had the misfortune to be number one before there was "real money" in tennis.

"Now, look at McEnroe, he's beginning to rake it in," Fenwick said. "He'll leave you the crumbs. A racket endorser, or sportswear salesman, or public relations officer for Adidas? You can't even be a sports *commentator* on the TV. . . . Okay, you speak very good French for a Hungarian, but not well enough for a Frenchman. And your English isn't good enough for the BBC, we all know how choosy *they* are. Nor is your German anything I can sell to Deutsche Fernsehen. You've got to straighten things out. You've lived like a star and you didn't even marry a rich woman! Now you'll have to earn some money, which you'll let me manage, and no throwing it away."

"In the meantime," said Istvan, "advance me twenty thousand."

Fenwick laughed. "I'm sure you'll pick up in time for the spring tournaments. How's Natty, anyway?"

"She could be working harder."

"Look who's talking. Is she coming back for Easter?"

"No. After everything you've just said, it doesn't sound like I've got time to look after her. Do I?"

24

Natty Kotany and Baba Bugatti were not very proud of having hitchhiked to Geneva. They had gone from a playboy's Ferrari to a container truck loaded with meat, finally leaving a pastor's VW beetle for the regular bus service between Lausanne and Geneva, which dropped them on the shores of Lake Geneva.

"The trip didn't cost us much," said Baba. "Just the short bus ride."

"Besides, we've covered our tracks well," said Natty. "The bus driver didn't even look at us. But we look pretty stupid with our ski gear and rucksacks next to all these boats."

"We'll get changed at the hotel."

"Let's hurry up and find one! I didn't know it was so cold in Geneva in March. From Gstaad, it sounded like the Riviera!"

They plodded along the verge in their moon-boots. Some seagulls wheeled above their heads, before swooping down over the wake of a heavy white ferry boat on the open lake, full of passengers for Evian. They walked

ILIE NASTASE

along past the gardens that sloped gently down to the lake.

"None of these houses looks like a hotel," said Natty. "We'll have to go further into town. We shouldn't have got off there."

"We didn't even know where the bus was going."

"Stop complaining," said Natty. "It's not snowing here."

"No, but it's going to rain!"

A speedboat arrived at a private dock. It bounced noisily on the waves, then slowed and settled lower into the water as it coasted to a stop. Natty thought of Istvan, who didn't like boats. It was his fault that she had spent the last ten days persuading her roommate, Baba, whom she called 3B, to run away from Edelweiss with her. She had decided to go AWOL when she learned that she would not be going to France for the Easter holidays because Istvan was tied up with some tournament. She did not even want to know where the hell it was. For months she had been waiting, trying to keep up with her schoolwork, pretending to listen to the advice of Herr Karl Brunner, her tennis coach. She had even agreed to put on her skis and had done a decent descent on the giant slalom. By showing that she could be reasonable, she thought that Istvan would see that she was a woman now and that it was time to take a serious interest in her career as a champion. She did not want to waste any more time in schools where she only met mediocrities.

3B Bugatti was a sweet girl, fun sometimes, but not interested in much, and Natty had to put up with her frequent bouts of depression. But 3B was adventuresome, game for anything, and Natty had decided to strike a big blow. Istvan was lying low? This would make him sit up. . . .

THE NET

It began with a cunning brainwashing maneuver on a dozen girls in the class ahead of theirs who were ready to believe anything. Playing on 3B's admiration for her, Natty explained what fun it would be to arouse the jealousy of the stuck-up, pretentious, upper-class girls by making them believe that she and Natty each had a lover. A real one, not those goofy, horny ragazzi who hung around the ski slopes. 3B's would be as fair as she was dark. An American. A TWA captain, who spent his spare time flying the glaciers in Switzerland. Natty's would be dark with green eyes, another American, a polo champion who was also a rally driver in his Porsche Carrera. To set up the scheme, the two friends had spent a weekend at the Gstaad Palace. The girls refused to explain how they had managed to sneak out of Edelweiss after dinner to join Bill, the pilot, and Peter, the polo champion, at their hotel. All they would tell the enthralled girls, after swearing them to secrecy, was that after drinking champagne till dawn, the four of them agreed that Bill would come and pick up Natty and 3B in his snow plane and fly them to a mysterious Eastern country where Peter was playing a secret polo match. Then Bill would smuggle them onto his 747 to New York. The Porsche Carrera would follow in a cargo plane.

Natty kept things vague as to Peter's and Bill's particulars, but the older girls read between the lines and put together a fairly accurate picture. They were between thirty and forty and handsomer than Robert Redford and Paul Newman.

The waitress at the Hôtel Les Oiseaux du Lac thought that two young American girls were very lucky to be dining across from each other at a nice table with a view of the pier lights. She hoped for their sakes that their parents, who had been delayed by an air-traffic controllers' strike, would not arrive for another two or three days.

"Tomorrow, we'll eat in our room," said 3B, leaning across the immaculate white tablecloth. "I don't like all these people *looking* at us."

"It's in your imagination," said Natty. "Nobody's taking any notice of us. You're just not used to restaurants. Istvan and I used to eat out all the time."

An hour earlier, in their huge, twin-bedded room with lacquered woodwork, they had prepared with the utmost seriousness for the ceremony of dinner. They had unpacked their somewhat crumpled outfits of young-girls-from-good-families kilts, moccasin loafers, and three-hundred-dollar cashmere sweaters. "You're not even thirteen," 3B had said wistfully. "I'm over fourteen, and I look like your little sister."

"Just as well! You didn't even dare go in and talk to the woman from the hotel."

"It's not that I was scared. I was afraid we wouldn't be able to afford it."

"But this isn't as expensive as the Palace, where we met Peter and Bill."

They had burst out laughing, then fought over the hairbrush. "Should we wear lipstick?" asked 3B.

"Definitely not. And we'll only drink milk. We're not here to attract attention."

Now Natty, feeling a little sick after her dinner of salmon trout in cold milk, watched 3B with disgust as she struggled with her peach melba.

"How can you eat such revolting things?"

"Lucky there are two of us," muttered 3B. "How do you know the owner hasn't called the police?"

"They'd be here by now. And anyway, why should she

THE NET

deprive herself of two nice, credit-card–carrying clients like us? Come on, let's see you laugh. We're not doing any harm."

"Oh, aren't we? What about my parents? What about Istvan Horwat?"

"Serves Istvan right."

"Don't talk so loudly. The man next to us can hear."

"No he can't. He's sticking his knee between that girl's thighs. I bet she's a whore."

"Shut *up!*"

Natty smiled angelically and looked around the room. Two ladies sipping herb tea returned her smile.

"I could do with some herb tea. Do you want one, 3B?"

"Lime blossoms to make us sleep?"

"No, mint to help digest that vile fish. I hate the sea."

It was raining solidly. Fog hung over the lake until midafternoon, and Natty and 3B lazed about in their room, lying on the beds, their Walkmans clamped to their ears, working their way through their supply of magazines and chocolates, which they renewed every evening in town before dinner. They had to eat at the hotel, since the owner had put them on the modified American plan, breakfast and dinner at Les Oiseaux du Lac.

From time to time, Natty went to sit in the Voltaire chair by the window and stared at the sinister-looking lake with the rain beating across its surface. She felt like crying, but told herself she had to hold out if she wanted to persuade Istvan of anything. She glanced at 3B, who was dipping absently into the box of chocolates. She was beginning to get on Natty's nerves. At Edelweiss they weren't together twenty-four hours a day. She found her constant presence stifling. But as she had dragged her friend into this lakeside ordeal, she would just have to put up with her. Anyway, maybe this was better than loneliness.

"If only there were a television in the room," sighed 3B, removing her headphones. "I'm sick of these tapes. Shall we go out and buy some more?"

"We've hardly got any money left. Just enough to buy a few drinks at the Café du Théâtre. We'll even have to cut down on comics and chocolate! Lucky we won't actually have to pay for the hotel!"

"How come?"

"They'll find us first. They'll manage."

"We could go to the movies."

"And stand in line in the rain? No thanks."

"There's no line in the afternoon."

"In Geneva all the films are lousy."

"Really?"

"Of course. Geneva's like Gstaad. Everything's lousy."

Natty sat stubbornly in front of the window and 3B lapsed back into lethargy. In another hour they could enjoy the noisy, smoky atmosphere of the Café du Théâtre.

Natty thrust herself from the armchair and went to stand in front of the bathroom mirror. The copious hotel dinners and the boxloads of candy had vanquished her skinniness. She thought she looked obese, almost as bad as 3B. She could hardly do up her skirt, and her blouse gaped over her chest.

Her plump cheeks made her triangular face look heavy. The previous evening, as she had walked past the mirrors in the hall and the shop windows in the street, she had barely recognized herself. She pinched her thighs in disgust. Only her legs remained slim. She may have been five

THE NET

inches taller than 3B, but she would rather die than let Istvan see her in this condition. He hated fat women!
"3B."
"Mmm?"
"You're right. Tonight we'll buy some tapes. No more chocolates and sweets. Besides, I'm not having dinner this evening. I feel too sick."
"Can you see me sitting in the dining room on my own?"
"We can go to the movie theater after the café, instead of coming back to the hotel. Get dressed. They must be there by now."

"They" were the regular patrons of the Café du Théâtre, a little bar that Natty and 3B had discovered the day after their arrival in Geneva, while they were looking for the confectioner that the waitress at the Oiseaux had told them about. To get shelter from the driving rain and the gusts that flattened them against the facades of the banks, they pushed open the door whose dimly lit, cathedral-glass panes gave them the reassuring impression of warmth and intimacy.

It was a smoke-filled lair of café Marxists, the most devalued film directors of the district, Geneva's gurus of psychoanalysis, mediums of postpostsurrealist poetry, and exponents of worldist politics. Intimidated at first, they gradually allowed themselves to be tamed by these bearded young men who smelled of perspiration and tobacco. Taken in by Natty's height, they offered the girls beer. They soon treated them like old friends. Drunk after the second pint, Natty and 3B floated up into the higher spheres of awareness. Natty asked the bartender for some cigarettes, to fit in with the others. She could make out strange faces through the haze but couldn't understand much of the obscure speeches, which only made her admire them all the more. They must have studied for years, these guys! Someone asked her what she did.

"I'm a philosophy student."

"In Geneva?"

"No, in Paris."

"At the Sorbonne?"

"Yes."

"So you're on vacation, then?"

"No, the lecturers are on strike."

She replied with such assurance that the bearded young man, wrapped in his own genius and the smoke from his pipe, contented himself with a knowing nod. His neighbor, who seemed more perceptive, asked her how old she was.

"Seventeen. I'm in the first year."

A psychoanalyst declared that it was shameful to fill young minds with an out-of-date science. A stormy discussion followed, dominated by the high-pitched voice of a disciple of Jean-Luc Godard's, who was referred to as "my fellow countryman" although Natty had no idea why. Nor did she understand why they constantly talked about class struggle and asked her if they fought in Geneva schools.

Seeing 3B come out of the toilet looking very pale, Natty gave her the signal to leave, promising to return the next day.

The Swiss police are among the best in the world, but it was only on the sixth day that a Jesus Christ lookalike, an informer of Inspector Kozinski's who sat half-bored to death amid the regulars of the Café du Théâtre and bought them his weekly round of drinks, wiped his

THE NET

steamed-up glasses and looked more carefully at the so-called philosophy student and her sister. He drained his glass of Fendant and made for the telephone booth.

Thirty-five minutes later, Natty and 3B were in an interview room at the police station.

In vain Inspector Kozinski tried every trick he had learned during his twenty years in the profession, switching from kindliness to threats, sucking on his pipe like a kind daddy or pointing it at the two fugitives like a gun. But all he could get out of them was the story he knew already, from the report made by his colleague Weinberg who had gathered statements from initially reluctant, then excitedly forthcoming Edelweiss pupils. What he wanted to know was, Where had the two seducers gone? And what were their names? 3B, trembling, had trouble saying more than three words at a time, knowing that the next interrogation would be in front of her parents. Natty's mind, however, was elsewhere. She impatiently awaited Istvan's arrival. She declared that they had just called their lovers Robert and Paul, because they looked like Robert Redford and Paul Newman. They said they actually called themselves Peter and Bill, but she and Miss Bugatti didn't know their real identities. Besides, they had no wish to send either man to prison for abduction of a minor; they had been very nice.

Inspector Kozinski, she knew, did not believe a word of their jaunt to New York any more than of the polo match in an Eastern European country, to which Natty had added, watching the policeman's face redden, a flight over the Andes in a plane of unknown make and a night among a Californian sect who sprinkle powdered hashish over brown rice.

As for Madame Rosenwald, the owner of the Hôtel Les Oiseaux du Lac, her heart sank when the police came to see her, after telephoning twenty or so Geneva hotels. All she could say was that the girls stayed in their room all day. They were so well brought-up, they were waiting for their parents to arrive . . .

It was not the first time that Kozinski had been burdened with an incident involving the jet set. But Istvan Horwat's adoptive daughter was one of the most awkward cases in a career that had mainly consisted of avoiding the bumps in the road.

25

"I didn't lodge a complaint," Istvan told her. "Nor did Miss Bugatti's family. But the law will be out looking for this famous Peter Redford and Bill Newman, if they do actually exist."

Sitting on a molded plastic chair in the departure lounge at Geneva-Cointrin Airport, where the flight to Paris had just been announced, Natty pretended to watch a baby trying to walk, hanging onto a folding stroller. She glanced at Istvan out of the corner of her eye. He sat stiffly and looked almost sinister in his black coat.

"Who's going to pick up my things from Edelweiss?" she asked. "It's not because I can't go back there—"

"I don't give a damn about your things. What I want to know is what really happened. You just said the first thing that came into your head."

The baby slipped and fell to the terrazzo floor howling, while the stroller came crashing into Istvan's knees. He kicked it two or three yards away and then, embarrassed, went over and apologized to the mother who reassured him with a smile.

"It doesn't matter. Do you also play soccer, Monsieur Horwat?"

In the plane, Natty sat with her face pressed to the window. She was disappointed. The adventure had come to an end too easily. Istvan would have difficulty finding a boarding school for the third term, but he always got what he wanted. Next year, though, it might be the same thing all over again. He was furious, of course, but he looked as sure of himself as ever. She hadn't given him enough of a fright.

There were only six of them in the first-class cabin, including the young woman and her baby who were sitting just in front of Istvan. The baby climbed up the back of the seat to smile at Natty. He cried when his mother made him come back down.

Istvan said nothing to thank the hostess when she offered him champagne. Natty did not want a thing. She watched Istvan sip his drink.

"What are you looking at me like that for?" he asked.

"Nothing. I was thinking about something, to do with the baby. The trouble with this business is that I'm not on the pill. And since I'm a woman now, you never know—"

"What, you . . ." Incredulous, Istvan took her by the shoulders and made her look at him.

She shrugged. "Yes, I'm 'fully formed,' as 3B puts it."

"Since when?"

"Over six months."

"You didn't tell me," he began, then realized how silly it sounded coming from him.

"I didn't have the chance. You only spent two days in Gstaad at Christmas and you were with your model all the time."

THE NET

She's right, Istvan thought, I haven't been thinking. I don't even see her grow up. If anything happens to her, it'll be my fault. Old Sandor said it's not enough to sign checks. I've got to look after her. Thieu's right, too. She's got her own room in the apartment. I'll find a local school for her. When I'm not there, Thieu will keep an eye on her.

He nodded, his mind made up. Then he spoke. "Natty, I've made a big decision."

"What."

"You won't be going to boarding school anymore."

She turned to him, eyes suddenly wide open. "Ever again?"

"Ever again."

"Do you swear it on your tennis racket?"

"If you like."

She hugged him and buried her head in the crook of his shoulder, showing him an affection Istvan was happy to rediscover. He did not know whether she was laughing or crying. Her mouth came close to his ear, and she whispered:

"We stayed in our hotel room all the time eating chocolate. That's why I'm so fat. The only men we met were the cretins in the café. What's more, I don't think they liked women at all. You know, I've only ever seen one naked man in my life, and that was you by the swimming pool in the bathroom. So you've got nothing to worry about."

26

Thieu did not have to look far to find a school near the apartment: all he had to do was cross the Avenue Robert-Schuman. Which meant there was no need to accompany Natty. The Vietnamese was a little sad about that, for it would have been his responsibility—Istvan was busy in the morning with his gymnastics and in the afternoon with his training at Roland-Garros. He would have liked to walk beside Natty, watching over her, even though now she was taller than he. It would have felt as if he were accompanying his own daughter to school. He would have elbowed his way through the huddles of pupils gossiping on the pavement, waited until the doors opened, and left only when he had seen her safely inside. Of course, a very small part of him knew it would not have been like that. Natty would have gotten rid of her bodyguard as fast as she could, so she could chat and laugh with the others. The best he could have hoped for was that she would have let him drive her to school and drop her at the gates.

As a special favor, Istvan Horwat's daughter had been

THE NET

accepted at the Collège Dupanloup for the summer term, before being enrolled for the next school year. She studied her schedule with Istvan. They had to find time for Natty's tennis lessons between Istvan's training sessions and Natty's classes.

"If Roland-Garros is too busy, we'll use Jacques's court in the Rue Ribeira," said Istvan.

"You won't be too tired?" asked Natty. "An hour's jogging, two hours of gym plus two hours at Roland-Garros every day . . . Practicing with me on top of all that is a lot!"

Istvan smiled. The "on top of all that" enchanted him. He loved it when Natty took herself so seriously that she thought tiredness might prevent him from going out on the court with her. It gave him hope. He had got her back. Now he had to make sure he didn't let her go again.

On Wednesdays, Saturdays, Sundays, and sometimes during the week after school, Natty put on her tennis outfit and went to watch Istvan train at Roland-Garros, which was just opposite the Collège Dupanloup. She never forgot to take her racket. Just in case.

Between five and seven o'clock, she found him battling against Connors, Tanner, Panatta, or Noah, depending on who was passing through Paris. It was a calm and happy time. She did not think about skiing, Gstaad, or her escape anymore. She found things more to her liking at the Avenue Robert-Schumann apartment now that Istvan was keeping Carla at arm's length before the series of tournaments in preparation for the big onslaught of the French International and Wimbledon, then Nice, Rome, and Monte Carlo. When he left to play abroad, Natty, as the mistress of the house, felt responsible, and would not allow herself the slightest whim. "You've become very reasonable, miss," said Thieu one day when she declined to accompany Istvan to Nice so as not to miss an afternoon's lessons just before the weekend.

"Yes, do you remember the fuss I kicked up before going to Edelweiss, when he went to Palermo with that awful Collins woman?"

"He'll be going away a lot during April. Who will you play with?"

"He hasn't left yet. But there's Jacques. He said he'd be happy to train me. Besides, when they start to prepare Roland-Garros for the tournament, I won't be able to set foot on a court. You may as well get used to driving me to Rue Ribeira." She gave him a smile. "By the way, have you noticed that Istvan means business? He goes to bed at ten o'clock."

"Since you've been living here, miss, he's started working again. It's very nice."

From then on she no longer told Laurence Germain and Sophie Imbert, her new schoolfriends, that she was going to hit a few with Istvan, but rather that she was going for a training session. Laurence and Sophie, who took a few lessons at the Racing Club on weekends, no longer tried to invite Natty; she belonged to a different universe. They were even afraid that she might come and watch them play one day, and the champion's daughter was likely to be unsparing in her criticism. Natty appreciated their deference, but she was very fond of both of them. She had never had two friends at the same time before. Laurence and Sophie had been to nursery school together, and they lived in the Rue du Château, in neighboring apartment blocks. Their fathers were lawyers—partners in the same firm, in fact—and their mothers shared tastes in swimming pools, sunbathing, and Yves Saint-Laurent in small

THE NET

doses. Listening to them talk, Natty thought they sounded like twin sisters. They were both of average height. Natty could look down on them.

One day, after school, Natty managed to get them into Roland-Garros to watch Istvan's training session. The two girls had never seen a tennis star at such closer quarters before. From then on, her friends' admiration knew no limits.

One cool April evening, as they were leaving for the Racing Club with their tennis bags, Natty asked if she could go with them.

"We didn't dare *ask* you," Laurence confessed, obviously delighted. "But if you want . . . You know, we share a coach. One week he teaches Sophie for an hour, and the following week it's my turn. So we're not all that good . . ."

Natty went, and noticed immediately that Laurence's and Sophie's fathers, in their spiffy Ryker outfits with their custom boron rackets, were falling over themselves, sweating like galley slaves to impress her. The sad thing was, it seemed lost on the two daughters. Maybe that was a blessing. She even offered to go a couple of sets with them.

"You go first, Laurence," said Sophie. "I'll watch. I won't be the only one."

So Sophie had noticed . . .

As soon as they began knocking up, bystanders began commentating. "It's Horwat's daughter." . . . "She's thirteen." . . . "She's already a junior seed." . . . "She's *excep*tionally mature for her age. . . ."

"Shall we play a set? Is that all right with you?" asked Laurence, proud of her last forehand. "We've got the court for three quarters of an hour."

"If you like," replied Natty.

ILIE NASTASE

Laurence's and Sophie's coach, two courts away, was giving a "luxury lesson" to a woman in her sixties who liked to drag him to the bar to tell him about her season at the beach, or at Bobet's. As he picked up the balls, he glanced at his pupil and Natty, who had just begun their game. He was fond of Laurence, but thought with a tinge of sadness that one day she would end up just like his too-talkative elderly pupil. A nice girl, but not very sporty, not really talented. She looked as though she were there as a foil for Horwat's daughter, whose play shined for its elegance as much as for her calm and concentration. She doesn't make mistakes, he thought. He knew she was bound to become a great player; he'd seen them before, young like this, getting started. He'd like to have her for a pupil, see what he could do with her, how far he could take her.

Natty surprised herself by suddenly deciding to get the thing over with as soon as possible. She played to win, and forgot about the pleasure this little match gave Laurence, who rushed from one side of the court to the other, charged with enthusiasm. Natty hit the ball solemnly, without worrying about Laurence's weakness. It was unlikely she would win a game, or even a single point. What a drag, she thought, I'm going to beat her 6–0. It'll go on for twenty minutes, and then we'll go and I'll get her an orange juice.

From the very first service, she realized that Laurence had difficulty returning the ball. Too bad. When it was Laurence's turn to serve, Natty sent back a powerful forehand, or a backhand right across to the other side of the court. Or she would do a drop shot to make her opponent run. Natty won one point after another: 1–0, 2–0, 3–0 . . . even her risky shots were successful. Laurence's serves began to fall in the center of the court. Natty, running up

THE NET

to the ball, would send back an unreturnable forehand or a backhand along the line.

Laurence was very happy to play with Natty. She knew that Natty got regular training but, even so, she had hoped to do better. She had thought, a little naively, that she would manage to play a decent game, especially if Natty didn't take it too seriously. Now, more than ever, she realized they were a world apart. She felt discouraged, and mixed up about her passion for Natty's father, who became more and more inaccessible with every shot Laurence missed.

When they switched sides, she dragged her feet. Perspiring and exhausted, she let her racket dangle dejectedly between volleys. She did not see how she could avoid losing 6–0. On the verge of tears, she picked up the balls more slowly, as if her delaying could postpone the outcome.

I'm going to make a fool of her, thought Natty. We're 4–0 already. In front of all these people, it's too brutal. And too easy. What would Istvan say if he could see me putting Laurence off tennis, when all she wanted was to play one decent game and see what she could do?

Laurence stood downcourt, looking back at her, a brave picture of misery. She was tough. Showing no sign of anger, she waited stoically for Natty's serve.

I can't carry on this massacre, said Natty to herself. It's unworthy. There's still time to let her win a game, or even two. Chin up, Laurence, I'm going to play to your forehand. It's your only chance. At least don't serve any more faults . . .

Very gradually, so that neither the Racing Club spectators nor Laurence sensed what she was doing, Natty eased up on her game. She was careful not to start playing badly; she simply let Laurence win some points on her forehand. On these forehands, she went up to the net, which allowed Laurence to hit passing-shots or lobs. A few of them were genuinely impossible to return. She started to be able to say with a shrug, "Good shot."

Natty felt better, and she smiled when she saw how Laurence felt having won a game. She decided to let her win another, then decided that she had been generous enough. Having proved to herself that she had the control of an adult, she began to attack her opponent's backhand and won the set 6–2.

"It was nice of you to let me win those two games," said Laurence when they were back in the changing room.

"Hey, come on," Natty said, "you won them. I didn't realize you had such a good forehand. It's not bad, you know. I mean, we're both only thirteen." Some cold April air had found its way into the changing area, and against its chill Natty wrapped herself in a towel and followed Laurence toward the steaming showers. "Besides, I learned a couple of things out there that I've been meaning to work on."

Natty hung her towel on a free hook beside the shower-room doorway. The warm cataracts beyond had turned it into a portal of swirling mist. Smoothing her hair back with her hands, she stepped over the threshold.

PART 2

27

He's a kid, thought Istvan. A kid as tall as me.
He shared the public's curiosity about the seventeen-year-old German coming onto the court with him.
Seventeen. Almost the same age as Natty.
Did Rainer Ritter expect to reach the quarter-finals of the French Open at Roland-Garros?
Istvan watched his rather arrogant, unexpected opponent.
The "Westphalian Gunner," the journalists called him. Looks nice enough. A boyish face. The German Federation didn't want him to compete at Orange Bowl. He won it in a personal capacity. One would think he'd be more athletic. He looked a little heavy. But be careful, he must be very powerful. The most bothersome thing was his eyes: he had the vacant yet totally concentrated look of a killer.
If I win the toss, Istvan thought, I'll let him serve. Let's see how the gunner opens fire.

* * *

"Ritter to serve. Play!" the umpire called down from his chair.

His first service surprised me, Istvan thought. So did his last ace. Most of his serves are in, and the ones that aren't are followed by aggressive services that are almost as dangerous as the first. . . . This kid's very good. Perhaps a little too good. That time I couldn't make it to the net in time.

"Forty–love!"

Istvan could hardly believe this was possible. Ritter was pulling aces out of his racket handle, while he hadn't won a single point.

"Game Ritter. One–love."

All right, Istvan thought, my service now. There was a lightning return, and Ritter looked amused. He smiled when he hit the ball. Jesus.

"First set to Ritter, six–three," said the umpire.

Sitting on his chair during the pause, Istvan rubbed his head with his towel. He massaged his cheeks with his hands, then worked on his arms and legs.

He was too fast for me, that's all there was to it. I didn't have time to concentrate. I was a spectator. I didn't get into the game. He's half my age and he's won double the number of games. It's all wrong, the world's upside down.

Nine games later, the umpire pronounced again.

"Second set to Horwat, six–three."

Istvan had himself back to square one. It was working. Ritter would go a long way, but not this time. Istvan knew he had to beat him 6–2, 6–3. A good match in four sets.

But Ritter was playing as if he'd *won* the second set, not rattled in the least. He was hammering, bombarding. He was going all out, holding nothing back.

THE NET

And it was going on too long. Incredible, Ritter's returns. And he always seemed to get the first service in now. How many aces already?

We're heading for a tie-break, Istvan thought, it feels too close. Is there a storm brewing, or is it me?

Istvan took him, finally, 15–13. But his legs felt tired, like those of an old statue.

Rainer Ritter won the tie-break 7–2 and with it the fourth set. Istvan could hear the spectators' silence. He applied himself to calmly repeating the familiar movements, giving himself time, time . . . He rolled the ball in his hand, bounced it three times, adjusted the strings on his racket although they didn't need it, tied up a shoelace.

They all think the German's going to knock me out, he thought, sensing the mood of the crowd. So don't let them see how tired I am. Hell, I can't feel it anymore.

Istvan faced losing his chance at the semifinals. Ritter looked a little less sure of himself, Istvan thought, though it was hard to tell for certain. He seemed less precise. And in the last set, there was no tie-break. No tie-break!

"Seven–all."

I'm going to get him. I'll finish him off in five minutes or not at all.

"Eight–seven."

The storm hasn't burst. The storm . . .

"Nine–seven."

Then: "Game, set, and match to . . ."

Was it really over?

"All the same, you did win," said Natty, who was still pale.

28

Standing in the box that Istvan had insisted on renting at Roland-Garros, despite Fenwick's complaints about the extravagance, Natty greeted a smiling Istvan. This really was even better than the players' box. Istvan had showered and was wearing a strange mauve-and-black track suit that made him look as if he were in mourning and emphasized his drawn features, the shadows under his eyes. He suddenly looked vulnerable.

Cora Gordon had held Natty's hand during the tie-breaks and the agonizing fifth set, knowing that she was feeling every second of Istvan's suffering. She gently chided her: "Buck up. You're reacting like a little girl."

Jim Gordon had insisted on staying close to his wife. He had not said a word during the entire match. He felt his generation was at stake. He had gotten no further than the second round. Livia Fabiani had given her invitation to her new lover and didn't know where to put herself. She asked Natty if she could sit with her.

"Of course," replied Natty, who looked regal in a turquoise dress. "Istvan's old friends are always welcome."

THE NET

She toyed with the gold Rolex watch—Istvan had given it to her for her sixteenth birthday, before taking her to Maxim's for dinner—as if it were a lucky charm.

"You gave us quite a scare," said Jim Gordon, embracing Istvan. "Natty nearly fainted."

"I knew you'd win," said Laurence, who also got up to kiss the winner.

"That Westphalian Gunner couldn't beat you," said Livia Fabiani.

"Can we change the subject?" asked Istvan.

Laurence Germain sat there almost glued to Istvan, staring straight ahead and wondering if the next match would begin soon. Bauer, Ritter's coach, slipped into the French Radio box to talk quietly to his young star. Both men smiled as they glanced across at Istvan. Natty had the feeling they were talking about her. For the last two days she had been wearing her hair in curls, which had been fun at first but now made her self-conscious. Maybe the hair was what they were laughing at. Well, screw them. Rainer Ritter could think what he liked, she didn't care.

The crowd rose after the second quarter-finals. Istvan looked up at the spectators, before whom he'd had such difficulty beating Ritter. He felt an overwhelming weariness, but he faced them. So many eyes were turned toward him. Natty took his arm, leaving Laurence behind with Jim Gordon, who was explaining some of the intricacies of Connors's game to her.

A few yards in front of Istvan, in the stampede for the exit, Ritter was elbowing his way through to join Holgersson, the Swedish player his own age, who had broken his wrist in a motorbike accident before the tournament. Despite his cast, Holgersson's wild Parisian nights were the talk of the town. Ritter, who had already recovered from the match and was laughing like a kid on vacation, intended to have a good time that evening with the Swede and his friends.

Istvan and Natty passed them without turning around. The familiar sight of a group of fans rushing toward him eager for autographs inspired a smile in spite of his fatigue.

"One day, you'll be the one signing tennis balls," he said to Natty, who let go of the champion's arm to leave him to his admirers.

People ran and jostled. Istvan waited resolutely. But the throng passed between them without seeing them. Disconcerted, Istvan turned around; Natty stood rooted to the spot. They were reaching out toward the German, a few yards behind.

Natty slipped her arm back through his and led him away. She wanted to cry.

"We'd better wait for Jim and the others," said Istvan frostily. "We'll lose them in this crowd."

29

Istvan awoke in one of the hotel rooms he camped in during his nomadic existence. In London, the management of Claridges, where he liked to stay during Wimbledon, always tried to give him the same room. He was appalled that the bed was so short. Because he was under six-foot-three, he was apparently not entitled to a special bed, as General de Gaulle had been. He tossed and turned in his sleep, although on awakening he did not recall having dreamed. Even when he was not struggling with his watery nightmare, he woke up with his feet hanging out of the bed. It gave him the unpleasant sensation of being a corpse waiting to be taken to the morgue.

Before he opened his eyes, he crawled back to the center of the bed. As soon as his feet found shelter under the covers, he leaned over to grope around for the pillows he had flung to the floor during the night. He leaned up against them, switched on the bedside light, and looked at the time. It was always earlier than the time he had requested an alarm call. He went over the up-coming day: the number of hours' training left before the tournament opened, his opponent's score in the first round, the need to avoid a tiresome female admirer whom he would have given in to the previous evening had it not been for Natty's determination to bring him back to Claridges by ten o'clock.

Natty had a knack of knowing when he was awake. She knew he needed ten minutes in the morning without talking to anybody. When that time had elapsed, she phoned his room. The year before, Istvan had noticed that she had lost her little girl's voice for good.

He let the phone ring three times before answering.

"Istvan?" There was always a note of anxiety in her serious voice, as if Natty were afraid of getting the wrong room. "Have you surfaced? . . . Good. Then I'll have them bring two English breakfasts to your room. I'm on my way."

He got up, drew the curtains, and adjusted the shower to maximum strength. It was the same problem as the short bed: the jet was never strong enough for him.

He had just finished shaving when Natty knocked on the communicating door. Three knocks, like letting the phone ring three times. It was their lucky number, supposed to make the day go well. Once again her timing was right. The bacon and eggs were cooked while Istvan was in the shower, the toast was grilled while he shaved, and the giant tray was at the door when Natty came in and kissed Istvan good morning on his cheek, which smelled of eau de cologne.

"We'll have breakfast on the bed," she decided. "Make yourself comfortable, I'll set it up."

She put the *Guardian* and the *Daily Telegraph* to one side, poured the tea, sugared hers but not Istvan's, and put salt on her eggs but not Istvan's. She found the darkest pieces

THE NET

of toast for him. He watched her, amused by this ritual that she seemed to adore.

"Don't you order chocolate anymore?"

"It's fattening."

She kneeled on the carpet beside Istvan, who allowed himself to be served by blond Natty in a blue track suit. She had a way with toast and marmalade.

Natty stretched out her long legs, then jumped up onto the carpet with both feet together. She went to the window and opened it, switched on the radio, and went into an aerobics routine.

"It's too violent," said Istvan. "You'd better do gymnastics, something low impact."

"One, two, and three! . . . Gymnastics gets on my nerves," panted Natty. "Four, five, and six! . . . You've already told me to stop swimming because it sets up the wrong muscles for tennis."

"Wear yourself out then, and that'll be the end of it. Anyway, this morning, I'm the one who's training. Hey, turn the music down, the phone's ringing."

He answered it ill-humoredly. He hated being disturbed in the morning, during his time with Natty when they talked about everything and nothing, sometimes arguing, but always ending up friends.

"It's for you," he said, covering the mouthpiece with his hand.

"For me? Who is it?"

"The hero of Queen's. Do you want to talk to him?"

"Why not?"

"She's coming," he said into the phone. "And congratulations again for yesterday . . ."

Istvan took a track suit and tennis shoes from the dressing room and went into the bathroom to dress. He left the door open, but it didn't get him anywhere because Natty, as usual, answered only yes or no when she spoke into the telephone. He was dying to know what Ritter could want from her. Queen's must have gone to his head for him to dare call Natty, and what was more, before nine o'clock. And in *his* room! So far, when they had met, he had just shaken her hand, as he had Istvan's, without hanging around. A few friends had mischievously told him that the German had been caught unawares by Alan Davidson, the famous photographer of the "Gang of Four" London paparazzi, while he watched Natty train, dumb with admiration. Beware the power of the Gunner's concentrated fire, they had said. Istvan, who abhorred vulgarity, merely shrugged. The previous evening, at the Bedford Pub, he thought that Ritter was going to speak to Natty, but Holgersson's female bodyguards were in the way. He was slightly drunk, and contented himself with shouting something in English that could not be heard above the din. . . .

"I'll have a look," Natty was saying. "The papers are here. I'll call you back about this evening."

"So, will you read me that article in the *Guardian?*"

"It's not very complimentary to you."

"What have they got against me? What's the name of the guy who wrote it?"

"John O'Neill."

"Never heard of him. Read."

Natty shook her head and held out the newspaper to Istvan, who skimmed over the report on the Queen's tournament and began to read aloud, slowly, when he reached the end:

" 'Istvan Horwat had great difficulty knocking Rainer Ritter out at Roland-Garros. One could almost say that

THE NET

the young German player won the match. His win at Queen's against the South African number one, Kriek, who played a very good game, confirms that we'll be hearing a lot more about Rainer Ritter. Yes, if we recall the drawn-out tie-breaks of his quarter-finals match at Roland-Garros, we can only conclude that we are witnessing a well-known phenomenon: the young celebrity, less laden with trophies, rises, while the old celebrity falls.'"

They looked at each other in silence for a few seconds. Without commenting, Istvan carefully folded the newspaper and put it back on the bed.

"While he was at it, didn't Ritter tell you how much his odds had risen at the bookmakers?"

"No, what are bookmakers?"

"A British and American peculiarity. Specialists who take bets, particularly on tennis. For example, for Wimbledon, after Queen's, Ritter must be at twenty to one. The odds on Krieck are something like fifty to one."

"I don't understand."

"It's simple. People will bet a lot of money on Ritter, who's the favorite, at least in the second round, because they know he stands a good chance of winning. The better a player is, the lower the odds are. It's the same with horses. I know an American champion, Bobby Riggs, who's in his sixties. All his life, he's made his living from betting. He even started up the first bets on scores, by backing himself. Do you understand? One year, he won the men's singles and doubles and the mixed doubles at Wimbledon. He said, for example, 'I'm going to win the third set seven–five, lose the fourth six–three, and win the fifth six–two.' He had to fulfill his forecast . . ."

"That sounds weird," said Natty pensively.

"You see, at my age, I've only got a one-in-forty

chance. The odds are forty to one against me. But when I won at Roland-Garros, I was at three to one."

Istvan broke off and sat lost in thought for a few moments, then concluded abruptly:

"That means, if I ever win the Grand Slam, about three bettors out there would get rich."

30

Natty wondered if Istvan would notice that for the first time in her life, she was wearing high heels. He would not want to make himself look ridiculous by forbidding her to go out with Rainer Ritter, but she sensed that he was annoyed.

She did not want to admit to herself that she had accepted his invitation partly to let Istvan know she was ready for a life on her own. Whatever he did, she felt he did not pay enough attention to her and insisted on treating her like a teenager, which she almost wasn't anymore.

After several attempts, she chose an outfit that was simple but provocative enough to make Istvan's blood boil. It was her first real date and she wanted to look beautiful. Anyway, since Istvan flashed around in a black track suit all day, why shouldn't she start wearing the same color? She had patiently explored several Knightsbridge boutiques to assemble all the elements of her outfit.

In front of the full-length mirror in the bathroom, she assured herself one last time that she was ready to show herself to Istvan. From the front, the black silk velvet dress was modesty itself, done up from the knee to the neck, her waist barely denoted by a belt. A simple cape of the same light velvet was slung negligently over her shoulders. It was an almost austere outfit, but one that was transformed the minute she took off the cape. In back, there was a revealing slit reaching down almost to her buttocks. Istvan probably wouldn't think to look under the cape, she hoped. But the black stockings should have an effect on him, along with the dark-red lipstick. She had chosen a discreet perfume: Yardley lavender, which was hardly discernible. She had had her curls straightened and her hair was held in place by a wide black velvet headband that made her look even blonder.

She smiled at the mirror, surprised at the result. She had never looked so beautiful. She lingered in front of her reflection, unable to understand why she had gone to so much trouble.

"The bride wore black," grumbled Istvan. "What is the fancy dress in aid of?"

He walked around her looking like a couturier furious at the failure of one of his designs. For the time being, he did not seem to have tumbled onto the cape trick. But coming closer to Natty, he protested.

"Don't you think you're tall enough? What do you think you look like with those heels? They make you lean forward. Given your height, you look better in flats."

Natty did not reply. Nor did she look ashamed. And Istvan was forced to look at her this time. She concealed the pleasure she felt under his gaze.

The black suede shoes did not fail to achieve the desired effect. They fascinated Istvan like Cinderella's slipper.

"Walk a few steps."

THE NET

Natty obeyed, feeling ill at ease.
"Are you thinking of going far in that getup?"
"I have to start sometime. Don't you want me to go out?"
"Of course I do! I said yes. You could have worn something else, that's all. Don't come back later than midnight. I won't be able to sleep. By the way, where's your Westphalian taking you?"
"To Covent Garden, seeing as you didn't want to go."

At half past seven, the violins had finished tuning up. Natty had told Rainer Ritter that she knew Adolph Adam's *Giselle* by heart, although in fact she had seen his name for the first time on the poster outside. She was surprised by the solemnity of the audience and the discipline of the orchestra. On the few occasions when she had set foot inside a concert hall, it had been on compulsory school outings, a good occasion for giggling, swapping dirty jokes, and sticking chewing gum on the seats. Covent Garden was no laughing matter. She remembered that certain pupils at Roedean were forever repeating that their parents had season tickets. They tried to clumsily reproduce the movements of the dancers they had admired at the ballet.

Natty was not impressed with Rainer's awkward manner as he sat rigidly next to her. Until then, she had only seen him in tennis clothes—his combat gear—or in a track suit. With his navy-blue suit and his gaudy tie, he reminded her of the ski instructors they used to invite up for the end-of-the-winter-sports-season party. They would arrive all dressed up in their Sunday best. He looked even pinker than usual, and the smitten looks he kept giving her did not help matters. She told herself that if she bumped into his ex-girlfriends, she would not know where to put herself.

Istvan would laugh at her if he could see her escort leaning forward, his hands resting on his knees, his trousers riding up his legs revealing red hairy calves above his socks. She thought, to reassure herself, that she preferred dark-haired men after all.

Throughout the performance, Rainer looked as if he were lost in a dream world: he sat impassive and rigid, turning to smile at her from time to time. There was no point her telling herself that in all honesty, she was the one who had brought him there, prompted by a stupid childhood memory and the magic ring of the words, "Covent Garden." She could not help wishing that he had overridden her and suggested something more fun than this masterpiece of romantic ballet.

She wriggled in her seat. She was cold, despite the season. She put her cape back on and sighed. The never-ending pas de deux was driving her to distraction.

Ritter admired Natty for coming to see a ballet she already knew so well. She was as cultivated as she was beautiful. She wasn't like all the other women players who invaded Wimbledon every year but didn't even know where Covent Garden *was*.

He would never understand anything about music. No more than he could read all the way through a thriller. He knew that Natty had been to the best schools, in England, Switzerland, and Paris. She was lucky to have old Horwat for a father, a lord of tennis. He had known how to deal with things, he hadn't tried to make her into a tennis animal from the age of eight. He didn't have to, it was happening anyway. Still, she was lucky to be able to sit

THE NET

still like that and watch a ballet. It had already lasted two hours and didn't look as though it was likely to end for a while. He clenched his fists on his knees and tried to follow the match.

3

Drowsy from *Giselle*'s long sleep, Natty and Rainer were abruptly brought to their senses by the crash of thunder. A violent summer storm burst as they came out of the theater. Caught in the crowd scrambling for taxis, they waded through the puddles. Natty nearly fell over and clutched Rainer's arm. He ignored the rain streaming down his face and for the first time took Natty's hand. He helped her toward the only free taxi and the pair of them, laughing like children, outraced the soaked theatergoers who could not compete with their conditioning.

As they were getting into the cab, an elderly English couple appeared and stepped into the taxi from the other side. They all ended up inside.

"We've been beaten by the senior citizens again," muttered Natty.

Rainer replied with a groan. He had just withdrawn her hand from his to catch her soaking velvet cape as it slid from her shoulders, when the Englishman said:

"There's plenty of room, and you won't find another taxi in this rain. May I suggest we share this one?"

THE NET

"Oh thank you!" replied Natty.

Rainer looked disappointed. For the last hour he had been shifting in his seat, not even trying anymore to follow what was happening on stage, waiting for the intimacy they would share at the restaurant. He might perhaps find the words to express to Natty what he had felt for her ever since he first set eyes on her. Now he had to try to find something pleasant to say to this charming gentleman who had seen him on television and was full of praise for his powerful service and crosscourt backhands.

"But I didn't think you'd beat Kriek. You'll go a long way."

"Our son, Edward, was in France for the Roland-Garros tournament," added the lady. "He told us you nearly beat Horwat."

"That's not true!" broke in Natty so sharply that the English couple did not dare open their mouths again.

"She's right," Rainer said to bridge the silence. "I knew that I couldn't beat Horwat. But I did what I could."

Rewarded by a look from Natty, he had the crazy idea of hugging her. But the moment passed.

Their clothes had not had time to dry before the taxi dropped them outside the Gloucester Hotel and continued on its way with the charming couple.

The head waiter, as dignified and starchy as the surroundings, asked them if they had booked a table, and under what name.

"We haven't booked," said Rainer.

Natty would have willingly slapped the head waiter's clean-shaven face for the way he was looking them up and down, as if they were refugees from the Salvation Army. Ritter, his wet hair plastered to his face, was look-

ILIE NASTASE

ing more and more ill at ease, and her dress was soaking wet and clung to her body.

The head waiter's verdict was not long in coming. "In that case, I'm very sorry, there are no tables."

"But I can see several empty," Natty burst out.

"Every table is booked, miss."

Natty was ready to turn on her heel when Rainer took the man's arm.

"Don't you recognize me?" he asked with youthful assurance. "I'm Rainer Ritter."

Natty wondered whether this emaciated majordomo with the face of a vampire really didn't recognize Ritter who, after the Queen's tournament, had received due honors in the press and on television.

"I regret I do not know you, sir," said the man impassively. "In any case, there are no tables, I'm really very sorry indeed."

Rainer stood rooted to the spot. Finally he turned to Natty.

"We're not going out into the rain again," he said.

"If you'd like to be seated in the bar, I'll come and fetch you when there's a free table."

"Let's go," said Natty.

"It'll be the same thing everywhere," said Rainer.

Natty followed him reluctantly to the softly lit bar. Hushed conversations were going on among the big leather armchairs.

"It's sinister," she said, starting to relax.

It can't be as sinister as Covent Garden, thought Rainer, his gaze following Natty's tall body as she made her way to the Ladies.

He had not thought such a beautiful girl could exist. He pictured her out on the court with her father. He had told Holgersson that she would be a great champion.

THE NET

"All I care about are her legs," Holgersson had replied, putting on a coarse accent. "Mind you, the rest isn't bad either. Her breasts are as round as a pair of tennis balls."

Outraged, Ritter, who usually found Holgersson's off-handedness amusing, had called him a sex maniac, good only for trailing around with his band of groupies who were ruining his health and would one day give him some uncatalogued venereal disease.

"Calm down," the Swede had said, shrugging. "We're not going to have an argument about it. Go to bed with her and that will be the end of it!"

But Rainer knew that if he got her into bed, he wanted it to be the beginning of something.

He began to recover his wits. As Natty threaded her way toward him, he took a ten-pound note out of his billfold and slipped it into the outside pocket of his jacket.

"Have you ordered?" asked Natty, lowering herself into her chair. "Stop looking at me like that!"

"You're very beautiful."

"I just did my hair. My dress is beginning to dry but my cape is still like a wet rag."

"How about some champagne?"

"Are you mad? I'm not supposed to drink alcohol. And you shouldn't either, just before Wimbledon."

"I thought you'd like to."

"I would." She smiled at him. "Let's."

Ritter stretched out his hand and placed it over Natty's, and then embarrassed, raised it to summon a waiter.

When the champagne arrived in two fluted glasses, they fell silent. Natty stared into the distance, making no effort to start up a conversation. Rainer wondered what she was thinking about.

"You're the expert on *Giselle*. Tell me, was it done well?"

"Very well. Merle Park in particular was marvelous." Natty remembered seeing the name on the poster.

"I thought she looked like a murderess," ventured Rainer.

The peanut bowl was empty. "I'd like something to eat," she said. "We're not going to stay here all night."

Rainer stood up and went over to the head waiter, who stayed imperiously where he was and watched the tall youth approaching. Natty watched them. She secretly hoped Rainer would knock the vampire out with a right hook. But no. Rainer had his back to her, telling the man something that seemed the right thing to say. In a moment Rainer was back.

"We can eat in three minutes. Do you want another drink while we wait?"

She shook her head. Once again, conversation dried up. Their silence was punctuated by a double sneeze.

"It's a cold," they said in unison.

They looked at each other and burst out laughing.

"I hope not," remarked Natty, "in the middle of the tournament season. I think it's just this bubbly."

Tournament—Rainer Ritter jumped at the word. At last he had found a subject of conversation that put them both at ease. They were in their element. Natty told him about the summers she had spent in the USA, about working her way up the ranking, about finally winning the Junior team championship that would put her in line to get to the Orange Bowl. Soon they were enjoying themselves, talking in raised voices, which was just not done in this sanctuary.

"Your table, sir," said an accommodating voice behind them.

THE NET

* * *

"Are you back already?" asked Istvan in amazement. He was lying in bed watching television.

"You told me not to come back after midnight, but you didn't say I couldn't come back before."

"Your dress is all crumpled."

"We got caught in the rain. You know, Covent Garden's brilliant! I'd like to go every evening."

"What did you do afterward?"

"Rainer took me to dinner at a restaurant. In a hotel, the Gloucester, do you know it?"

"Oh yes."

"We ate lobster and we talked about lots of things. Rainer's very cultured. You can tell he hasn't only played tennis . . . he's studied too."

"So. Now you're all for education."

"We came back early because of his training tomorrow. Otherwise we'd have gone dancing. He loves it. You didn't get bored all by yourself?"

"I had dinner with Connors. We came back at nine o'clock. We've got training tomorrow too."

"Right. Tomorrow. I didn't forget."

But she had forgotten, and she thought about that as she got into bed and drifted off to sleep.

32

"See you later on in the bar!"

Istvan left Panatta with his customary farewell and walked into the shower rooms before realizing that Panatta had not even heard what he'd said. He had been concentrating so hard that he was still in another world.

After being beaten by McEnroe, he had shaken hands and smiled and walked off the court with his usual casual step. He knew he had played a good match against the great Wimbledon favorite. This defeat was a victory for him, at thirty-six, against a player thirteen years his junior. He had won the first set brilliantly 6–4, felt his strength ebb a little during the second, which he lost at the tie-break, but after that had not been able to do any better than 3–6, 2–6.

In the relative privacy of the shower, he wondered whether any of the spectators had realized what it had cost him to achieve that result. He had put on more of a show than ever for the journalists awaiting his demise. They probably had some choicely offensive articles already prepared on the theme of the old champion on his

THE NET

way out. He kept up appearances in front of the spectators, formerly accustomed to his successes, and also in front of Natty, Fenwick, and Ritter, who had been eliminated in the first round by Schappers, the Dutch champion, ranking 160th. True, Ritter had been unlucky. The wind was very strong, and the ground was so slippery that the match should have been canceled. He had not had much sleep and had not been able to stand up to Schappers's powerful, even game.

Playing opposite McEnroe in particular, Istvan projected the image the public had come to expect. He seemed to be silently laughing at the world, to find all the shots easy, to concede his own faults with a smile.

For years, he had hidden himself behind this protective screen. Deeply melancholy at heart, he had adopted the mask of the incorrigible joker. But in fact he followed a ruthless regimen, hardly ever drinking alcohol, keeping his weight in check, counting the number of hours of sleep he got, forgoing female companionship as much as possible, contriving to deceive everybody in the world as to his real nature.

He could not stand visible effort or obvious asceticism. That looked forced. Everything had to seem easy, as if it were natural. At least during that match against McEnroe, he had managed to make the spectators laugh on occasion.

They had seen nothing but fire, he told himself, adjusting the shower jet. If they only knew that for two weeks he had been going to bed earlier than Natty, while the gossip columnists imagined him in nightclubs where he had never set foot.

But McEnroe hadn't been taken in, nor were the friends who were watching. Nor was Fenwick; he looked worried. Perhaps he wasn't expecting such a good result.

Good result! How much longer would he be able to

keep up such an effort, more than he thought he'd be able to muster. He had done his clown act better than he had opposite Ritter at Roland-Garros. No doubt because he was getting older and preferred grass; it was less tiring. All the same, if every tournament required such concentration, he wouldn't be able to sustain it for long. An effort like that is torture. Nobody could keep it up forever.

The article in the *Guardian* that Rainer told Natty to read annoyed Istvan—that John O'Neill was such a devoted R.R. fan that he made excuses for him when he was knocked out by Schappers in the first round. He would have written differently, Istvan knew, if he had wanted to encourage Istvan to fight like a lion against McEnroe.

Istvan had a vision of journalists goading him toward mortal combat, thrashing him with strokes of their pens.

"Oh look, you're in white." Natty was waiting for him outside the changing room.

She took his arm. He breathed in the smell of her freshly washed blond hair.

As he walked through a group of players who congratulated him on his match, he put his arm around her waist, spun her round, then walked off with her toward the bar.

"Aren't you tired, Istvan? You looked great during the match, very relaxed. After the first set, I thought you were going to beat McEnroe. Even after the tie-break in the second set . . ."

She stopped and placed her hands on Istvan's shoulders. In her eyes he read a touching confidence.

"Next time, you'll beat him."

He smiled and started to walk on, but she stopped him, her hands tightening on his arms.

THE NET

"Next time you'll beat him, won't you?"

"If there is a next time," he answered without really looking at her.

He kissed her forehead and broke free, waving at Connors who was calling him.

"They said they were ordering champagne," said Natty, "as if you had won."

"You see," said Istvan, "I was right not to wear myself out."

"I don't like it when you joke all the time. I never know what to think. Sometimes I think you're making fun of me, that you say the first thing that comes into your head."

"Even when you were little, I never said the first thing that came into my head."

33

"This evening I feel as if I'm on vacation. Since I've been eliminated, I'll take you out."

"I can't hear a thing!" shouted Natty. "I'm in the bath. Open the door!"

Istvan obeyed and recoiled immediately. It was a long time since he had seen Natty naked in the bath. He left the door ajar and retreated quickly to sit on the bed, pushing aside a pair of panties, a bra, two or three skirts, a pair of trousers, and a few sweatshirts that fell onto the floor.

"I said we're going out this evening. The porter has got us two seats at Covent Garden . . . Can you hear me?"

"I went there the other day."

"I know, but tonight they're doing Frederick Ashton's *Vain Precautions.*"

"Will you take me out to dinner afterward?"

"Yes, I told you, we're celebrating this evening."

"Hold on, I'm coming!"

He heard Natty get out of the water, then jumped as her hairdryer started up. He found it increasingly hard to bear the noise of appliances. Even his electric razor set him off every morning. In fact, he was becoming increasingly impatient with the whole unavoidable process of washing. And so he was always amazed at the pleasure that women took in soaking in the bath and shampooing their hair at five o'clock in the afternoon.

At last the dryer stopped. Istvan could make out the sound of Natty brushing her hair. Then she came out draped theatrically in a terrycloth American flag.

"Where on earth did you get that?" asked Istvan. "Is this a new version of the Statue of Liberty?"

"It was a present from Rainer."

"Him again?"

"He gives me lots of presents. Are you angry?"

"Why?"

"You could be jealous, at least, when a boy gives me presents. After all, you're a man, I'm a woman . . ."

"That's obvious from the mess in your room!"

"I was trying to decide what to wear to go for a drink at Queen's."

"With Ritter?"

"He's very nice."

She disengaged her right arm from the flag and bent over to pick up her bra and panties from the bed. She turned her back to Istvan, let the flag hang loosely, and began to get dressed.

"When I phoned, you didn't tell me you were getting ready to go out," he said.

"I didn't know you'd made any plans for us."

She let the flag drop to her ankles, picked it up, and flung it round Istvan's shoulders.

"You can look at me, you know," she added. "There are uglier women around."

"If everybody says you're beautiful, it must be true."

"So what shall I wear for Covent Garden? The same as the other day?"

"I thought you were going to Queen's?"

"Would you rather I did? Then you could have an early night. Make up your mind. I'm not going to stand here half-naked for an hour."

"Isn't Ritter coming to pick you up?"

"We were supposed to be meeting there. I'll call him and break the date."

"It was brilliant."

Natty took Istvan's arm, snuggled up to him, and walked with her face upturned toward the stars.

"Where are you going? The car's here."

The beautifully restored old Daimler limousine had drawn up as near to the theater as possible. Natty climbed in and unfastened her black velvet cape.

"I like feeling the leather against my bare skin," she said. Then she began raving over Frederick Ashton's ballet. Suddenly, she broke off and looked at Istvan with a worried expression.

"You haven't said a word. Did you like it?"

"Of course I did."

"You weren't bored?"

"At times I found it rather noisy."

"Oh Istvan, how can you say that? You were with me, but maybe you'd rather have been somewhere else?"

"Not at all. You're forgetting that it was my idea to go."

She looked so disappointed that he put his arm around her. He caught sight of the chauffeur's expression in the mirror. An odd mixture of curiosity and feigned indifference. He had often driven Istvan since his arrival in London; but he did not know that Natty was his adoptive daughter.

THE NET

There's another one who's taken in by the Horwat legend, Istvan thought. The great champion, knocked out of Wimbledon in the second round because he spent more time on girls than on training. Istvan couldn't blame him. He was the one who had created that legend. Why should it bother him? Because he was with Natty? He ought to find it amusing. The driver must know that Natty was very young, despite her dress and her black stockings. Especially since, to please Istvan, she wasn't wearing any eye makeup and hadn't even put on any lipstick.

Natty wondered how she even could have thought that the head waiter at the Gloucester Hotel looked like a vampire. His engaging smile did not reveal any unusually long or pointed canines.

"Delighted to see you again, Mr. Horwat," he said. Then, bowing in Natty's direction, "Would madame like to follow me please . . ."

"Did you book?" asked Natty as they studied the menus.

"You know very well I never bother to book in London. Why, did Ritter make a reservation? I'm not surprised. That's what your generation's like. Computers. As a matter of fact, I was wondering why you wanted to come here. I was going to take you to Wheelers. It's much more fun."

"I thought it would be the logical place to come after Covent Garden. I'm going to go fix my hair. Will you order for me?"

"What do you want?"

"Whatever you like. The same as you."

Istvan watched her walk off. Several people in the room were staring at her. He imagined her on the stage at Covent Garden.

She could have been a dancer, he thought. Now she was going to be competing at the Orange Bowl. He followed his thoughts for a few moments, then suddenly looked up. Natty had resumed her seat opposite him so discreetly that he had not heard her approach.

"Aren't you eating? What were you dreaming about?"

"I thought you'd given up wearing makeup, but I see I was mistaken."

"Doesn't it suit me?"

Istvan tilted his head to the right, drew closer to Natty, then sat back and assayed her purple mouth and her eyes, which she'd enlarged with a few strokes of the brush.

"It suits you very well," he said at last, "except that it makes you look ten years older."

"Two at the most. Dracula called me madame, I don't want to disappoint him."

"Dracula?"

"It's the nickname Rainer and I gave him. Come on, let's eat! I'm happy with you. I'm hungry."

"A fruit juice and then we're going back," Istvan said. "I may be free, but you've got to go to bed early."

"Orange Bowl in October, I know, I haven't forgotten. I'll just have a bowl of oranges . . ."

Istvan winced as they stepped into the hubbub at Tramps. The rock music exploded in his ears. Natty dragged him onto the dance floor.

"I feel more at home on a tennis court," he shouted in her ear.

He wheeled around, bumping into a redhead who laughingly protested. He had just received a great clap on the shoulder. Typical of Rainer Ritter.

"I thought you were at Queen's," Istvan shouted to him after apologizing to the redhead.

THE NET

"We've just come from there," Rainer yelled. "Can I borrow Natty for five minutes?"

Istvan felt choked and blinded by the cigarette smoke. He could not see any free tables. He elbowed his way to the bar, suddenly tired. He ordered a vodka and Coke, and tried to spot Natty and Rainer amid the crowd.

It was not difficult to spot R.R. He flailed around like an out-of-control semaphore, flinging his great arms out at nearby dancers. Natty was helpless with laughter.

Istvan found that there was no longer anything graceful about her, that she was writhing around in an almost obscene fashion. He forced himself to admit that she was no worse than any of the other girls he could name, and told himself he was an old fool. He certainly felt like one, standing there holding Natty's cape.

34

"You have a talent for remaining friends with all your ex-girlfriends," Natty said. Mary Collins had just invited Istvan to watch the Orange Bowl tournament from the CBS box.

She added, "If you ditched *me,* you'd never see me again."

Natty was not bothered by the heat of Florida in October. After making a major contribution to the American victory in the world Junior team championship, she was quietly heading for the finals of the individual championship at Key Biscayne.

She remained indifferent to the phenomenal excitement of the Orange Bowl fortnight, where the best young players—the under-sixteens and the juniors, generally escorted by their parents or coach—were stirred to a frantic competitive pitch.

When asked if he had been expecting Natty's steady progress through the preliminary rounds, Istvan replied with an enigmatic smile. In truth, he was at a loss for words. If he thought about it, after making sure that

THE NET

Natty was asleep at their hotel in Miami, lulled by the throbbing of the air conditioning, he had to admit to himself that, deep down, he had thought that she would put up no more than a decent fight. Perhaps because, despite everything, Fenwick's words—"training not intensive enough"—were ringing in his ears. He was amazed that Natty's results confirmed his theory: harmonious development from childhood, and never any excess. Since she was little, he had never wanted to overtrain her or tire her. He even restrained her half the time. He did not regret it. If she had been playing three or four hours of tennis a day since the age of ten, she would already be worn out, with all due respect to Fenwick.

Then it came to him in a rush that all this was too good to be true, and he was afraid. After Natty's performance in the team championship, Fenwick had obviously changed his mind. Now he could not find enough superlatives to praise Natty Kotany's playing. The manager did not miss a single match of hers. He paid close attention to the public's enthusiasm: over the last two weeks, she had become the most beautiful girl in Florida, according to one journalist who wrote, with down-home familiarity, that after all, she had been born in New York and she had just turned seventeen.

Istvan had advised Natty firmly not to read any articles mentioning her and not to watch television before the end of the Orange Bowl. She obeyed him in everything with a docility that astonished him, given her character. She seemed to be living in a state of permanent concentration, eating correctly, sleeping the right number of hours, answering everybody with a smile and from a certain distance.

Istvan, on the other hand, could no longer sleep.

He was grateful to Mary Collins for letting him shelter in the CBS box, to escape from the fussing of his friends, Jim and Cora Gordon, which he found as exaggerated as Countess Balanska's fanaticism. She had arrived for the final, together with Livia Fabiani.

"It's quite a little family reunion," repeated Gordon. "We're thinking not only of the child but also of her parents, Istvan."

"You're not thinking of her escort very much," said Livia. "You're very nice to him."

"Ritter? He wears everyone out with his enthusiasm."

Keeping aloof from the group, Istvan took a morose pleasure in remaining alone with his anxiety. The bustle of the CBS crew isolated him even more from the others, and that was fine.

His familiar nightmare had been claiming him almost every night since he and Natty had arrived in Miami. And every morning, after he was awake, he battled the premonition that Natty would not reach the final.

This pessimism was something he was not able to allay despite everything—Natty's results, which had been faultless since the beginning of the team championship; the opinions of informed observers, which were increasingly favorable; and the journalists, who were singing her praises, even if they did say more about her physique than her game. As a matter of fact, that was one of the reasons for his anxiety. Did not Natty's image conceal shortcomings that would be revealed during the final?

He became obsessed with Charlotte Larbaud, the top French junior. From the beginning of the tournament, he forecast that her precision would take her into the final. And in his moments of despondency, which he had always managed to mask with his offhand antics, he began to doubt his methods. There was the interview that Char-

THE NET

lotte Larbaud—or rather her mother, who spoke on her behalf—had given to Mary Collins. Charlotte had been playing without a break since the age of six. By the age of eight, she was training for two hours a day. At twelve, three or four hours. She was already a "professional," as her mother put it with a practiced smile. At thirteen she had won the Orange Bowl under-sixteens' championship. If Natty did make it to the finals, Istvan thought, what would she do against this keenly bred and trained specimen?

The final arrived. Natty was in it.

"Do you mind if I join you, seeing that Mr. Horwat is already here?" It was Madame Larbaud.

Mary Collins darted Istvan an apologetic look. She had no reason to send the woman she called in private "Amadeus Larbaud's mother" packing.

For Istvan this was finally the waking nightmare. The one that confirmed his premonitions. The mother had come to goad him with her unwelcome presence in his CBS refuge, knowing that in a few moments, Natty would be slaughtered on the court by Charlotte Larbaud.

He moved away from the camera stand that stood between him and the platinum-haired, very model of a possessive mother. Her suntan was too dark and her low-cut dress feigned modesty, while the smile on her painted mouth was forced. As Istvan stood there, the mouth moved. It was saying, "Just because our children are opponents doesn't mean we can't speak to each other."

Good God, it was too much—now she was coming on to him, stooping to conquer before her daughter had even won.

"I'm one of your greatest admirers, Monsieur Horwat. And Charlotte is delighted to be playing your daughter in the final. But . . . she's not really your daughter, I believe?"

Istvan did not answer. The match was about to begin and the crowd was already quieting down.

Madame Larbaud's smile faded slightly, but she went on. "When Charlotte won at Orange Bowl five years ago, it was against an American girl. By the way, Miss Collins, you haven't anything against the French, have you?"

"No," replied Mary. "Why?"

"You cut three-quarters of Charlotte's interview. The most interesting parts."

Behind them stood a tall, thin correspondent whose huge straw hat covered his ears and seemed to be held on by his sunglasses. "They're about to start," he said, hoping to put an end to the chatter.

"Just one thing, monsieur," said Madame Larbaud. "I like what you write very much. Would you like to have lunch with us tomorrow? You'll have a great article. I can't promise you exclusivity, but . . ."

"We'll see."

"Now everyone be quiet," snapped Mary Collins, her notebook on her knee, already concentrating on the court.

Istvan closed his eyes.

He opened them to find that Charlotte Larbaud had won the toss and was going to serve.

She served an ace.

He swore he would not look at the mother's face again during the game. He could feel the smugness in the prissy way she clapped. He gritted his teeth.

He could hardly breathe. He tried to forget that this was the final. Now that the action was under way, he became the coach again, judging his pupil's game.

And he dissected Charlotte Larbaud.

In the background, the mother bored everyone within

THE NET

earshot with admiring comments on her daughter's volleying, serves, and lobs, and tales of other matches. Charlotte dominated the first set and took it 6–4. But Istvan read the signs, saw through to the poor kid whose knees were already bandaged, who was feeling the pain of the tennis elbow that came from playing when she should have been resting. He saw the signs of distraction and despondency as the youngster kept glancing up to the CBS box and her gushing, unseeing mother.

This is what it did to these kids. Charlotte was *afraid* of failing. Her life, at only seventeen, hung on this Junior world title, just as, for year after year, it had depended on competition after competition.

Doubtless she knew, as everyone did, that her mother had arranged a huge celebration for all the managers—anyone of any importance in the game—wagering seventeen cases of champagne on her victory. No wonder the pressure was showing.

Istvan couldn't do anything but feel sorry for the kid, even if she did look like a lost and bewildered robot. Instead he switched his whole attention to Natty, admiring the contrast and grateful for it, win or lose.

Natty looked at nobody and nothing. She sipped a little water, found a fresh headband, and calmly went back to her place. She bounced the ball from her racket three times on the very hard court of Key Biscayne, where the air shimmered with the heat.

She was leading 5–4 in the second set.

But she quickly changed that to 6–4 and set-all a few minutes later. Then a rally of crosscourt backhands from the baseline brought the spectators to their feet, applauding.

"Istvan," shouted Rainer Ritter. "It's the Horwat backhand!"

Holgersson was prodding Rainer to make him sit down. "Want to bet with me?"

"What?"

"That your American girl loses the third set."

"Forget it! You only say that because you haven't been able to play for six months. Or because Natty sent you packing. Is that it?"

"No. Watch."

"Two aces, two!" shouted Charlotte's mother.

"Quiet!" said the journalist in the straw hat. "You're not at a football stadium, lady."

Istvan wondered how Charlotte Larbaud had been able to place those two aces. To him it seemed as though she was breaking down, like someone put together from spare parts.

"Are you daydreaming, Natty, or what?"

He was thinking out loud. Mary Collins turned around and put a finger to her lips. "Shhh!"

Suddenly the French girl missed a powerful but not impossible forehand drive of Natty's.

"It's her contact lenses," groaned her mother. "What with this heat and the perspiration, she's a real martyr."

"Then she should wear glasses like everyone else," retorted the man in the straw hat. "In any case . . ."

"In any case what?" yelped Madame Larbaud. "Are you against her, too?"

As if to admit defeat, Charlotte looked in the direction of the stand. A plea for help.

"Two games all," announced the Italian umpire.

* * *

THE NET

Istvan would forever remember the voice of the umpire shouting over an avalanche of applause:

"Miss Kotany is the winner, four–six, six–four, six–two!"

In front of him, her face a mask of pain, Madame Larbaud was grief-stricken. If at least she could cry, thought Istvan.

He brushed her aside, vaulted the front of the VIP box, and ran toward the net where Charlotte Larbaud was sobbing in Natty's arms.

"Ian, don't miss that!" yelled Mary Collins to McGill, the cameraman who was following in Istvan's footsteps with the hand-held camera on his shoulder.

"Stop it!" screamed the mother, scratching the arm of the journalist who tried to restrain her from running onto the court. "You want to humiliate her! Charlotte! You're making an idiot of yourself! I'm coming! Get away from that bitch!"

Ian McGill could not have hoped for a better start to his career as a cameraman. Istvan Horwat hugging the two Orange Bowl finalists.

As soon as she felt Istvan Horwat's hand on her shoulder, Charlotte Larbaud stopped crying.

"It's not her fault," said Natty, "she couldn't see a thing."

"No, that's not what it was. Since the beginning of the second set I've been aching all over. My mother doesn't understand. What will she say?"

"She won't say anything. I'll talk to her if you like."

"You're a great player," said Natty. "You're tired, that's all."

"Incredible!" yelled Ritter, pushing into the center of the commotion. The stewards helplessly let them through before forming a wall to keep back the crowds. "Unwahrscheinlich!" Ritter said. "Natty's world champion, and you spend your time comforting the loser!"

"Shut up, Gunner," said Natty. "She's my friend. So be a sport." Then, looking about her: "We're going to get changed. We're allowed to, aren't we?"

35

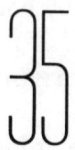

"I'd've liked to have traveled with Charlotte," said Natty, "but her mother told me where to get off."

"Me too," said Istvan. "Yesterday evening, I tried to talk some sense into her about her daughter's training. She took it very badly. Forget it."

When they changed planes at Kennedy Airport, the group of friends dispersed. Cora and Jim were staying in New York; so was Mary Collins. Livia Fabiani was going on to Paris.

Madame Larbaud hugged her daughter to her so that she would not get caught up in the rowdy crowd of youngsters returning from the Orange Bowl, exhausted but very excited.

Rainer Ritter kept as close as he could to Istvan, which was a good way of not letting Natty out of his sight.

The better-off citizens of the Republic of Tennis soon transformed the first-class cabin into a nomads' caravan. The crew watched the parents, who were a little out of their depth among the Orange Bowl generation, the coaches, satisfied or disappointed, and the managers, who sat apart from the others talking about everything except the best players whom they had earmarked for a possible contract.

Istvan let Natty have the window seat and settled down beside her.

"We're taking off in five minutes," he said. "As soon as we've had dinner, you can go to sleep."

"But it isn't seven o'clock yet. And I'm not hungry."

"You're shattered. You can eat what you like, then it's good night."

"What about you?"

"I'll stroll over to the bar while you go to sleep."

Ritter, sitting two rows behind, was suffering Holgersson's ill humor.

"May as well give away free seats," repeated the Swede, "the company could have booked us on the Concorde. Do you realize it'll take eight hours to get to Paris in this fat-assed so-called wide-body?"

"I love planes," said Ritter. "I never get bored. I think, I dream."

Holgersson burst out laughing and studied R.R. as if his friend were a curious insect.

"That's a new one," he said. "Rainer thinks. Rainer dreams. Don't forget the service, please!"

"And when do you take up your service again?"

"My training's more or less all right, as you saw. I'm going to get back into the swing of things gradually, starting with an invitation tournament in some dead-or-alive hole, I can't even remember what it's called. Look, here's our little snack. Did you see the hostess's legs? Whoops, excuuuse me! The love-sick knight only has eyes for his lady."

* * *

THE NET

"Aren't you cold?" Istvan asked Natty. "Do you want a blanket?"

"Later. I'm fine for the time being."

She took Istvan's hand and held it to her cheek.

"See, I'm warm."

Istvan pictured Natty on the court, the day before, at Key Biscayne, concentrating on her game, indifferent to the outside world that began thirty feet from where she was standing, so grown up in her attitude, in her game. . . . In that instant, in his mind, she became a child again. The blue of her eyes had deepened as she contemplated unknown ghosts on the other side of the dark window. Was she thinking of Jane and Màrton? He recalled her words after her victory the previous day: "Papa must be proud of me, mustn't he? And mommy. Natasha Kotany, world champion . . ."

That was when it had occurred to him to send a telegram to her grandparents in Hungary. How many times had he reproached himself, but only fleetingly, for not speaking to her about her family more often, as if he wanted to keep Natty all for himself.

Deep down, he thought, I'm nothing but the coach of the new Junior world champion.

"You're bored, Istvan," murmured Natty without shifting her gaze from the window. "That much I can tell."

She turned around and shaded her eyes with her hand.

"I bet Livia's at the bar getting herself chatted up."

A half-bottle of Saint-Emilion had gotten the better of Carl Holgersson, exhausted by the last few minutes in Miami. He had called it burying his life as a bachelor. He was going to start playing again and had sworn to follow a strict regime once he left Florida. For now, the whimsical

ILIE NASTASE

Swede had burrowed under his airline blanket. Rainer Ritter could at last lean forward and contemplate Natty's profile silhouetted against the window.

He was still staring at her when he saw Istvan get up and make his way to the bar, perhaps to join that woman who made a fortune from writing tennis novels. Frau Ritter had bought one for her son once. He hadn't been able to get through it.

Natty had a blanket over her legs and had tilted back her seat. "I was dropping off," she said when Rainer sat down next to her.

"Can I stay for five minutes?"

"If you like."

"I like."

Natty smiled vacantly.

"Are you happy?" asked Rainer.

"It's beginning to dawn on me. This morning when I woke up, I told myself I'd dreamed the whole thing. Yes, I'm happy."

Ritter took the risk of putting his arm around Natty's shoulder. He was afraid she would shrug him off. But she simply let herself slide down a little, and settled into his shoulder.

He leaned over and kissed her cheek.

"One day, you won't only be the Junior champion, but world champion . . ."

"What about you? Next year you'll already be number one . . ."

"And here we are, the pair of us, modestly sitting here."

Rainer took advantage of the moment to kiss her again, this time on the lips. She could not make out his features very well, so close like this, in the dim light. This evening, he had the face of her new victory, not his own recent ones. She was not accustomed to being courted so inti-

THE NET

mately. Her heart beat wildly and her body rebelled, but she was floating on a cloud of glory. No, it wasn't so unpleasant being kissed by R.R., the young prodigal, when you'd just won Orange Bowl. The obvious had happened. Their story had begun.

She felt gentle, offering herself to him. He slid his hand under the blanket. She closed her eyes and let him caress her.

In the silence of the dimly lit cabin, Istvan looked down the long rows of inert sleepers. He was working his way back down the aisle from the bar when he saw Rainer and Natty kissing. He cast around for an unoccupied seat, and tried to smile for them. Quickly he succumbed to the weariness that he had kept at bay at the bar. He only wanted to wrap himself in a blanket and sleep. He already had an appointment with his nightmare.

They lost all sense of time, kissing, whispering, falling silent with their own thoughts, drowsy, wrapped in their own world.

"I don't know what Istvan's planned," she said. "I'll have to talk to him about it."

"Why?"

"I've already missed a month of school."

"Are you going back to school?"

"Most likely... Yes, I think so... It's my senior year."

They fell silent and kissed again. Rainer's hand was still there, touching. She felt a gentle squeeze on her arm.

"Look," said Rainer, "dawn."

The sky ahead of the plane was pink, while behind it, the night was still black. With his fingertips, he parted the strands of hair that had fallen down into Natty's eyes.

She shook herself, emerged from the blanket, and stretched. She looked around, suddenly alert.

"What's the matter?"

"Istvan . . . where is he?"

"He's still asleep, like everyone else."

Natty got up, smoothed her dress, and nearly stumbled when she caught her foot in the blanket. She inspected the rows of seats and examined the abandoned bodies in the dim light, Istvan's among them. "They all look like corpses."

"Look at the sky, it's more fun," said Ritter.

She smiled. "Can you get my bag down?"

He reached up, unlatched the overhead baggage compartment, and took out the white bag embossed with the initials I.H.

"I'll give you one with R.R. on it," he said, while she rummaged for her makeup kit. "R.R., like Rolls-Royce, of course!"

"What about just N.K. My name's Natasha Kotany, isn't it?"

36

The Collège Dupanloup welcomed Natty back with a surprise party after classes were over. Istvan was invited too, and watched proudly as she was the center of attention amid the petits-fours and fruit juices. After a speech celebrating the virtues of sport and of striving in general, the headmistress took him quietly to one side.

"I was wondering, monsieur," she asked anxiously. "Will Natasha continue her studies up to the baccalauréat?" It was the exam that haunted every schoolchild in France, right up to the age of eighteen.

"Do you think she's capable of it?"

"Oh, no doubt. And we will help her—we'll arrange her timetable so that she can continue her training."

"The tournaments will create a problem."

The headmistress smiled dismissively. "Then we can give her extra lessons to help her catch up."

On the short walk home, Natty was glowing, and Istvan put an arm around her shoulder. "They were all talking about the Orange Bowl as if it were something extraordinary—but it was only the natural win of a very talented player." She leaned into him. "All the same," he went on, "I think it's important for you to complete school this year."

"Don't worry. Everything's fine. I'll give it a try."

They were silent for a few steps. "Something else..." he said.

"Yes?"

"I'm going to phone Fred Stolle this evening."

"Who's he?"

"An old Australian champion. Nowadays he's a very good coach. Just what you need."

"Don't you want to train me anymore?"

"You're big now..." He stopped in midsentence, stared at Natty, and went on with a forced smile. "I mean tennis-big. Very big. You don't need to have me with you all the time anyway, do you?"

Once again, a short silence. He faltered, casting around for the right words. She sensed that he was thinking about what had happened that night on the 747, and she spoke quickly.

"Of course I need you. You're the one who wants to get rid of me: school, this new coach..."

"No, Natty. I'm being absolutely serious. With this world title, you're beginning a champion's career. I've tried to teach you everything I know. Not only technique, but the values of this sport to which I owe everything, and which I love passionately. But I'm not a teacher. It's not my profession. At the level you've reached, you can no longer be my pupil. From now on, your mentor will be Fred Stolle. As for the rest—"

"The rest?"

"Yes, we have to discuss money matters. So far, I've taken care of everything. But you're going to be rich. You know the kind of money there is in tennis these days.

THE NET

Much more than when I was your age. As far as I'm concerned, all that's never mattered much to me. We're going to have to get Frank Fenwick to deal with your affairs. I'll get him to draw up a contract."

"Stolle, Fenwick . . . Are you retiring or what?"

"I most definitely am! Very soon. But a player needs a lawyer, an accountant, someone to manage PR. I can't take care of everything."

"I understand, Istvan. Okay to the coach and manager. All the same, this is really weird. I'm the one who's suddenly aged, aren't I? It's getting chilly. Let's go home."

37

By ten o'clock on Sunday, Natty had finished her first training session with Fred Stolle. Istvan had suggested that he not accelerate the rhythm she was accustomed to.

"I saw the results of your method at the Orange Bowl," Stolle told him. "Don't worry, I won't force the pace." He gave an implacable little grin. "That comes later."

The program for the rest of the day was carefully planned. Now she was going to try to finish her French homework before lunch. While she was flicking through the dictionary of quotations to fill out a rather empty page, Thieu came to fetch her from her room. Rainer Ritter was on the telephone.

"I'm taking you out for lunch," he said. "Okay?"

"Yes, but not too early. I've got to finish my homework first."

"You can finish it later. I'll pick you up at eleven-thirty. We've got quite a way to go."

"Make it noon."

"A quarter to twelve then."

And he hung up before Natty had time to protest.

THE NET

* * *

When he came, it was in a taxi.

"Why didn't you come by car, Rainer?"

"I haven't found one I like yet," he replied. "They're all alike. Even Rolls-Royces aren't what they used to be."

The truth was that he had flunked his driving test twice.

"Move over a bit," said Natty. "I can't breathe. Are we going very far?"

"It's a surprise."

The taxi turned off to the right into the part of Le Bourget Airport reserved for private planes. Rainer paid the taxi driver, then led Natty into a glass-walled office and shook hands with the two men who were waiting for them.

"Everything's ready, Monsieur Ritter," said one of them. "We can go."

"Are we flying?" asked Natty. "Is that your surprise? You're crazy! What about my work?"

"We're flying in *my* plane." said Ritter. "We can come back whenever you like."

He took her hand and made her run with him to a twin-engined Cessna. On the plane's side the black letters R.R. stood out above two crossed white tennis rackets.

"It's *better* than a Rolls, isn't it?" he said.

"Is it really yours?" she asked, impressed in spite of herself.

"It's in my father's name, but I paid for it. I've made loads of money this year. Do you like it?"

"It's a lovely toy. Where are you taking me?"

"That's the second surprise," he said, leading her up the steps into the cabin. He let down the partition that separated the six seats from the cockpit. He opened the door of the bar.

"But you don't drink any of that!" exclaimed Natty, counting the bottles of Scotch, vodka, rum, and mixers.

"It's for my guests. Do you want some tomato juice? There's champagne too."

He poured out the tomato juice. Glass in hand, he showed Natty all the refined features of his toy. The seats that pivoted around to face a folding table in the center; the boxed-in video concealed between the windows; the luxuriously appointed lavatory.

"You could go around the world in this," she said dreamily. "Come on, tell me, where are we going?"

He grinned. "For the time being, we're going to watch a film."

"Mademoiselle, every time Rainer phones us, he always mentions you. He always said he was sure you'd win the Orange Bowl a year after he did!"

Herr Ritter turned off onto the autobahn interchange road, following the signs to Münster. Burly, ruddy, with hair even redder than his son's, he drove his Audi Quattro with the precision of a rally driver, and nearly as fast. Natty did not know much about him except that he was a lawyer, his wife a painter, and that Rainer was their only son.

"I named him Rainer," he added in a confidential tone, "because when I was at the university, I was mad about the great poet Rilke. Rainer Maria Rilke. Do you know Rilke, mademoiselle?"

"No."

"Rainer never wanted to open his *Letters to a Young Poet*. At his age, I'd already read it five times. Unfortunately, my son is only interested in tennis."

"It's hardly unfortunate, given the results," said Natty.

"True, yes, of course. And when I realized, I put him in

THE NET

the hands of the best coaches in Germany. I paid handsomely so that they would devote themselves to Rainer. They did, and he devoted himself, too."

Whether he meant it with satisfaction or regret, Natty couldn't be sure.

Natty soon found the visit . . . overwhelming was perhaps the word. For one thing, there was the constant refrain of Rainer, which threatened to swamp her. For another, the predominant color in the big house was white—walls, carpets, tablecloths, everything—giving it a lack of warmth and welcome. White was Frau Ritter's favorite color. Her paintings were immaculate surfaces broken up by the occasional red, black, or orange square.

And then, before sitting down to lunch, Natty had to let them show her Rainer's room, lined with posters of champions, cluttered with trophies and rackets, each of which had played an historic part in his career as a champion. She stood a little stiffly in the doorway, not knowing what to do with her huge glass of Seven-Up.

Herr Ritter, who sounded like a fast-talking commercial, enumerated the stages of Rainer's life, from when he cut his first tooth. Rainer listened with a modest smile. His mother, who did not understand much English, stood in silent agreement, wearing the same smile.

Tired of the general rapture, Natty was relieved when the maid interrupted them to announce that lunch was ready.

Eva, the snub-nosed young serving girl, wearing a blue dress and white apron, covertly eyed Natty. Every time she came to the table to serve, she glanced at the champion for a second. They must have been about the same age. Her fine face was weighed down by her heavy braids. Natty wondered for a moment if this blond girl was another of Rainer's little trophies. Boredom always made her spiteful, and she wondered, too, whether the heavy, bland cooking was responsible for R.R.'s massive shoulders.

She had lost her appetite and sat there smiling politely, with a faraway expression, picking at her food under Frau Ritter's disapproving gaze. But Rainer was in seventh heaven. He stopped describing the Orange Bowl for the umpteenth time only to boast about the virtues of his plane.

Natty felt numb, almost paralyzed on her white leather chair. She felt a little giddy. She found it hard to understand what was happening to her.

Had she really believed she was in love with Rainer? She remembered when it had started, in the joyous moments after the Orange Bowl, when she was overcome by waves of happiness that she was the world Junior champion. She hadn't known which end was up, then. And she did not have much of an idea now, either.

She did not dare look at him. She found him pinker, in the warmth of his family, than ever. Something akin to nausea overtook her as she tried to banish the memory of his kisses and caresses.

She could no longer stand anything or anyone in this dining room, which was more like a hospital where they dissected her with questions to which she barely replied, or gave the wrong answer.

Rainer had promised her a surprise. What a surprise! She was prisoner of a family lunch that was more like an engagement celebration.

Her anger welled up. She had trouble restraining it, and the effort was making her head spin. No, she was not in love with Rainer, and engaged she never would be. She

THE NET

should have stuck to her first impression at Roland-Garros.

She resented Istvan for having abandoned her, for not having sat close to her in the 747. He should have understood that she wasn't in a normal state the day after such an emotional upheaval. She was up in the clouds, and he had left her to make a fool of herself in the clutches of this German.

She was no longer listening to a word they were saying. She was planning what to say to get Rainer to take her back to Paris. Something tactful, like: I told you I had a lot of homework for tomorrow. . . .

38

"You're back very late," said Istvan. "It must have been a long lunch. . . . Where did you go?"

"Don't ask. To Münster!"

"Münster?"

"Would you believe it? He wanted to show me his toy plane, this carpeted airplane with two propellers and R.R. all over it, and tennis rackets for a coat of arms!"

"So that's how he managed to lure you home . . ."

"You think it was a little trap to get me into bed, is that it? Quite the opposite. There was Daddy, Mommy, and even the maid. A genuine intimate family engagement party. The *big* trap. I felt so cornered, I couldn't swallow a thing."

"Sit down and explain."

"There's nothing to explain," said Natty sinking onto the sofa. "I wasn't expecting any of it, that's all."

"Weren't you?"

"What's that supposed to mean?"

Istvan looked at her with a mocking smile.

She leaped to her feet again as quickly as she had sat

THE NET

down. "I'm going to change into a pair of jeans. I'm fed up with this engagement dress!"

"I still don't get it. Aren't you in love with Rainer?"

Natty grabbed a lamp from the coffee table, almost tripping over the cord, and brandished the lamp above Istvan's head.

"Say that again," she cried. "I'll break this over your head!"

"Calm down! I've seen you with him. Don't tell me you don't love him."

"One more word like that and I'll kill you!"

"All right, all right. But if you're getting upset, it's because you care about him."

"You're joking! He's a kid. He doesn't know what a girl is! That's why he needs them easy. I've never been in love with him, never!"

Istvan got up in turn, took the lamp from Natty's hands, and put it back on the table.

They stood facing each other.

"I've often wondered," she murmured, "why I wasn't interested in boys like the other girls. Whenever they came near me, I always found something wrong with them. They always repeated the same nonsense, they were all the same, they were wasting their time and they wanted to make me waste mine. They were worse than Rainer, they disgusted me. At least he's a great tennis player. But that isn't enough. Have you ever wondered what goes on in my head when I'm not on the tennis court? I wasn't happy. My only moments of happiness were when I was facing you across the net."

With tears in her eyes, she put her hands on Istvan's shoulders. He remained silent, steadfastly looking at her. Minutes seemed to pass before she spoke again.

"It's too stupid, you haven't understood a thing. I told

myself you'd realize in the end. There'll never be any other man but you in my life. Do you hear me?"

She let go of his shoulders and stared down at her feet, suddenly shy.

"I was waiting for it to dawn on you, Istvan. I told myself that twelve was too young, thirteen, not old enough. Then I was fifteen, the same age as Juliet in the play. And then sixteen, and you still didn't notice a thing. Haven't you understood that ever since the first day, you have been the only man in my life? Shut up! I'm certain of it! I can wait for years until you wake up and face it. Maybe you'll be an old man, hardly able to walk, you'll go to concerts and listen to your Liszt, you'll mistake the violins for tennis rackets, but too bad. I'll be there! And you expect me to fall in love with the first idiot who runs after me."

"Go and change into your jeans," he said hoarsely. "Let's go out for a walk." Something was telling him they should leave the intimacy of the apartment, be among people.

The gates of Roland-Garros were open in the November twilight mist. The blurred shadows of the last departing employees melted into the distance, and the Federation offices, which were still lit up, shed a ghostly light.

The center court was empty. And like all empty stadiums, it seemed vast—just the opposite of the way childhood houses seem tiny when visited years later. The many destinies that had been played out at the foot of the stands left an aura of tragedy and mystery, as a woman's perfume lingers in a room she has left.

The net had been removed. It must be in my nightmare, thought Istvan. The mist eddied above the tarpaulin covering the hard courts. The moon was already out between

THE NET

the clouds in the darkening sky. Natty followed Istvan, and she sat down with him among the eerie terraces. He had not said a word since they had left Avenue Robert-Schumann. Then he took the plunge, speaking firmly.

"You've got to be sensible. At your age . . ."

She looked at the tarpaulin-covered court, the great emptiness of the stands. It all felt unreal. Nothing made any sense. He was only eighteen inches away from her but he seemed too far away to hear.

"Do you understand, Natty?"

Then the word again.

"Will you be sensible?"

She shivered.

"Are you cold? Let's go home."

He drew closer and put his arm around her shoulders.

She shivered even more.

"You're frozen," he said.

She turned her face toward him. She brought her lips close to him. He did not move while she kissed him, long and hard, hungry for his mouth.

Istvan worked the buttons on the remote control. He went back to the same channel several times, turned up the volume, lowered it, tweaked up the color, went back to black and white and adjusted the contrast. Finally he pressed the off button and the television picture collapsed into darkness, the screen glowing for a few moments in the night. Only the blue night light remained on next to the big round bed.

He closed his eyes.

The jumbled television images lingered, danced, began to spin.

He half-opened his eyes to put a stop to this frenzy and rediscover his familiar surroundings.

ILIE NASTASE

The door had opened onto the lighted corridor. Was this the memory of an image he had seen on the screen earlier, or the beginning of a dream?

No, the door really was open, and Natty's silhouette appeared. She stood in the doorway wearing a baggy T-shirt. He held his breath, his heart beating wildly. She walked toward the bed. The light from the corridor threw shadows on her body, emphasizing every detail through the thin cotton.

She leaned over him, brushed his cheeks with her hair and slid under the sheet.

"Don't pretend to be asleep," she murmured as she removed her shirt. "I know you were waiting for me."

PART 3

part 3

39

The DC9 began its descent over the lagoon. Natty, her face pressed to the window, followed the contours of earth and water on the plain, the undulations that outlined, on the gray-and-brown surface, a moving map.
The plane tilted, wheeling on its left wing. Natty slid toward Istvan's armrest. He leaned toward her and tightened her seatbelt, which she had only pretended to fasten to placate the stewardess. She took advantage of this double movement to put her arms around his neck. The plane wheeled over to the right sending them both, intertwined, leaning against the window.
"We're going to land on the water," she said.
They stayed cheek to cheek, watching the dull, blue-green surface, mottled by rain, approaching rapidly. Natty put her hand over Istvan's as it gripped the armrest. She made him take it off and placed it on her knee. She could feel how cold it was against the warm silk of her stocking.
Istvan relaxed when the wheels touched down on the runway.

"Anyone would think we were landing on an island. Where's Venice?"

"We're going to take a boat," replied Istvan.

They ran through the rain to the jetty. A Riva with a varnished mahogany hull bobbed up and down on its mooring line. A man, with a little boy at his side, watched them arrive well ahead of the other passengers, who were breathless and slithering all over the wet planks as they piled into the vaporetto.

Istvan asked the pilot of the Riva if he was free.

"We're going to the Gritti, and I'll keep you for a week."

Natty stood in the boat trying to make out the city in the distance. All she could see was a hazy dark line blurred by a drizzle that reminded her of the English coast. She sat down on the seat and put her head on Istvan's shoulder.

"I'm happy," she said.

She smiled at the little boy, taken with his blond curls and angelic look. It was a face that reflected her own happiness.

"My name's Antonio," said the man. "He's my son, Giambattista. His mother works all day, the school's closed because of the scarlet fever, so I'm keeping him with me. He's very well-behaved, you know. He only speaks when spoken to."

"A real cherub," chorused Natty and Istvan, and both burst out laughing.

"You're right," said Antonio. "Love's no secret in Venice."

Istvan held Natty tight as the Riva gathered speed. She kissed him and licked the salty taste of the spray from his lips. Then they drew apart to look at each other.

THE NET

Istvan smiled at Natty, whose light eyes took on the blue-green of the lagoon.

"Natty . . ."

"Are we there?"

"No. I'm looking at you. There's still a long way to go."

The launch kept up its speed, and presently an endless wall loomed up before them, unreal in the light pink-and-gold mist and the pale sunlight. The rain, the waves, and the clouds had vanished as if by magic. And surely, by more magic, the wall would open.

"Istvan!"

She sat close to him. The little cherub moved over to make room for her.

"Wait," said Istvan, "you'll see."

A gap had opened in the clear sky.

The noise of the engine was no more than a muffled throbbing.

"Venice!" exclaimed Natty. "It's Venice!"

"You see," said Istvan, "the sky's blue now."

"We're very honored to have you and Signora Horwat stay with us, signore."

At the reception desk in the Gritti, the man leafing through the register without looking up announced with a smile, "I've booked you the suite that Count Visconti occupied during the filming of *Death in Venice*. If you wish to have lunch here . . . The porter booked you a table just in case."

"You did the right thing," said Istvan.

They followed the man to the elevator. Natty looked about her, enthralled by the baroque decor. Istvan burst out laughing and leaned toward her. She gave him a quick kiss, under the blasé eye of the man who was holding open the elevator door.

They did not linger to admire the view from their window, which the porter had pointed out to them with pride. As soon as they were alone, Istvan swept Natty up in his arms and carried her over to the bed.

Much later, they found themselves alone in the deserted dining room beside the Grand Canal, which was also deserted at this hour when everyone was having a siesta.

"Anyone would think this town was abandoned," said Natty. "Abandoned to us."

40

Istvan awoke first and slipped out of bed. He drew back the double curtains and opened the shutters. He inhaled the cold air. He remembered one hot May when he had come to Venice with a girl whose name he had forgotten. Damp had attacked the Danieli, where he had stayed. The smell of sludge had risen from the canal. It was a sickening memory.

Venice in December suited Natty. Since they had crossed the lagoon in the rain, there had not been a cloud in the sky. The sun cleansed the facades of the buildings. The great dome of the Santa Maria della Salute, on the other side of the Grand Canal, was so clear that it seemed very close.

Natty slept naked in the overheated room. Istvan had had to get used to this temperature. Normally it gave him a headache, but she liked heat, and, by her side, he did not suffer from the slightest headache.

He contemplated her asleep, on her stomach, her blond hair spread over the pillow that she hugged to her. He watched her gentle breathing. How could she be so chaste and so shameless at the same time? He resisted the impulse to touch her, for fear that she would move. He felt that if he took his eyes off her, she would escape him and vanish into the lagoon like a creature of the water.

"Me, too," Natty had said to him the previous evening, guessing his thoughts. "I'm always afraid that you'll vanish into the mist, behind these ghostly buildings." Hand in hand, intertwined, standing, sitting, they were inseparable. Then she added, reassuringly, maternally: "But you mustn't worry from now on. I'll be able to find you anywhere."

He could not get over his amazement that he had never been so happy. Happy, simply happy. The great moments of elation in his career, taken for the strongest feelings of happiness that he would ever experience, seemed to him remote and unreal.

Sometimes he realized with horror that if Natty had been as blind as he, they could have spent their lives side by side, leaving each other and uniting again without the word love ever being uttered.

"Those pink reflections on the black water of the canal are lovely."

He had not heard her get up. Standing alongside him before the window, draped in a bathrobe, she pretended to be shivering. She spoke very fast, eagerly reminding him of their day's plans.

"I want islands," she said, in the same tone of voice as if she were saying, "I want to make love."

The previous day, she had found the Lido beach too sad, with its locked bathing cabins and black, freezing sand. Antonio the boatman had suggested taking them to see the Murano glass blowers.

"Afterward," he had said, "I can take you to Torcello.

THE NET

We'll come back in the early afternoon, before it gets too cold."

"All right. Tomorrow," Natty had said without asking Istvan's opinion.

She closed the window and went to the telephone to order breakfast.

"Let's get dressed quickly, Antonio's waiting for us."

She had already flung off the bathrobe and was running toward the bathroom. She turned round to blow Istvan a kiss. He had never seen her so spontaneous, so adult and so alluring at the same time.

Natty did not take the time to have a bath. Through the door, which she had left open, he saw her, standing in the bathtub, cautiously manipulating the shower so as not to wet her hair, singing to herself, enveloped in a cloud of steam.

She put the hideous multicolored glass clown from Murano down on the table.

Sitting at the Café Florian, with cups of steaming hot chocolate, they were dreaming. They glanced at the tourists hurrying toward the basilica of St. Mark's. In this Mecca of romanticism, they looked like two nineteenth-century German travelers, the master and his young disciple. Natty had thrown her cape over the back of her chair. Two elderly Venetians had put down their coffee to gaze after her when she came in, on Istvan's arm. Perhaps they thought she was a young boy, with her hair tied back, her knickers and her black velvet jacket, her stockings and black shiny moccasins. Istvan had never seen these clothes before. When she was getting dressed to go to Torcello, he had been troubled by the unexpected metamorphosis of this young sportswoman. For an afternoon, she had erased her body. He caressed her hand, overwhelmed to find, in this vague femininity, the passionate gentleness of their most intimate moments, and in their silence, the violence of their love.

"In fact, we're not doing any sightseeing," said Natty at last. "You know, I've realized that the Doge's Palace, the museums and all don't interest me in the slightest. What I like is when we follow the zigzags of the launch going backward and forward from one bank to the other, or when we pass the facades of the buildings."

"I prefer our room," said Istvan.

"We're very bad tourists! But when we come back to Venice, we'll still have lots of things to discover . . ."

They skimmed through the city dazed by happiness. They contemplated a funeral procession on the lagoon as they passed it off the island of San Michele. Giambattista crossed himself. Antonio slowed down so that they could see the coffin, the priests, and the family in the gondolas decked with black, maneuvered by men dressed in black, like the mythic boatmen of the underworld.

They only had eyes for each other. Locked in their exclusive love, which Istvan refused to call passion—he did not like that word; it evoked for him all the fleeting affairs he had had before Natty—they saw around them nothing but a film set alive with extras. An incredible shared selfishness set them apart. They felt unassailable, invulnerable.

"What about having dinner at Harry's Bar?" asked Natty.

"If you like, but we're going back to the hotel first."

4

Doubtless they were awful tourists, as Natty had said, but they were no worse than the succession of lovers who had seen Venice and lived out their stormy passions or melancholic reveries, conventional honeymoons or epic disasters.

The city bewitched and transformed them.

A souvenir photographer caught them on a narrow bridge where two people could barely pass one another. The Polaroid image showed them holding hands, cuddling up together. She was laughing because a gondolier had bent down at the last minute to go under the bridge, yelling at his passengers to do likewise. Istvan was smiling and leaning toward her. That night Natty had put the photo on the bedside table, next to the glass clown.

"What on earth were you telling me, before that gondola went past?" she asked.

"I don't remember . . . probably that I love you."

Now, as they sat on the red velvet-upholstered seat of the gondola they had hired to follow the little canals that were off limits to motorboats, their whispering was accompanied by the lapping of the dirty water, which swamped the ground floors of secret buildings and rotted the posts of the tiny bridges. They penetrated gardens of shadows turned brown by the winter, where it looked as though nobody had ever ventured.

Natty buried her hands under her cloak, dreaming of other landscapes, hearing the bells of horses harnessed to a troika, in the snow—an image she remembered from one of her childhood story books.

When Istvan dozed off after making love in their room, her whole body felt the joy of having been made for him and having given herself to nobody but him. She had never found Istvan so handsome. And she knew she was worthy of him. The suitcases of useless clothes were no doubt a last fit of adolescent uncertainty and anxiety. A mask she no longer needed. Istvan told her in vain that Venice was the city of masks, of appearances, but such deception was foreign to her. The winter sun in its metallic blue sky dispersed the shadows on earth as in heaven.

She wanted to know Venice, having heard the name so many times. But she knew that the legendary city of love would not give her any more than any other place. It was Istvan's presence that mattered.

"Do you want to go to La Fenice? It's just round the corner from the hotel. We're always walking past it."

They were finishing dinner, the hotel lights reflected in the Grand Canal.

"What's on?"

"Vivaldi. I thought you liked redheads! Vivaldi had very red hair apparently. The porter offered me two seats."

"We said we'd have an early night."

THE NET

Istvan shrugged mischievously. "As you wish," he said. "But I'm not making a very good job of educating you."

"Music studies aren't important. It's on the curriculum at college."

"Where, incidentally, you should be at this very moment."

"Listen to who's talking! Who's playing hooky from his tournament in Milan?"

Istvan stroked Natty's breasts as she slept with her head on his shoulder. She opened her eyes and mumbled a few incomprehensible words. She looked at him for a few seconds, then closed her eyes again, still smiling. He could feel her breath on his neck.

He found it hard to accept that the next day they would be crossing the lagoon for the last time in Antonio's boat, turning their backs on the ramparts. He gently freed himself from Natty, got up and switched on the desk light, then took out of the wardrobe the little casket he had hidden under a pile of shirts that afternoon while Natty was having a siesta. He opened it and looked at the Renaissance ruby set in a bracelet that looked as if it had been made for Natty's wrist.

"A unique piece," the old jeweler had said. "A Renaissance bracelet—doubtless the lady is worthy?" There was a twinkle in his alert eyes at the question.

"A princess!"

A faraway look came over the old man and he nodded appreciatively. "Si, signore."

Istvan had given up trying to convert the millions of lire into dollars. He only wished the night were over so that he could fasten it around her wrist. He was fascinated by the symbol on the gold-and-iron bracelet: a man's iron gauntlet holding a woman's hand fashioned in gold. The hands were entwined. A marriage of roughness and refinement, of strength and grace . . .

"No," he said to himself walking across the room. "I'm not waiting until daybreak."

He went over to the bed. Natty had adopted her favorite position—she lay flat on her stomach with her arms around the pillow. He gently disengaged her left hand.

The clasp snapped shut in the silence, and Istvan's hand lay on top of Natty's.

When she began to wake up and sensed rather than saw something on her wrist, she thought it was part of her dream and closed her eyes again. Then, clasping the bracelet in her right hand, she realized that it was real. Istvan, standing by the window with his back to the Grand Canal, seemed not to see the tears running down Natty's cheeks. She leaped up and flung herself into his arms, repeating with a nervous laugh that she had never worn a single piece of jewelry and that she would never wear any other.

After breakfast, accelerating away from the hotel, Antonio remarked gloomily, "It will rain soon."

"Of course," said Natty, "because we're leaving."

"When you come back," said Antonio, "just leave a message at the Gritti. That way you can be sure I'll come to meet you at the airport."

"Who knows if we'll come back," said Istvan.

The Riva sliced through the rough water, which had turned a brownish color and begun to ripple. Natty, standing with her cape billowing in the wind, looked like a figurehead. She did not seem to feel the cold. But Istvan turned up his coat collar.

As the boat drew away from Venice, Istvan realized

THE NET

that his love for Natty had taken on, in the space of a few days, a dimension that made him feel giddy and at times crazy.

I must leave her now, when we get back to Paris, he said to himself. But I won't. Because it'll kill me.

42

Natty had left Istvan at the entrance to the changing rooms. She tried hard to smile, but her eyes were full of tears.

"Come on," he said, "think of this as a great day for me."

She gave him a hurried kiss and ran off.

Yes, a great day. The outcome of a decision that he had considered and weighed for a long time. On the occasion of the first round of the international championship at Roland-Garros, he was going to play what would probably be his last match in a Grand Slam tournament.

The idea of saying his farewell to tennis in this stadium where he had won his first Grand Slam had gradually taken shape during the winter, when he had only played in minor tournaments with mixed pleasure. Since the second round at Wimbledon the previous year, he had done nothing, he kept telling himself. Nothing. And this last match at Roland-Garros he was only playing thanks to the wild card that the organizers of the Grand Slam tour-

THE NET

naments reserve for five good players so they can avoid the preliminary heats.

During his sleepless nights, he had turned the question endlessly over in his mind. His love of tennis, which had been his whole life, pushed him to carry on, to persevere, in spite of his inevitable drop in the rankings. Surely what mattered more than anything was to play, whatever the level of the game, and accept the uncertainty of the outcome? To face the public at the major tournaments, even if it meant hiding his weaknesses behind a good-humored facade, by acting the clown, as Natty called it? Was not greatness to continue practicing one's discipline, even if one's strength had diminished and even when, as everyone knew, a champion was old at thirty-five? To accept such humility, after having reached the highest level, rather than trying to leave an impressive image at all costs? For a boxer, one fight too many might make him a life-long invalid, or even kill him. It's understandable when they stop. But Istvan's pride demanded he play one last great match. No doubt because he saw himself through Natty's eyes.

He still found it hard to realize that the match, which in a few seconds would pit him against his friend Jimmy Connors, was bound to be his last. Natty, who had been informed of his farewell at the same time as everybody else, confessed that it did not surprise her. She had had a vague premonition that winter. And yet, right until the last minute, she had not wanted to believe it.

He drew back the tarpaulin that hung between the changing rooms and center court. The sun dazzled him. He shaded his eyes with his hand. The weather was close. The stormy air was electric. He tapped the ground with his foot three times before entering the arena—a superstitious tournament ritual that he now enacted for the last time.

When he won the first set 6–4, Natty clutched the arm of Frank Fenwick, who was sitting next to her in the stand. Connors was in tiptop form, but Istvan had overshadowed him.

"Why does he want to stop?" she exclaimed. "Frank, did you see?"

"He might even win the second set, maybe . . . but after that . . ."

"What?" she asked indignantly.

"Tiredness, Natty . . ."

It was rare to find every seat taken in the Center Court stands at Roland-Garros for a first-round match.

"It's as full as for a final," Natty said. "They've all come to see this."

For the first time in a long while, Fenwick had nothing to say. He had followed and managed Istvan's entire career, greatness and decadence, and he saw in Natty, whom he had known since childhood and was now managing, the female equivalent. Tennis careers were short enough that he would probably still be here in twenty years to see the same thing happen to her.

"Second set to Connors, seven games to five!"

Fenwick glanced at Natty, who was staring out at the court. He put his hand on her shoulder. "Don't forget I want to see you in the quarter-finals here. And even better, I hope!"

She did not answer, but kept her eyes riveted on Istvan. Suddenly she was overcome with a violent antipathy for Connors, whom she had always liked. Instinctively, she focused all her despair on Istvan's opponent, who was in the process of beating him.

THE NET

"You know that all the papers are talking about you," Fenwick went on. He did not know why he said that. He should be keeping his mouth shut, concentrating on hanging onto his job, conducting the reassuring waltz of future contracts. He did not recognize the sound of his own voice; it was faltering and distraught.

He was experiencing Istvan's drama strangely. He had seen plenty of fallen champions, handled a few, too. But for him, Istvan was something special. Perhaps the last tennis artiste, not yet computerized or biomedically maintained like a racehorse. Besides, the whole justification for this last show was that fury that made him wrest three games from Connors in the third set. Connors wasn't letting him off lightly, but had understood, with a fellow champion's intuition, that Istvan's last match had to be one of the toughest, one of the best, in the history of tennis.

His elbow brushed against Natty. She was trembling. He leaned toward her. He bit his lip. He rummaged in his pockets for a handkerchief, but found only filing cards. Finally he ventured onto territory where he had never been before and wiped the tears from Natty's cheeks with his big hands. What's gotten into me? he thought, as he realized that he was crying too. He rubbed his face on his jacket sleeve. And, ashamed at being ashamed, he looked around to make sure that nobody had seen F.F. crying.

He was amazed to see a lot of handkerchiefs being discreetly folded away. Fifty yards to his left, Rainer Ritter, who had not been seen in France all winter, was standing, ashen, his face tense. What did the gathering storm remind him of? His own match against Istvan the previous year?

Fenwick had resented Ritter ever since the German, through plain clumsiness, had ruined the publicity operation surrounding him and Natty, the couple of the year. But he could only admire the compassion of the future number one as Horwat slipped behind in the fourth set.

"Game, set, and match to Mr. Connors," said the umpire, "four-six, seven-five, six-three, six-two!"

The spectators were on their feet, cheering Horwat as if he were the winner of the final. It was a storm of ovation and applause.

Connors jumped the net and took Istvan by the shoulders. He looked in his eyes for a few seconds before embracing him.

The clamor grew even louder when the umpire, contrary to custom, climbed down from his perch and went onto the court to shake Istvan's hand. The crowd, undecided, did not quite dare invade the ground, but a flock of tennis personalities rushed up, R.R. at their head, to embrace Istvan Horwat.

Natty did not let go of Fenwick's arm. She made him keep apart from the tumult. The television cameras congregated in the middle of the chaos. They followed Chatrier, the president, who offered Istvan the golden keys of the Stade Roland-Garros. The journalists jostled each other, calling out in different languages. Natty, overwhelmed, paralyzed, contemplated this mixture of smiles, tears, and gestures. She could hear nothing but a general din, and she felt giddy. She thought she would faint.

Then she pushed Fenwick aside and rushed into the middle of the crowd, elbowing her way through to fling her arms around Istvan's neck. He kissed her and slipped the symbolic keys into her hand.

43

"You still don't regret putting away your racket?" asked Fenwick.

"This is no time to think about it," replied Istvan with a smile.

They knew each other; their small talk was designed to break the tension that belied the tranquillity of the clear blue Wimbledon day.

"Lucky it rained last night," said Fenwick. "Natty's been complaining about the dryness of the grass over the last few days."

"I should have stayed at the hotel," said Istvan. "It's unbearable. I'm looking at the court but I can't see it."

Earlier, Fenwick had said to Natty, "You've reached the final. You will win. It's Natasha Kotany's Wimbledon."

She had replied simply: "I'll beat that Czech woman."

A journalist had found the phrase: "A Czech against the Hungarian." One almost expected to see it posted on the scoreboard. When Mary Collins used it in front of her, Natty snapped, "I'm American, but it doesn't matter."

To the *Guardian* reporter who pointed out that her opponent was three years her senior, she said, "I count points, not years."

She was handling it all with a remarkable maturity. Since Istvan's farewell match at Roland-Garros, where she had been beaten in the semifinal by the American number one who went on to win the tournament, Natty had not stopped concentrating on a single goal: she would win Wimbledon.

Now, this was the day.

The tension of the dressing room, waiting for two o'clock. The official fussing around, more nervous than the players. The bouquets. The attendant carrying their gear for them onto the court, the curtsey to the royal box, the toss, the warm-up volleys. The relief of the first serve.

The Czech, the favorite at two to one, won the first set fairly easily. The odds on Natty were fifteen to one. Fenwick repeated that these odds were ridiculous, but so much the better: he had placed his bet. Although Natty's progress to the final had been sure, he was beginning to have his doubts.

Istvan's anxiety was contagious. He was going to bring her bad luck with his negative vibes. Yes, it would have been better if he had stayed at the hotel. He probably looked like a football player's wife who had come to encourage her hero but was worried about his getting hurt.

"She'll win the second set," said Istvan in a voice from beyond the grave.

"Jesus," said Fenwick. "The Czech didn't serve a single fault."

"Nor did Natty!"

"They'll be at it for a week." Frank lapsed into silence for a few minutes. Then: "Even if she loses, she's already

THE NET

got heaps of contracts, you know. The sponsors are fighting over her. She's already rich."

Istvan wasn't really listening. "I know," he said, his attention on the court below.

"The next point is, what about you? What are you going to do?"

"Later, Frank."

Both men concentrated on the game. Then Frank said gloomily, "You're not going to become her gigolo-businessman cum racket-carrier, are you? I'm the businessman, remember."

"Do you think this is the time to talk about it? Look at that ace! The Czech didn't even see the ball! One more game and the second set's hers."

Istvan was breathing very heavily. He was listening to the spectators cheering Natty, who had just won an interminable but fast-moving rally. Applause that grew louder as Natty ended the game with a crosscourt backhand passing shot. Istvan heard R.R. shout, like at the Orange Bowl, "It's the Horwat backhand!"

"She's going to win, Frank, she's going to win!"

"Yes, fine, just let your Hungarian girl play," groaned Fenwick, who knew he was perhaps a little jealous of all this passion. "I'll make you an offer. If you want, you can work with me. You could look after your champion's affairs as a priority, but in an office."

"You get on my nerves, Frank. Mary Collins has already offered me a job with CBS—look! Did you see the wisdom of that lob?"

"I see everything. What I see right now is that the Czech is winning two games to love. And Natty's coach, old Stolle, over there, is looking pissed off."

"Shut up!"

"Steady, my man." CBS? Had he heard right?
"I want her to win!"
"So let it be!"
Natty had just equalized, two games all. Fenwick, his elbows on his knees, his head in his hands, did not say another word. This CBS deal—if there was one—hadn't gone through him. Where was the percentage in that?

Istvan felt alone and distraught. He wished he could snatch Natty from this nightmare, run out and take her in his arms and get her away from this uncompromising girl who was now leading 3–2.

Istvan looked down. Fenwick's shoes crossed over each other, uncrossed, fought between themselves. That was when Istvan realized that the phlegmatic Texan was as anxious as he was. He asked him gently, "F.F., do you think she's done for?"

The giant shrugged his shoulders. He did not reply, which was as worrisome an answer as any.

Natty had won the second set 7–5. She wondered if it was fear that was making the Czech perspire: she had changed her headband three times already. Natty could not stand her mechanical game. She was going to derail that precision, turn it into a pile of old iron. Yes, by the end of this third and last set, the Czech would be ready for the scrap heap.

She thought about Istvan, lost up there somewhere in the crowds to which she was oblivious. Had he understood that the Czech robot was beginning to rust? Perhaps not. It was a feeling she had from inside the fight . . .

Well, you'll see, Istvan, my love.

Like a man. I'm going to play like a man.

That'll please Fred Stolle, she thought.

From the other side of the net, the resistance began to

THE NET

weaken. Natty was leading 4–3. Then 5–3, after a series of deep volleys and beautifully judged lobs that transformed the Czech into a frantic runner.

Fenwick felt Istvan grip his arm.

"She's going to do it, Frank!"

"Shut up, I'm getting superstitious . . ."

A clamor arose from the stands following a double fault from Natty. Nerves? Surely not, not now, not so close . . .

After the interminable anxiety, the end came quickly.

"Game, set, and championship to Miss Kotany, four–six, seven–five, six-three."

Istvan was too full of emotion to utter a sound. He could only watch as she put on her cardigan and waited for the presentation, cool and barely smiling yet.

Frank, however, found himself chanting above the crowd's roar, "Number one. She's number one."

44

They were sitting, waiting for the gas station attendant to finish. He was a young boy, and kept hovering around the hood, sponge in hand.

"He's nuts about cars," said Natty.

"No, it's you he's looking at."

Istvan lowered the power window. "Could you check the oil too, please."

The boy wiped away the mosquito carcasses. He leaned toward Natty. He obviously recognized her. His nose got squashed against the windshield for a moment as he lost his balance.

He put the windshield wiper back in place, fumbled in his pocket, and brought out a Total notepad that he gave to Natty.

"Can I have your autograph, please, Miss Kotany . . ."

Natty wrote her name. He thanked her with a smile.

"Thank you," he said, giving Istvan the change. "Have a good journey, Mr. Kotany."

45

The whirlpool sucked him with increasing violence toward the net of his nightmare. He wanted to yell. His mouth filled with water. His eyes rolled upward, staring back at him, multiplied by the crowd of sea monsters that, for the first time, had appeared out of the abyss, waiting for the prey to be imprisoned in the net. But as soon as it closed around him, the horror gave way to a strange peace. Numbed, he no longer felt like struggling, or shouting. The countless green eyes hypnotized him. He let himself grow torpid, become paralyzed. He savored this anesthesia, as if it were a death he himself had willed. He made no effort to disentangle himself from the mesh that was choking him. He adapted to his empty lungs. He no longer needed to breathe. Freed from all vital necessity, he let himself drift in the water, which had suddenly become calm.

He finally picked up the telephone. It took him a moment to recognize Thieu's voice, which was insisting, "It's Miss Natty. She's in Budapest . . . at the airport."

He closed his eyes, vainly seeking the peace of his dream. He clenched the receiver. He was shaking. He had to control his voice. He took a deep breath and managed to utter:

"Natty, darling, I can't hear you very well . . ."

She was babbling: "The plane for Paris is going to take off, my love. I'm on my way. Three days away from you, I was lost . . ."

"How are Sandor and Erzebet?" he stammered.

"Fine. What about you? Are you better? I love you. I love you, Istvan."

They were cut off.

Istvan, who hated lies, had had to scheme to remain alone for these three days before making the most heartrending decision of his life. He had postured a little about the feelings of Natty's grandparents; emphasized the new woman champion's duty to go and see them to share her joy with them. Then he had invented a toothache at the last minute so that she would go alone.

Grotesque, but necessary.

In the bathroom mirror, he met again the eyes of his nightmare monsters, but they had lost their power to hypnotize. They were simply tired. Their gaze lingered, desperate.

Istvan applied himself to going through the usual motions, to beginning this horrendous day.

There was not much time left for him to disappear.

To methodically organize a state that would be irreversible: the lack of her, the big void.

The previous day, he had telephoned Mary Collins in New York. He accepted the offer she had made him at Wimbledon. Istvan Horwat would do commentary for CBS at the U.S. Open at Flushing Meadow. He would join

THE NET

her at once, to learn his new job. He would just call back at eight forty-five and confirm his arrival by Concorde, so that she could meet him at Kennedy Airport.

He thought that if he was going to commit suicide, he would proceed exactly the same way, with the ritual precision of everyday actions. Refresh himself under the shower. Put up with the drone of the razor, ignore the shadows under his eyes, the little wrinkles at the corners of his eyes. Dress lightly. It was hot in August in New York.

Natty would be just nineteen at Flushing Meadow. He thought of the party he and his friends had held there for her last birthday.

Then his heart began to beat faster, as he thought about what it was going to be like to see her again, since she was playing in the tournament.

Yes, but they would no longer be together. And watching her develop from a distance would be hardest of all. His loneliness would be unbearable. All the more so because she would probably not remain alone. There would be no shortage of suitors now.

He must not think about Natty. Absolutely no more.

It was up to him to lie horribly, so that their special love would not be reduced to a caricature—unworthy of them—of the old champion installed in the golden palace of a very young celebrity.

No, Natty, it's not a gigolo-businessman, or a daddy-lover cum racket-carrier that you love. He picked up the phone.

"Hello, Mary, I hope I didn't—"

"No, I wasn't asleep. I was waiting for your call. I'll be there. See you later."

She would be there. For a long time, no doubt.

Had she already thought about the wedding invitations, Mary Collins, journalist, CBS star, to her colleague, Istvan Horwat, ex–world's champion tennis player?

May as well get it over with quickly.

"Thieu, give this parcel to Miss Natty."

"She'll be here soon. Aren't you going to wait for her for lunch?"

"I'm in a hurry. She'll understand."

I don't want to spend my life with you. I'm very fond of you, but I'm not passionately in love with you . . . My life is complicated.

That was the beginning of the first draft, which he had torn up.

I love you, Natty, I've never loved anyone but you, we're crazy, both of us . . .

Torn up. Too true, that time.

Natty, soon you'll be nineteen. You'll be number one for years. I'm . . .

He tore it up.

Natty, your glory lies ahead of you. I don't want to be by your side, reminded of what I used to be when you were born . . .

Scraps of paper crumpled at his feet.

"A present, Thieu? But where is he? What's he doing?"

"He didn't say it was a present. He said, 'Give her this parcel, she'll understand.' He was in a hurry."

Natty went into Istvan's room. As empty and huge as the center court at Roland-Garros on a winter evening. She bit into the wrapping paper, which had been clumsily taped. There was a sheet of writing paper wrapped around a small box.

Your life belongs to you, Natasha. I bid you good-bye, as I said farewell to the Grand Slam tournaments. Apparently CBS can't manage without me.

THE NET

She screwed it up into her hand.

"She will understand," he had said to Thieu.

But how could she? The man who had been the center of her childhood and then of her life as a grown woman, the man who so many times and so tenderly had sworn his love for her . . . could he just call a taxi to the airport and fly out of her life to New York or Timbuctoo, it didn't matter—and she would understand?

"Your life belongs to you, Natasha." No, Istvan, it belongs to *you.*

Slowly the tears came, until they were uncontrollable. It was a cold shadow she had to pass through. An hour passed until she was exhausted and she fell into numbed sleep.

When she awoke the note was still in her fist, damp and crumpled. She let it drop onto the carpet, and her mind turned to Flushing Meadow again. It would be the hardest competition she had ever faced. With this loss darkening and crushing her, she would have to go on court, round after round, to outthink and outmaneuver her opponent, expected to win . . . locked within the white bounds of the court beyond which no other world was supposed to exist. And this time she really would be alone.

Yet, even as she felt the tears welling up again, she realized that he would never leave her completely. Wherever she played, she knew in her heart he would be there, somewhere in the crowd, watching, encouraging . . . loving her like the awkward parent he had once been, and now would be again.

She noticed the box around which the note had been wrapped. Written on it in felt pen was simply, "For Natasha Kotany—Istvan Horwat." Inside was a brooch. Perhaps three inches long, a representation of a tennis net in gold filigree, a tiny racket fixed at an angle in the middle, the net cord hiding the clasp.

She fell asleep again, the brooch fast in her hand.